ULRICKA'S GAMBIT

Ulricka's Gambit
The Assassins of Harmony: Book Two
Copyright © 2022 by Jamie McNabb
All rights reserved

Cover design by Allyson Longueira
Map design by Brandon Swann
Cover art copyright © Roberto Atzeni | Dreamstime.com

Ebook ISBN: 978-1-948447-15-7
Trade Paperback ISBN: 978-1-948447-16-4

Published by Soapbox Rising Press

Ulricka's Gambit

The Assassins of Harmony: Book Two

Jamie McNabb

SOAPBOX RISING PRESS

The Metropolitanate of The Inland Empire and The Holy Oregon

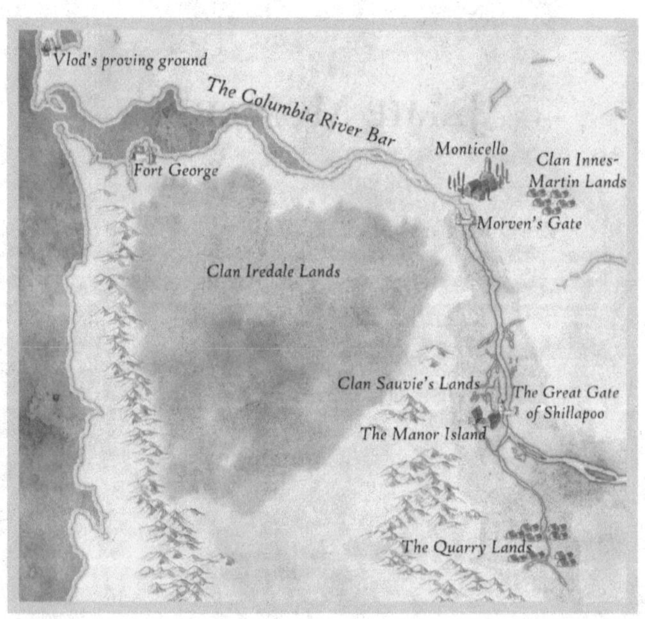

Lower Columbia River

The Metropolitanate of The Inland Empire and The Holy Oregon

Upper Columbia River

ONE

Astrident knocking rattled the door to the Mother Metropolitan's sitting room in the Saraswati Palace.

Her Beatitude, the Most Blessed Ulricka, Mother Metropolitan of the Inland Empire and the Holy Oregon, now in the fifth year of her reign, looked up from the Senet game she was about to lose to Her Eminence, the Most Reverend Shabnan, Crone of the Cathedral Henge of Eileen the Immortal.

The two women's eyes met in anxious anticipation.

Was this, finally, the news they had been waiting for?

No one but an officer of the Cathedral guard would dare to hammer in such a manner, and no one but an officer of the Cathedral guard could be entrusted to deliver such an important message.

Surely, this could not be another report of failure, not at this absurd hour.

Throughout the evening and deep into the night, one after another, the messengers had announced the near misses or the catastrophes in the guard's hunt for one old priest. Was another such announcement about to be dropped into Ulricka's lap, or would this be the message that Ulricka had been praying for?

"Come!" she said. Her voice reflected her twenty-eight years of life, her five years in office, and her four successful pregnancies—four babies carried to term and thus four children bestowed upon the Cathedral. Her tone was reflexively determined, accustomed to command and certain of obedience.

The door swung open, and an officer entered.

A figure loomed in the passage behind her, excluded and blocked. She was a runner, an adolescent in a woman's uniform. If all went well, she might live long enough to grow into it.

The runner dodged around the officer and bolted into the room.

The girl was all arms, legs, and excited eyes. She reeked of grime and sweat. She was menstruating, too, and the rotten-fish stench of it simmered beneath the rest. She'd have to change her pad soon or she'd stain her kilt.

Given the recurrent, heretical itch to reinvent lost technologies, or to make up new ones, why was it that no one ever sought to reintroduce cotton pads or, better still, tampons?

Perhaps it was because those who did march to that drummer had other things on their childish minds.

Currently, rumor had it that one of the downriver magi had taken it into his head to figure out a way to harness horses to a capstan, much as it was done in sawmills and flour mills, and then use the power generated to drive the wheels of a wagon or to turn a set of paddlewheels on a boat.

What was the point? Horses pulled, rowers rowed, and sails propelled. Anything else threatened the Harmony.

The runner bowed.

Why was it always things like self-propelled wagons and boats with neither sails nor oars? Why not looms and lumber mills and, for the sake of argument, machines to dip candles?

The runner came to attention.

Ulricka answered her own question: no cheap cotton. The Columbia River Basin had a temperate climate, and because it did, cotton couldn't be grown locally, not in any commercially viable volume. Cotton had to be brought in overland by caravan. Therefore, cotton was an expensive luxury.

As for raising it elsewhere on the continent, the volume of labor needed to grow it in commercially viable amounts simply didn't exist.

And that was *before* considering the additional amount of labor that would be needed to process the raw cotton into useable products, like cloth, pads, tampons, and summer-weight garments.

The runner stood mute, her eyes fixed on the wall behind Ulricka.

A routine intelligence report had mention—in passing, for the love of heaven!—that Vlod of the Iredales was trying to use the pressure of steam to push water through a pipe.

Steam as a motive force! It was nothing but an invitation to heresy, upheaval, and death.

Thora, the previous mother metropolitan, ought to have done away with that runt years ago, but she'd missed her chance, and her subsequent, half-hearted attempts had been bungled affairs at best.

Well, Ulricka thought, what hadn't been done might still be done. Like his father, the runt might even be persuaded to light his own pyre.

Why didn't the runner speak? Was she waiting for permission?

No, she couldn't be that silly, not on a night like this.

Then again, maybe she could be.

Deciding to rescue the poor child, Ulricka asked, "What do you have to tell me?"

The runner caught her breath, then blurted, "Your Beatitude, Colonel Chiharu sends her devotion. She is pleased to inform Your Beatitude that the traitor Jinhai has been found in the Sacred Grove."

The words had spilled out in a jumble, like a dozen kittens being dumped from a wicker basket.

Ulricka and Shabnan shared a look of triumph.

"May the Goddess bless Colonel Chiharu," Ulricka said. "She is not to break contact but neither is she to capture him. I shall join her shortly."

"Yes, Your Beatitude," the runner said. She bowed and hurried out.

The officer followed, but at a dignified pace.

The door closed with a sharp click.

Ulricka swirled her winter cloak across her shoulders and closed the clasp. She hooked a quiver of arrows onto her belt and picked up her favorite bow, the laminated recurve she used to hunt elk.

A gentle delight in the foibles of youth flared in Shabnan's eyes. "You are Dianna in the flesh," she said.

"Don't blaspheme. We shall need Her blessing."

"No disrespect was intended." Shabnan reached for her own cloak. "Will you murder him?"

"I must," Ulricka said. "Both him and his handlers. The Cathedral's safety depends upon it."

Shabnan cocked her head to one side. Deciding to speak, she said, "Yours too."

"I'm a cipher," Ulricka said.

Shabnan shrugged. "What about the baby you're carrying?"

Ulricka's hands went cold. "How did you know I'm pregnant? I've barely just figured it out myself."

"I am the Crone of your Cathedral. How could I not know? Your court will rejoice."

"They aren't the ones who'll have to bring it to term and then deliver it."

"Hence their great joy. Other women's babies are such a delight, don't you think?"

Shabnan opened a drawer in the base of the Senet board and moved to sweep the pieces into it.

"Don't," Ulricka said. "I'd like to finish that game."

"You can't possibly win."

"I have my hopes."

His Honor, the Venerable Jinhai, Archdeacon, Protopriest, and Archthurifer of the Cathedral Henge of Eileen the Immortal, ran south through the Sacred Grove. The ancient oaks stood thick on the ground, and he found that he had to dodge between them.

It reminded him of playing soccer in his youth, of moving the ball down the field. He would pivot and dart this way and that, risking his knees and his ankles, and all in an effort to avoid the players on the other team, in a desperate drive to get close enough to the goal to kick the ball past the goalie and into the net.

The roots of the trees bulged beneath the grass. They made it dangerous for him to run in the dark, but he had no choice. He would either make his rendezvous or he would die.

A wall loomed up sixty meters ahead of him. Made out of rough stone, it was less than a meter-and-a-half high. It was a demarcation rather than a barrier, like a decorative railing on the edge of a scenic clifftop.

Beyond the wall sprawled Maryhill, the city that served the Cathedral and its precincts.

If Jinhai could make it over that wall, if he could accomplish that much, then he might be able to disappear into the town's warren of streets and alleys. There, he might be able to elude Chiharu, and having eluded her, he might—May the Gods and the Generations grant it!—be able to reach the Columbia River and rendezvous with Ziellottes, his handler.

Jinhai had only one purpose: to warn the clans about Ulricka! The Cathedral, no, the entire province, hung in the balance.

His right boot came down wrong and slipped on the wet grass. Jinhai stumbled, nearly falling, but he regained his footing and plunged on into the night, on into the shadowed maze.

Just then an arrow struck one of the oaks, ahead and slightly to the left. It had missed by less than a quarter of a meter.

He recognized the gold-and-purple fletching. Ulricka had joined the hunt!

Had she shot wide deliberately?

No, not Ricki. She'd missed.

Jinhai stole a glance back. His pursuers were gray-black shapes, as silent and as quick as wolves, coming on among the trees.

Looking back on what had happened, Jinhai decided that the crisis had begun two days earlier. It had sprung like a slow-moving bear trap.

The senior librarian had informed him that he had been unable to locate the book that Jinhai had asked him to bring up from the closed stacks.

The book in question was *The Council Crest Grimoire*. It wasn't a terribly important book, but Jinhai had wanted it to clear up one or two points in his current research. That research was into the influence, if any, of the cave cults and mountain covens on the early origins of the Cathedral's present-day liturgical practices. Had there been carryovers, and, if so, what was their meaning, recognized or otherwise?

The librarian's failure to locate a requested volume was not in the least unusual. Library staff often returned volumes to the wrong shelf.

However, *The Council Crest Grimoire* was not a popular volume. Indeed, as far as Jinhai was aware, he was the only researcher who had any interest in it. Thus the staff would have had little or no opportunity to misshelve it since the last time Jinhai had accessed it.

The book, logically speaking, ought to have been in its correct place on the correct shelf, rather than in the wrong place on the wrong shelf.

Stranger still, the librarian had not offered to conduct a search for the book. Moreover, he had flatly refused to grant Jinhai access to the closed stacks in order to search for it for himself. It was an unheard-of slight to a senior member of the Cathedral's clergy.

Yesterday one of the junior thurifers had failed to appear for a mandatory rehearsal. She had sent no note of explanation, no request to be excused, and no apology.

Under normal circumstances, such behavior might well have resulted in her dismissal, and she would have had to have known that it might; nevertheless, she had dared to do it.

Then, at midmorning today, Howahkan, another of the Cathedral's protopriests, had sent word that an unavoidable conflict had arisen, forcing him to cancel their working lunch.

Their working lunches were nothing of the sort. Rather, they were once weekly times when they could gossip for a couple of hours, all the while eating and drinking as they never did otherwise.

Over the years, Jinhai had found it necessary to cancel two or perhaps three times—he couldn't remember exactly—but Howahkan never had. Never! If he had died the day before, his corpse would have kept the appointment.

And yet, he had sent his excuses.

Significantly, Howahkan had not suggested another time.

As Jinhai had thrown Howahkan's note into the stove in his apartment, his mind engaged what appeared to be a growing threat.

Had he put his foot into a trap? Had he put his weight on the pressure plate? Were those the sounds of the jaws swinging closed?

Perhaps.

Taken individually, the events were meaningless. However, taken as a group, they forced an inescapable conclusion. The Cathedral guard were asking questions and dropping hints. They were isolating Jinhai from his colleagues. Doubtless, they had already begun to demonize him. They were making him a target for arrest, for the stake.

But if their intent was to arrest him, why hadn't they? Why the cat-and-mouse games?

That wasn't much of a question. They wanted to know how much he'd revealed. They wanted to snap him up with his hands dirty. They wanted him to lead them to his contacts, to snap them up as well.

That being the case, their only choice was to play him on a long line. But they had both waited too long and had moved in too quickly.

It was understandable. The situation was both fluid and murky. It was like hunting carp with a bow and arrow. Easy enough to do in clear lake water, but when the river's shallows were muddy and the fish had gone deep, success was largely a matter of luck.

Jinhai had not been so silly as to believe he could evade them indefinitely, but neither had he expected them to discover him so soon.

The last of Howahkan's note collapsed into the flames, like the final parts of a heretic's burning corpse.

Jinhai took several deep breaths and recited a calming mantra. This was not a convenient time to panic.

He reasoned that the guard would not be ready to strike for several more hours, perhaps not until dawn.

Dawn was a good time for such goings-on.

And, too, despite their lust for heroics, they were a sluggish lot.

No, all in all, he had ample time. The wood wasn't piled around his legs just yet.

He coded what would of necessity be his final report. He finished with an urgent request for extraction and a promise to bring out as many supporting documents as he could.

He'd been unable to obtain originals, but he had collected a surprising number of intermediate drafts and working copies. These had been passed around and traded back and forth, like any documents in any bureaucracy, never mind how limited the distribution. As a result, several of them were complete with handwritten marginal notations.

Handwritten by whom?

He recognized Shabnan's handwriting and Ulricka's, and he could only think that the rude masculine scrawls were Narmer's.

The documents themselves made interesting reading, to put it mildly. It was the notations that cinched Jinhai's gut.

He double-sealed his final report in an official clergy-confidential envelope.

Luckily, his handler, Ziellottes, was in Maryhill on unrelated business, so the normal delays would not come into it. Jinhai had no idea what that business might be. Ziellottes was a man of many talents, many interests, and few revelations.

The canons permitted no one to interfere with the delivery of a clergy-confidential envelope and no one other than the envelope's designated recipient to open it.

As a result, even an officer of the guard would think twice about intercepting such a message.

But what about Colonel Chiharu, the guard's commander?

Jinhai tapped the envelope against the palm of his left hand.

Clergy confidentiality offered scant protection from the likes of the good colonel, but it might hold her at bay long enough.

If she had any shred of hard proof, the sort of evidence that would allow her to violate clergy confidentiality, she would have already arrested him. Besides, if she were in fact playing him on a long line, she would let the message go through, hoping to catch his contact at the other end.

Ziellottes would be safe enough. No doubt he, or his agents, had installed numerous cutouts along the way.

Yes, the message would to be safe enough.

Jinhai went down to the rectory office, picked one of the duty couriers at random, handed him the envelope, and sent him on his way.

Goddess bless!

Two

Jinhai's answer arrived at midafternoon.

Ziellottes' instructions were succinct. He and Jinhai were to rendezvous at a specified time, well after dark, at one of the lesser used cargo docks.

Jinhai must be prepared to travel fast, light, and unseen. Ziellottes was most explicit on those points. Speed meant life.

Therefore, he could pack only one small rucksack.

In a sense, this was a shame.

The night would be cold and clear, so he hung his winter cloak next to the door, where he would be unlikely to forget it. That done, he turned to his packing.

A man of sixty-two, he had spent forty years in the priesthood, twenty-three of them as a protopriest and archthurifer.

He loved the way of life in holy orders, but it had led him to collect a shocking number of odds and ends. He had never realized how shocking until he had them spread out and faced the task of selecting which few to take, picking out these and setting aside those.

He sorted through awards and certificates, amulets and insignia, religious medals, and his ceremonial robes.

He discarded every one of them.

It was not only his life that was at stake.

But then he came to his personal thurible and hesitated.

The thurible was silver and brass, ornately worked. It was both the symbol and, as it were, the vehicle of his principal office: Archthurifer of the Cathedral Henge of Eileen the Immortal. It was a magnificent object, a work of art in its own right, but, on balance, tragically, it was far too heavy to take along and meaningless outside of the bounds of the cathedral. He added it to the pile of rejects.

His throat stung, and his eyes filled with tears. He blinked them away, but he couldn't blink away the burning in his stomach, his racing heart, or the oily sweat that had formed on the palms of his hands.

Was he truly doing the right thing?

He kept one book—*The Wheel of the Year, a Manual of Offices and Occasional Prayers*—and the string of prayer beads his family had presented to him on the occasion of his ordination to the priesthood. His father had insisted that the beads were over six hundred years old, a true family heirloom.

The story was that a jeweler had fashioned the string from a Roman Catholic Rosary, way back in the earliest decades of the Second Creation. The jeweler had chosen a silver labrys, that immemorial symbol of the Goddess, to replace the image of the crucified Jesus; and, naturally, the centuries had changed the meaning to the image of the Queen of Heaven from Mother of God to Mother Goddess.

Jinhai's father had delighted in pointing out that such transformations proved—Proved!—that the Goddess had brought true knowledge out of humanity's ignorance.

So many things had been unearthed and returned to the light, returned to their original, pre-Christian, pre-patriarchal meanings!

Jinhai placed the book and the beads in his rucksack. He added a few items of clothing, his razor, his toothbrush, and his medicines. Finally, he stuffed the papers—those damning papers—in on top. He closed the flap and latched it. He gave it a pat for luck.

At this point he had nothing to do but avoid arrest and wait until it was time for him to leave for the rendezvous.

He changed out of his robes.

He'd almost forgotten to.

How had he managed that? Was he so old that his memory was failing?

His robes, being white, would never do, not at night, but his hunting clothes would serve. With those on, once the sun was down, he'd be as close to invisible as humanly possible.

He marveled at the cold simplicity of walking out: pack a bag, change his clothes, and leave. One, two, three, done. It seemed to him that his life had raced by him, that it had left him behind. One day he had been a child playing on a river beach, and the next he was an old man, a traitor, running for his life.

Had he ever been anything in between?

Perhaps he had always been a traitor, deep down. Perhaps Ulricka's machinations had merely brought it to the surface.

No, he couldn't blame her, not in that way.

As for the rest of it, he didn't *feel* as though he had grown old. He didn't *feel* as though he were running away for his life, not his true life. He didn't *feel* as though he had betrayed the metropolitanate. He didn't *feel* as though he were a spy, a traitor. He didn't *feel* as though he'd seen his opportunity, his pretext, and taken it.

He *knew* better.

The light spilling into his apartment through the windows was fading from the crisp brightness of a winter afternoon to the paler tones of the period between afternoon and sunset.

Jinhai's apartment occupied a fourth-floor corner, and his windows allowed him sweeping views to the north and east. He could see the Cathedral precincts and the southwest aspect of the cathedral henge proper: its outer ring and its nested inner rings. The cathedral was a forest of monoliths, posts and lintels, and braziers and torches.

Jinhai could not see the sacrificial altar, which occupied a place in the exact center of the innermost ring, but he would never willingly forget it, just as he would never willingly betray the Cathedral.

Ulricka was another story. She had failed in her duty. She was a traitor to the Cathedral, her province, and the people under her spiritual protection. If no one deposed her, the province was sure to end up crushed like a bug between two rocks.

To prevent this, Jinhai had willingly played the spy.

Not all, naturally, would see the situation as he did. More's the pity.

As good as by accident, just then, Jinhai noticed one of the guard's watchers. She was on the other side of the street, huddled in a doorway. She looked cold and impatient.

A second watcher joined her. They nodded to each other, and crossed the street toward the rectory.

Jinhai's heart jumped up into his throat.

They were early—much, much too early.

In his arrogance, he'd left it too long.

He grabbed his rucksack and fled from his apartment. His boots thundering on the treads, he raced down the service stairwell.

He was two flights down when he realized he had forgotten his winter cloak.

Now, the stone wall was clearer still. It was less than fifty meters ahead of Jinhai: a decoration, a hurdle, not a barrier. He was not trapped. They had not run him to ground. He had his rucksack, and inside it was ample evidence of Ulricka's heresy, of her betrayal of the Cathedral.

The golden light of Maryhill radiated beyond the wall. Once in the town, he would be able to escape Ulricka's jealousy and her revenge.

Jinhai sprinted forward. He dodged left and right, making an irregular zigzag path. He learned the trick from watching rabbits trying to escape a fox.

It hadn't worked then, and Jinhai doubted that it would work now. The rabbits had been young and agile, and yet they had failed. Jinhai was old and awkward...

An arrow *whirred* close to his head, less that a handbreadth off.

Ulricka had aimed with greater care this time. She had changed from guardian to huntress.

Jinhai could feel the weight of her gaze as she judged his movements. She was gauging his movements as though he were a fleeing stag, as though he were an afternoon's diversion.

The wall was less than forty meters ahead now.

The noise of hawkers, wagons, and horses called to Jinhai. They beckoned him forward. All he had to do was climb over the wall and lose himself in Maryhill's maze of—

The agonizing burn of slashed muscle and pierced organs ripped through Jinhai's chest. He looked down and saw the labrys-shaped head of one of Ulricka's hunting arrows protruding from the front of his robe. The arrow had emerged a finger's width below his sternum. Blood spurted from the arrow's blood grooves.

Jinhai lost control of his legs, and he fell. His momentum pitched him forward.

His head reeled, and his eyes refused to focus.

But he retrained his grip on his rucksack.

Blood surged up the back of his throat, choking him.

So here it was: death.

Ulricka had chosen to kill him rather than arrest him.

It made perfect sense. She could not afford for anyone to hear what he might confess, as confess he surely would.

Yes, that had to be it.

His silence might accuse her, but it could not prove her duplicity.

Chiharu was nothing if not an evidence hound. She would follow wherever his confession might lead...and be damned to the consequences.

He, however, would not live long enough for her to question him.

No matter.

Chiharu had only to search his rucksack. There she would find ample evidence to set the bitch alight!

He must hold on to it. He must!

Ziellottes. What about him?

Had Ulricka already captured Ziellottes? Had she already murdered him, too?

It was possible. And it would explain why she felt free to murder Jinhai *before* he'd made his rendezvous.

Or was it that Jinhai had angered her to such an extent that she had decided to take her revenge on him personally?

Never one to tolerate much in the way of disagreement, that one.

She was a proud little bitch, through and through.

He'd tried to warn Thora, but, alas, to no avail.

None...

Jinhai hit the ground.

His shoulder twisted into the wet grass.

The lights of Maryhill glowed above the wall.

A new terror gripped him.

Because he was dying accused of treason and heresy, because his flight convicted him, the Cathedral would refuse to write his name into *The Dirge Common to the Cathedral Henge of Eileen the Immortal*. As a result, the Goddess, the God, the Gods, and the Generations would turn their backs on him.

For him, there would be no memory eternal.

He would cease to exist.

His fate would be annihilation.

Nonexistence.

Absolute and unending.

It was his own doing.

He deserved no less for his failure to dissuade Ulricka from the course she had chosen, for losing his faith in her integrity and sagacity and, finally, for betraying her.

Why had he done it? There was the fate of the Cathedral and province, yes, but had it not also been because Ulricka had struck Thora down in the rite of succession?

Surely not!

It was impossible that he had been that childish.

Thora's time had come. She had outlived herself. Thora and her court had accepted it, and Thora herself had nominated Ulricka to succeed her. There had been no conspiracy and no betrayal. Ulricka had acted righteously.

How pious he sounded, as though he believed every word.

And he *did* believe them, every last one of them. Of course he did. While at the same time, he knew them to be utter lies, every last one of them.

The bitch had murdered his beloved Thora.

His blood fanned out across the grass.

So what was the truth?

Why had he thrown his life away?

No, he was dying because he had underestimated two things: Chiharu's tenacity and Ulricka's despair.

He redoubled his grip on the rucksack's strap. Surely a woman of Chiharu's merit would recognize its importance.

———

Ziellottes said, "He isn't coming."

The pier hid their canoe. She was light and fast, and had three seats. Ziellottes occupied the seat in the stern, while Farran, his hired agent, a local man, occupied the seat in the bow.

Above and around them, the pier was a black latticework of pilings, braces, stringers, and planks. A dilapidated ladder led down toward the water.

"He might come," Farran said.

"We can't wait any longer."

"What about the treaty drafts he promised?"

"Another day," Ziellottes said. "Besides, we don't need the exact wording to know the gist."

"But—"

"The gist will be enough," Ziellottes said.

He slipped the blade of his paddle into the water.

They maneuvered away from the pier and turned downstream.

As Ziellottes paddled, the waterproof wallet bandaged to his body worked against his ribs. By morning, he'd have a raw spot.

He felt ashamed for thinking of it.

Compared to what that old priest was going through, a raw spot was less than nothing.

The wallet contained Jinhai's final dispatch. In it he had summarized the current state of Ulricka's negotiations with Narmer.

A nonaggression pact was in the works, or perhaps they'd call it a treaty of mutual defense. Conceivably, they might limit themselves to a memorandum of understanding.

Whatever the specifics, if Ulricka were to conclude any such agreement with Narmer—or with anyone else—it would mean that she had abandoned the Cathedral's centuries-old policy of strict military neutrality and had decided to take sides.

Militarily.

Not that the Cathedral had much of an army.

In those waters, however, it wouldn't need much of an army. Whomever she sided with would have, for that very reason, an overwhelming advantage.

Narmer.

The name alone was enough to turn Ziellottes' stomach.

The man had schemed and plotted his way up the ranks of his clan's military, higher and higher.

In due course, he had staged a coup and installed himself as chieftain of the Pasco-Burbanks. At the same time, as one ambition had been fulfilled and another had come into the light, he had changed his name from Kerrderwynn to Narmer.

Now, as his adopted namesake had done with the Nile, his plan was to gobble up as much of the Columbia as he could.

Only the Cathedral Henge of Eileen the Immortal stood in his way.

But no longer.

Perhaps.

Depending.

A draft treaty was not a signed treaty, and a signed treaty was not an enforced treaty.

The downriver clans might yet have enough room to maneuver.

Enough time to avoid the catastrophe.

Therefore, Ziellottes had to leave Maryhill as soon as possible, even if it meant abandoning Jinhai, even if it meant leaving without the promised documents.

The rumors had become fact or nearly.

The downriver clans had run out of time, and because they had, Ziellottes could not risk Jinhai's final dispatch, not even for Jinhai himself.

As much as he despised what he was doing, Ziellottes had no choice but to deliver that dispatch to the man who had paid for it, to the one man who would know what to do with the information.

THREE

Ulricka went down on one knee beside Jinhai.

The ground was cold and damp. It chilled her.

Around them the oaks of the Sacred Grove loomed like a ritual choir, but silent, its members dressed in black. Jewels twinkled in the uppermost reaches of their hair.

It was a fanciful notion, fetching in its own way, the stars twinkling through the winter-bared branches, but it was out of place in the midst of this night's business.

Jinhai struggled to drag himself away from Ulricka, to drag the rucksack closer to Colonel Chiharu, but the arrowhead caught in the grass.

He wailed in pain, and yet more blood dribbled from his mouth.

"Where are they now, old man?" Ulricka asked. "Where are the people who promised to rescue you?"

Jinhai glared up at her as though she had dared to interrupt his private prayers. "Beyond your reach."

"Let's try it another way, shall we?" Ulricka said. "Where were you supposed to meet them?"

Jinhai smiled. Blood covered his teeth. "I'll never tell."

Ulricka noticed the way Jinhai held his rucksack close to his body, protecting it.

Ignoring the rucksack, careful to draw no attention to it, she grasped the arrow instead. She tugged on it.

Jinhai gasped in pain.

"You shall!" Ulricka said. She could almost pity him.

"You have no right."

"You have no mind. You never did."

She steeled herself, and worked the arrow's shaft in a circle.

Jinhai screamed.

Tears, stinging and unwelcome, blurred Ulricka's vision. Why wouldn't the old fool tell her?

"Where are they?" she asked, and twisted the arrow through a second circle.

Jinhai's shriek filled the grove. He sounded like an animal caught in a hawk's talons.

Many in Ulricka's hunting party, for that was what it was, turned away.

Ulricka, too, would have turned away if she had not been the Mother Metropolitan.

Shabnan knelt beside her. "Cruelty is beneath your office."

Ulricka's tears trickled down her face. "As you say, but it is *my* office."

"You are the avatar of the Goddess."

"Which is why he must tell me."

"No, it is why you must show mercy and let him to die."

Shabnan's voice was cold and not to be ignored. She had spoken as Her Eminence, the Most Reverend Shabnan, Crone of the Cathedral Henge of Eileen the Immortal, as an official who exercised as much or greater power as any mother metropolitan ever would.

But the metropolitanate was Ulricka's. The decision was hers, as was the responsibility for the outcome. And yet, to torture Jinhai would draw undue attention. It would risk her exposure, and that she could not do.

She released the arrow.

As if at Ulricka's command, Shabnan directed the party to draw back.

It was the wise thing to do. There was no telling what the old man might say, what he might reveal.

It created an ideal opportunity, too.

Ulricka grasped the rucksack, and after a brief struggle, she tore it from Jinhai's grasp.

She handed the rucksack to Shabnan, who secreted it within her hunting cloak.

"You've lost, old man," Ulricka said.

"I loved Thora," Jinhai said, as though it truly mattered that he say it.

"We all loved her," Ulricka said.

"Not you, Ricki. You only fucked her."

Ulricka reached toward the arrow, but caught herself and refused to grip it.

"I loved her as much as any of you priests ever did."

"Your whoring after Narmer proves you didn't."

She felt the accusation as though it had been a physical blow. "Better a whore than a fool."

"You're both," Jinhai said. "Narmer will drown the province in blood. You're handing him the Cathedral's head on a pike."

"Gibberish," Ulricka said, but her stomach balled into a mailed fist.

A war *was* coming unless she could stop it. That much had been clear for months.

Ulricka had sought to maneuver around or through it. She had attempted to play the clans off, one against another. She had sought to remove the Cathedral from the center of the field.

She had tried, but she had fumbled, and now the game was as good as lost.

Her negotiations with Narmer had been, so far at least, one last, drastic effort to keep the various factions at one another's throats and thus avert a war, if she could pull it off.

The timing of the thing would be all important. If she could reveal her negotiations at just the right time and to just the right people, the ploy might work. If she mistimed it by as little as a day, one way or the other, a blood-soaked debacle would ensue.

But Jinhai's sense of moral outrage had intervened. He had gotten wind of her negotiations with Narmer, had misread them, and had decided to play the spy.

His actions threatened to reveal her negotiations ahead of time, and now nothing but his death would permit her any hope of success.

Why couldn't he have trusted her?

Jinhai attempted to lift himself up, but he groaned and fell back. Blood dribbled down his jaw and across his neck. He convulsed, gasped, and died.

Good.

She had silenced him.

That part of the whole miserable affair was behind her.

Rather than hope, or victory, or a sense of justice achieved, what she felt was a coward's lessening of terror.

Nevertheless, the certainties *had* shifted, and she had the satisfaction of having shifted them.

With Jinhai dead, it might yet be possible for her to protect the Cathedral. She might avoid being dragged from her bed, tried by a summary court, and burned alive. She might be able to bring her baby to term, to deliver another child to the Cathedral.

Success was possible…if she could regain control of events, rather than be controlled by them. If a decent number of the contingencies broke *for* her rather than against her, if she could keep her feet planted and her back straight, she might live long enough to finish out her reign.

Ulricka motioned to Colonel Chiharu.

When the good colonel was standing close to her, she said, "Scour the river."

It was a safe-enough command. By this time, Jinhai's handlers were far, far away, and nothing would come of the search. At the same time, if she hadn't issued the order, that lack of action would have raised eyebrows and set tongues to wagging and clicking.

Ulricka added, "They're not to escape. Understood?"

"Yes, Your Beatitude," Colonel Chiharu said, and dispatched runners to relay the order.

Ulricka closed Jinhai's eyes and held the lids down until they did not reopen.

She stood.

Chiharu asked, "What do you wish done with the corpse, Your Beatitude?"

"Tell the Mistress of Sojourners to inter him with all the honors due his rank and office. Tell her he died in a hunting accident."

Chiharu's face went rigid. "Yes, Your Beatitude."

The time had come to deal with that great, hovering *if*. Ulricka asked, "Before the watchers closed in, was he able to send a message?"

Chiharu looked away, then back. Her eyes were the color of black coffee. "He might have. We can't be certain until we've captured his handlers."

Stomach acid flooded up Ulricka's throat. It was hot and bitter, and it threatened to make her vomit. She forced the bile down. "Do what you can."

"Yes, Your Beatitude."

Ulricka entrusted her bow and quiver to one of Chiharu's lieutenants, and turned to leave.

Over her shoulder, she said, "Shabnan, walk with me."

The two women strode away from Jinhai's body. They went upslope through the Sacred Grove, back toward the cathedral.

Ulricka's legs felt as though they had lost the strength to carry her, but carry her they did, one step after the other.

Murder.

Escape.

Peace.

Was peace worth such a price?

It was a stupid question. Of course it was.

Her personal guard moved to follow, but with a shake of her head, she dismissed them. Let them return to their quarters. Let them get in out of the cold.

Shabnan fell into step beside her.

Ulricka said, "It was necessary."

"We make our own necessities."

"Not always."

"A comforting excuse, that."

"You don't believe me?" Ulricka asked.

"Not for a moment."

"Understood. I'm not sure I believe it, either."

Shabnan arched an eyebrow. "Was that the rosy-fingered dawn of wisdom, I just heard?"

"No, that was my bloody-minded conscience telling me off."

"Good for it."

As they walked on, the only sounds they heard were the rustle of their skirts and, from behind them, the murmur of the guards as they prepared for the removal of Jinhai's body.

Four

Ulricka had intended to return to her residence in the Saraswati Palace by the shortest route, which skirted the cathedral. Instead, she entered the outermost ring of the cathedral henge.

This ring was the circle of monoliths that people usually pictured in their minds whenever they thought of the cathedral henge. The cathedral was in fact much larger, both above ground and below.

She crossed to the Gate of the Immortals.

The guards came to attention, and one of the pair opened the gate.

Ulricka and Shabnan passed through and descended into the Victoria Chapel, the antechamber to the complex beneath the henge.

The chapel memorialized Mother Metropolitan Victoria, the first mother metropolitan to rule the Inland Empire and the Holy Oregon.

The Goddess had one of Her many altars here, and it was an article of faith that Victoria's relics rested within it.

Shabnan sprinkled a spoonful of incense into the altar fire.

The smoke billowed up, fragrant and reassuring.

Ulricka did the same, and allowed herself to savor the heady aroma. She watched the billowing smoke, gray in the lamplight.

A handful of moments later, with Shabnan at her side, Ulricka descended a second flight of steps and entered the crypt. Here, rather than incense, the warring aromas of embalming spices and decay burdened the air.

Ulricka crossed to the Dirge Grotto, the chamber where teams of dirge singers continuously chanted *The Dirge Common to the Cathedral Henge of Eileen the Immortal*. The *Dirge* was the sanctified roster of those considered to have died in a state of harmony with the Goddess. It was many hundreds of volumes long.

Beginning with the very first entry in the very first volume, the names were ceaselessly chanted, one after the other, until the last name in the last volume had been sung. Before the echo of that last name had died, the *Dirge* was begun again. Thus the memory maintained and the memorial perpetually offered.

Round after round, down through the centuries, the names of the righteous dead of the Inland Empire and the Holy Oregon were sung, ensuring their immortality.

A man and a woman stood at the lectern. They were dressed in white robes with black-and-gold trim. Open before them on the lectern lay one of the bound volumes of the *Dirge*.

The woman chanted the names, while the man watched.

When she grew tired, he would take over. When he grew tired, she would take over. The two of them were the moon and the sun, the cosmic balance, the earth and the hunter. They were the divine Harmony in microcosm.

They glanced up as Ulricka entered. They nodded their respects, but not for an instant did the woman stop chanting, nor did the man allow his attention to waver.

Ulricka listened for a time and then left.

She turned down a branching gallery and entered the scriptorium.

Shabnan followed, but stood off to one side, as though she were a bodyguard.

The chief scribe hurried over and bowed arthritically. "Your Beatitude. Vladika! What a glorious surprise! Welcome, welcome!"

His use of her honorific pleased her. It made her feel as though she had come among companions. "Ingvar! Hello, my old friend," Ulricka said, as brightly as she could. "What a pleasure to find you on duty."

Ingvar straightened up. "A minor problem with the latest update to the *Dirge*, Your Beatitude." He shrugged in self-deprecation. "I can yet wield a pen."

She let her smile fade. "Jinhai was killed in a hunting accident earlier this evening."

Ingvar gasped. "Oh, Your Beatitude, what a tragedy! What a blow to the Cathedral! How horrible! I didn't know him well. 'Hello' and 'How are you?' That sort of thing, but I knew him by reputation. He was a wonderful man." He shook his head sadly. "Any death is to be regretted, but he will be especially missed."

"He will indeed."

"Well, how may I be of service?"

"I'm here to forestall any confusion that might arise. You understand?"

His sympathetic smile told her that he did. Where better for idiopathic confusion to swamp the orderly progress of business than in a scriptorium?

"What may I do to help, Vladika?"

"Where is the newest volume of the master copy of the *Dirge*?"

His face went blank, and she damned her ignorance.

She hadn't used the correct term, and as a result, she'd confused him. Perhaps, she'd embarrassed him. Paper wasn't paper; it was a dozen different kinds of paper. Ink wasn't ink, pens weren't pens, and books weren't books.

She tried again. "The volume in which you first record the names reported to the Cathedral by the manor henges."

His face lit up. "Ah, *The Open Journal*, Your Beatitude."

And then she remembered the details of that long-ago briefing.

As the mortality reports—the lists of those who'd died—came in from the manor henges, scribes transferred the individual names into the current volume of *The Open Journal*.

Once the current journal had been filled, the chief scribe checked it over and renamed it, rendering it the newest volume of the master copy of *The Dirge Common to the Cathedral Henge of Eileen the Immortal*.

The chief scribe then took a fresh journal, its pages a snowy blank, from the bindery and designated it *The Open Journal*.

As though it were a memory exercise, Ulricka recited the sequence to herself: reports are recorded in journals, filled journals become volumes, and those volumes made up the one and only master copy of the *Dirge*.

"Yes," Ulricka said, "that's the one I wish to see, *The Open Journal*."

"As it happens," Ingvar said, "Zandrina stayed late to complete the day's entries, Your Beatitude. There's been a local outbreak of the measles upriver. Very bad. Quite distressing. You can imagine for yourself, Your Beatitude, what an outbreak of the measles must be like at this time of year."

She assured him that she could imagine it, and privately reminded herself to include the victims in her private prayers.

Ingvar guided her to a desk where an old woman was copying names from a sheet of paper, one of dozens, onto a page in a book that looked like an accounting ledger.

Ulricka smiled at her. "May I?" she asked, and took the pen from Zandrina's unresisting hand.

Ulricka dipped the pen into the ink well and wiped off the excess.

She moved to *The Open Journal* and wrote "His Honor, the Venerable Jinhai, Archdeacon, Protopriest, and Archthurifer of the Cathedral Henge of Eileen the Immortal." She wrote it in perfect order, immediately under the last name that Zandrina had entered.

Ulricka liked the way his name and titles sat on the page: not too near the top, not too near the bottom.

Jinhai now dwelt with the Gods and the Generations, if they would have him.

In a note to one side, she added, "Entered by my own hand and not to be removed on pain of eternal damnation. So and blessed let it be, Ulricka, MM."

She noticed their stares, their open-mouthed incomprehension of what she'd just done.

She returned the pen to Zandrina.

"Thank you."

The old woman nodded.

To Ingvar, the chief scribe, Ulricka said, "I will tolerate no alterations to that entry."

"No, certainly not, Your Beatitude. It will remain exactly as you have written it."

"Good. See that it does."

"Oh, yes, Vladika. Of course, Vladika. Of course."

Ulricka carried *The Open Journal* into the Dirge Grotto and set it before the Dirge singers. The relentless flow of names stumbled into silence.

"The last name," Ulricka said. "Chant it."

They bowed, and when she was seated on one of the benches, in unison they slowly and reverently chanted: "His Honor, the Venerable Jinhai, Archdeacon, Protopriest, and Archthurifer of the Cathedral Henge of Eileen the Immortal."

Their attitudes and the notes had been correct, but routine. Possibly because both her demand and her presence had thrown them off their game, but possibly because they were tired and bored.

"He was a righteous man," Ulricka said. "Try again."

"Yes, Your Beatitude," they said.

They arranged themselves anew and chanted.

This time, their voices played against each other. They danced together, solemn and rejoicing in the same moment in time. They lifted the syllables through the entire range of the *Dirge*. They purified the tones and struck the harmonics. They split and intertwined the melodic and base lines, the drone line, and they made of that single name an image of rapturous beauty.

The name ended.

The silence took hold.

The singers watched her, hoping to discover her reaction. Had they pleased her? Had they chanted the name as she'd wished them to chant it? Had they balanced ritual and performance? Had they adapted themselves acceptably to this breach in the Grotto's routine?

Ulricka suppressed a smile. Were they afraid of how she might react to their efforts? Did they imagine that she'd have them punished if she were not pleased?

She wouldn't, but how could they be certain of that? How were they to assure themselves that she was not a capricious sadist? How were they to know that power hadn't defiled her?

They weren't.

Which might be just as well, given what lay ahead for the Cathedral and the metropolitanate.

Ulricka said, "Well done. Thank you."

At her instruction, Shabnan retrieved the journal and took it from the grotto. The fall of her boots tracked down the corridor and into the scriptorium.

To the Dirge singers, Ulricka said, "I interrupted you. Please continue."

"Yes, Your Beatitude," the singers said.

The *Dirge* resumed its eternal flow.

The woman chanted.

The man watched.

Ulricka closed her eyes and listened.

The names and the melody glided through time, like white clouds drifting across a summer sky.

She drifted with them.

Shabnan reentered the grotto, but she did not sit down. It was time for them to leave.

Ulricka rose from the bench.

"Her Beatitude, the Most Blessed Thora, Mother Metropolitan of the Inland Empire and the Holy Oregon," she chanted in a strong, clear voice, and returned to the Saraswati Palace.

Later, an hour or two before sunrise, alone in her apartment in the Palace, Shabnan got into bed. Her eyes burned and her skin felt greasy. Her body ached with fatigue, and the clothes she had been wearing, even from across the room, gave off the odors of the Cathedral's morbid piety.

She blew out her bedside lamp, and stared into the darkness, reviewing what the day had brought: Jinhai's murder, his handlers' escape, and Chiharu's befuddlement.

Of greater importance was the rucksack. It had contained clothes and toiletries and keepsakes, but it had also contained various working drafts of the treaty Ulricka was negotiating with Narmer. That it had, meant, with any luck, that none of those documents had made it to Jinhai's employer. That in turn meant that the secret was safe. Conjecture abounded, but in the absence of hard evidence, Ulricka's enemies, the Cathedral's enemies, had nowhere to stand.

Of greatest importance had been Ulricka's actions and reactions: her resolve and her grief.

Ulricka, Shabnan decided, stood a damn good chance of amounting to something after all.

FIVE

Vlod, Magus to Edmund, crouched in front of his experimental boiler. He opened the door to the firebox and fed a piece of well-seasoned wood into the flames.

Steam coiled lazily from the pressure-release pipe at the crown of the water jacket. Soon the escaping steam would start to gush, and when it did, the boiler would be ready to play its part.

Vlod closed the firebox and ran his hand upward along the water jacket, which sat atop the firebox. It was a matter of stove and teakettle. The iron was hot and rough. The rivets felt like rounded screw heads.

As it came to the boil, the water sent a subtle vibration through the metal.

They ought to have used a better quality of plate, but of necessity they'd had to make do with what they could scrounge. Even then the costs had been outrageous, and their dickering had attracted a fair amount of unwanted attention. They found out that confidentiality is impossible when you're hauling a wagonload of scrap iron through the center of town. People were bound to notice, and they were bound to share the news that one of their chieftain's magi—You know the one!—was tinkering again.

Vlod felt dwarfed by his own creation. Part of it was his lack of height, but part of it was the boiler itself.

The contraption was two meters tall and a half meter in diameter. It was meant to create and direct the technically forbidden power of live steam.

It was dangerous stuff, then, both politically *and* physically.

The moment Vlod closed the release valve the pressure inside the boiler would begin to build. It was that pressure, when controlled and directed, that provided the legendary power of steam.

A frisson of terror gripped him. His heart pounded and his feet felt as though he were standing in a tub of ice water.

It wasn't too late to abandon the project. Was he trying to alienate Clan Iredale? Was he trying to end up like his father? Wouldn't it be better to put out the fire, scrap the boiler, and walk away? Wouldn't it be wiser to stick to the reading of entrails and leave the mechanical speculation to… to leave it to people who weren't living with targets on their backs?

Well, wouldn't it? Why not leave it up to an inquisitive old hermit, say, to some old coot living off somewhere in a shack in the wilds of Alaska?

The door at the front of the workshop banged open, banged closed, and Desmond, one of the Iredales' junior magi, dropped down on his haunches next to Vlod. Two years younger than Vlod, Desmond was round, soft, and displayed no trace of the incipient warrior-sage he had imagined himself to be at the Academy.

In falling prey to such romantic nonsense, Desmond had not been alone. At one time or another, all of the students and no small number of the faculty had pitched headlong into that inspiring delusion. It was good to see that at least one of them hadn't drowned in it.

As for Vlod himself, in spite of his years of service to Edmund, and in spite of knowing better, he still secretly hoped that either the sage or the warrior would soon make his appearance. He had come close while studying with Master Yokashima, but whether the academy's martial-arts instructor had been honing the warrior or the sage had yet to be determined.

Vlod found the prospect of spending the rest of his life in a state of never-ending incipience decidedly depressing.

Desmond stretched his hands toward the firebox. "I need your help."

"I'm a little busy right now," Vlod said.

"Oh," Desmond said. "Time is in short supply, I guess."

"You guess correctly."

"Sorry," Desmond said. He looked around, gaping as though he were seeing the inside of Vlod's workshop for the first time. He wasn't. "What's cooking?" he asked.

Desmond knew damn good and well what was cooking.

"Water," Vlod said.

"Steam, eh? What are you planning to do with it?"

This line of stupid-sidekick banter had to be a joke, or an attempt at one.

"I'm not sure," Vlod said. "I could squirt it into cold soup and produce a delicious hot meal."

"Sounds great." Desmond rubbed his hands together. "How long before the weather warms up around here?"

Vlod raised his eyebrows. "It's January. This *is* warm."

"Oh, yeah, right. My piss didn't freeze on its way into the pot this morning; therefore, it's a warm day. Positively balmy."

"Welcome to the Pacific Coast."

Desmond looked at the boiler and at the water tank it was attached to. "You work fast. A month ago this was a stack of parts."

"It's not that complicated."

"Says you," Desmond said.

Vlod watched as his friend pointed at each of the parts, traced the connections, and counted the control lines. He muttered to himself the entire time.

Vlod had built his boiler to apply steam pressure to a water tank, using a steam-feed pipe. The tank had a water-outlet pipe.

The idea was for the pressurized steam to push the water out of the tank through the water-outlet pipe, which ran several score meters up the hill behind the workshop.

At the end of its journey, the water would flow out onto the ground.

"Okay," Desmond said. "Indulge me. What's the point?"

"I've already told you: to use steam to push water uphill."

"Uphill to where?"

"The castle's cisterns."

Desmond shook his head. "Royden's going to love you."

"He already does," Vlod said.

Vlod opened the firebox. Flames curled out of the opening. He tossed in three pieces of wood, and closed the door.

The venting steam had left lazy coils behind and had hardened into a noisy gush, very energetic. The sound was like a kettle nearing an angry boil.

Vlod's two workmen edged away from the boiler. Their foreman, a man named Eakan, did not.

Desmond asked, "Can it blow up?"

Vlod shook his head. "Safety valve."

"What's that?"

"It's a hole in the top of the water jacket with a plug in it. A stack of weights holds the plug in place."

"And...?"

"If the pressure rises too far, it will overpower the weights, lift the plug, and vent the water jacket."

"How'd you come by that idea?"

"Liquor stills."

Desmond glanced at the workmen. "I've seen them happier."

"I haven't tested the safety valve, not under a working load."

"The fuck you say!"

"Professional hazard." Vlod shrugged. "A distillery blew up last year. The safeties had rusted shut. They aren't supposed to, but they do. They're supposed to be maintained, but they never are." Vlod pointed at the top of the water jacket. "We finished ours last week. Brand new. Ought to work."

"You say the nicest things."

"Enough beating around the bush," Vlod said. "I'm busy. What do you want?"

"It'll keep."

Eakan asked, "How long now?"

"We're almost there," Vlod said, and stood up.

The fire in the firebox crackled, and the exhaust gasses *whooshed* up the smokestack. The boiling water inside the water jacket hissed like rain on a cobblestone street.

Eakan had helped with the boiler's construction. As far as Vlod could tell, he wasn't about to show any lack of confidence. His pride in his workmanship wouldn't allow it.

Vlod wished he shared his foreman's resolve.

They had steam, lots of it. But how strong was the boiler? What would happen when he closed the release valve? Would the plates and pipes hold, or would they rip apart?

"We're almost there," Desmond repeated. "Don't we have somewhere *else* we ought to be?"

"Yeah," Vlod said. He pointed across the room to a low wall made of logs and sandbags. "On the other side of that safety barricade."

The escaping steam was now making an intense, wet roar.

"It's time," Vlod said.

Eakan rolled his eyes. The gesture said, "Damn right, it's time!" better than any words could have. With a wave of his hand, he dismissed the two laborers. They hurried out the front door.

Vlod, Desmond, and Eakan crouched behind the barricade.

Vlod called, "Everybody clear?"

No answer.

Eakan said, "They're gone."

An oily sweat broke out on Vlod's hands.

"Okay," he said. "Ready?"

"Yes, sir," Eakan said. "Ready."

Desmond nodded.

Red, green, and blue ropes led from the top of the device to cleats mounted behind the barricade. Vlod pulled the green rope, opening the valve that would channel the steam into the water tank once he closed the release valve.

Vlod poked his head over the barricade. There was no change in the boiler's outward appearance and no change in the sound it was making. He hadn't expected any, but it was prudent to check.

He pulled the red rope, closing the release valve. The sound of the escaping steam choked off.

Vlod ducked down.

He had to admit that he felt a lot safer with a stack of logs positioned between his head and his boiler.

Vlod could only guess at the specifics of what happened next.

The pressure inside the boiler shot up. The steam shoved its way through the steam-feed pipe and into the water tank.

This part of the process made a nasty metallic gurgle.

Almost at once, Vlod heard the water in the tank begin its trip up the hill.

"It works!" Eakan said.

"Maybe," Vlod said.

He cautiously looked over the top of the logs.

With a sudden, ear-splitting shriek, steam erupted from a joint in the steam-feed pipe. An instant later, a pinpoint geyser of boiling water burst from the side of the water jacket.

"Too much pressure," Eakan said.

"The safety ought to have popped," Vlod said. "Why in hell isn't it popping?"

"No idea," Eakan said.

"The plates aren't going hold," Vlod said, and crouched back down. "They can't. Too fucking thin."

"Shitty iron," Eakan said. "No better than rotten shingles."

Vlod pulled the blue rope.

He'd rigged the blue rope to open the release valve—red to close, blue to open. Nice idea, foolproof in its own way, but the blue rope didn't budge, and the release valve didn't open. Vlod pulled again, harder this time, but the valve still did not open.

"The valve's jammed," Eakan said.

Desmond's face turned the color of a boiled chicken. "Why'd it do *that*?"

"We'll have to take it apart to find out," Eakan said.

Vlod's heart rate jumped. He could feel it pounding in his ears, across the front of his face.

Never mind the release valve. Why hadn't the safety valve blown? It was a perfectly simple mechanism. And when it came to simple, why hadn't the water tank emptied? That would have allowed the pressure to vent through the steam-feed pipe, through the water tank, through the water-outlet pipe, and out into the open air.

What had gone wrong?

Pipes, boiler plates, release value, and safety valve: every one of them was utterly simple and each of them had failed.

Why?

Vlod damned his stupidity, his willingness to hurry, his negligence in cutting corners. He ought to have known his boiler wouldn't withstand that much pressure.

But how much was that? He had devised no reliable way to determine how much pressure he was creating in the water jacket. Moreover, he could only guess at how strong the plates were, how much pressure they could contain.

He'd been working blind.

He had built up the pressure too rapidly, and he had directed it into the water tank too suddenly. Rather than a manageable fault, he had created a full-blown failure.

He ought to have started with a low fire, and he ought to have closed the release valve in stages. Earlier on, he ought to have tested and retested each part separately, before assembling them into a boiler. Then, with the boiler in hand, he ought to have thoroughly tested it before connecting it to the water tank, which he only now fully realized was itself a pressure vessel.

He ought to have insisted on first-class plate, rather than settling for used plate and scrap. He'd tried to compensate by using thicker pieces of metal, but shit still stinks no matter how high you pile it.

Worst of all, he'd allowed himself to be fooled by the apparent simplicity of his contraption. Nothing about steam was simple.

A rivet shot from near the top of the boiler and *thwacked!* into a support post, cartwheeling away. The rivet had pulverized a patch of wood the size of a man's palm.

"Shouldn't we run for it?" Desmond asked.

"Not yet," Vlod said. He knocked on the barrier. "We're safe enough. It might not blow."

"Teach you that in 'magusing' school, did they?" Eakan asked. He grabbed a sledgehammer and vaulted over the logs.

A sound like a sword snapping, but incredibly louder, burst through the workshop. A deafening shriek followed, and live steam sprayed into the workshop.

It was none of Eakan's doing. There hadn't been time.

"The steam pipe's burst!" Vlod yelled, and leapt over the barrier. "Eakan, get down! Get down!"

"Come back here!" Desmond yelled.

Steam blanketed the boiler, while water shot toward the ceiling from the water jacket and flowed across the floor.

Eakan, a dark outline against the chaos, his sledgehammer raised to strike the release valve, approached the boiler.

Vlod ran forward.

Too late!

A deafening explosion smashed through the workshop. It ballooned the walls out, shattered the windows, and slammed Vlod back into the crude log barricade.

Six

The morning ground on toward the lunch hour, and Ulricka ground on toward the bottom of her paperwork. That hoped-for bottom was an illusion, one she confronted daily.

Thora had warned her about it. The province and its cathedral ran on paper. One would have thought that it was faith and prayer, but, no, it was paper.

Shabnan brought in a cloth-covered tray and shooed the clerks from Ulricka's office. She used one of her feet to nudge the door closed.

"I can't take a break now," Ulricka said, making an effort not to whine.

Shabnan set the tray on a table. "Nonsense. You have plenty of time."

"No, I don't." She put down her pen. "Oh, very well. What's on the menu?"

Shabnan pulled away the cover. Revealed were two cups of coffee and two plates of sugar-laden rolls. "Caffeine and carbohydrates."

Ulricka sipped her coffee. "Thank you," she said, and bit into a roll.

"I'm curious," Shabnan said. "Why the special treatment for Jinhai?"

Suddenly Ulricka's coffee turned bitter. "For a traitor, you mean?"

"Yes."

"I don't have any idea," Ulricka said.

That wasn't a thoroughgoing lie. Nearer to the truth was the fact that she'd done it because Jinhai and Thora had been close, and Thora would have wanted Ulricka to secure his place among the Gods and the Generations.

Ulricka had had other motives as well. Generosity? Mercy? An attempt to avoid a scandal?

Those fit, but they fell short.

"Not even a shred of an idea?" Shabnan asked.

Ulricka took a long swallow of coffee. "Let's say I can't see any reason why he shouldn't have to suffer through Eternity just like the rest of us."

Shabnan smiled. "Death is too good for him?"

"Not death, but annihilation," Ulricka corrected. "Everlasting, total annihilation."

"*Annihilation* is too good for him. I like the sound of that. Annihilation *is* too good for him."

"Annihilation is too good for most of us," Ulricka said, and prayed for a swift return to her paperwork.

The afternoon light filtered in through the windows high in the north-facing wall of the palace's indoor archery range.

The air was cold and still. The silence was complete.

Ulricka checked her stance.

She raised her hunting bow, the one she used to hunt elk, and drew the arrow back. She aimed, let out half her breath, steadied, and loosed.

As the arrow left her bow, the shot *felt* perfect.

The arrow streaked downrange, its arc shallow, the aim accurate.

Ulricka's will rode the arrow, guiding it, persuading it to strike home.

Thunk!

No luck.

The arrow pierced the target a hand's width to the left and two above the bull's eye.

Damn!

It wasn't her first stray.

She wanted to blame the arrows—bent shafts, bad fletching, poorly seated nocks—but the truth was that she was out of practice. She had slacked off. She had relied on deep muscle memory, but over the long haul, only practice would do.

If nothing else, her hunt for Jinhai had taught her that.

She missed both her first and second shots, and both had hit to the left. It had been unconscionably bad practice.

From the moment of her consecration, her hunts had become less and less frequent. They had devolved into rare treats, and archery practice had taken on the color of a self-indulgent luxury.

Ulricka shook off her asinine self-pity.

She nocked the tenth and last arrow of her current group. She drew, aimed, and loosed.

Thunk!

This time the shot was better, but it was still no prize.

She pitied any deer unlucky enough to be her target.

The group, the third of her current session, was abominable. The shots were scattered in a rotund, irregular pattern; although, it was vaguely elliptical, if she squinted. Seven of her shots had hit to the left, while two had gone high and to the right. The last had hit on the centerline but low.

She took solace in the fact that she had the range to herself. No one but the attendant was present to witness the spectacle.

Ulricka stood away from the shooting stand, and the attendant trotted forward to deal with the target.

Ulricka sat down on one of the benches that extended across the back of the range. She cradled her bow across her lap.

The door opened and Yingpei entered.

A sexual thrill tingled through her, jangling her thoughts.

Yingpei was young and handsome, blond and lean, well-muscled, with a dancer's legs.

She'd had him assigned to her personal escort several weeks ago, and so far, she hadn't regretted it.

She had yet to persuade him to seduce her, but that would come in time.

Her current baby wasn't showing yet, but she felt fat and unattractive. After the baby was born, however—after she had recovered her figure and felt desirable again—his seduction of her would be inevitable.

Yingpei ushered in a lieutenant of the Cathedral guard. She was old for her rank. Had she been a late enlistee? Had she come up through the ranks? She was older than Ulricka, but not by much, two or three years at most.

Unfortunately, a ruminant stupidity distorted the lieutenant's features. Making matters worse, much worse, she had afflicted herself with the slack pudginess that adolescent girls so often acquire and that so many women never bother to throw off.

In five or ten years, she'd be out of the military, slovenly and obese.

Regrettably, then as now, she would have no more control over her character than she would have over her body.

To the range attendant, Ulricka called, "Please finish that later."

The man bowed and hurried out though a side exit.

Ulricka turned to the lieutenant. "Yes, what is it?"

"Your Beatitude, Colonel Chiharu sends her devotion," the woman-child piped.

She actually *piped*. Like a teenager!

"May the Goddess bless Colonel Chiharu," Ulricka said.

"Searches of the river and of the shoreline have failed to locate Jinhai's handlers. A thorough investigation has established that the traitor Jinhai—"

"No one is to call him that," Ulricka said.

"I apologize, Your Beatitude."

"No one. Ever. Is that understood?"

"Yes, Your Beatitude."

In the periphery of her vision, Ulricka caught the flash of Yingpei's smirk and his instant suppression of it.

To the lieutenant, Ulricka said, "Continue."

After a brief dither, the child said, as though repeating a memorized speech, "A thorough investigation has established that, uh, Jinhai, the deceased protopriest and archthurifer, managed to convey a message *before* the Guard attempted to arrest him."

What, Ulricka wondered, had Jinhai reported and how accurately had he reported it?

Apart from the draft treaties, which she had intercepted, he had had nothing to report but summaries and appearances. Ulricka had meticulously crafted both for Narmer's benefit, but could anyone outside her inner circle penetrate her ruse? Would they be able to discern her purpose through that blizzard of innuendo and qualification?

Ulricka asked, "Has Colonel Chiharu found copies of his reports?"

"No, Your Beatitude, but we've found the remains of his codebooks and several fragments of a draft. We can't be certain of what."

"Anything else?"

"We've traced his movements, Your Beatitude. We have a witness who saw him pass an envelope to one of the couriers in the rectory office, who in turn passed it to an operative named Farran, and—"

"Why wasn't Farran arrested on the spot?"

"The watchers were hoping to follow him, but he evaded them."

Why wasn't Ulricka the least bit surprised? "Very well," she said.

Amateurs!

Ulricka, Shabnan, and Chiharu had spoken only of Jinhai's "handlers," but Ulricka was convinced that Jinhai's handler was none other than Ziellottes.

Ziellottes was the basin's premier digger of data, swapper of secrets, and, as it was often said, doer of deeds.

Ziellottes!

What she wouldn't give to have a score of people like Ziellottes on her staff.

Dream on!

He was one of a kind, and he was not on the market.

She sighed.

Perhaps one day he'd discover an inner vein of piety that he had hitherto not suspected.

Why not?

It worked the other way around often enough.

She sighed again.

When it came to Jinhai, what had happened was plain enough.

Only two questions remained. First, how would Ziellottes' employer interpret Jinhai's final report?

Incidentally, how many reports had Jinhai sent, and over what period of time had he sent them?

Ulricka had no reason to believe that he hadn't sent dozens and every reason to assume that he had.

Second, who employed Ziellottes? Or was Ziellottes his own man, ferreting out here and selling there, serving his own interests rather than the interests of any particular clan or group of clans.

The answer to that question was vital. It could be—

But she was running ahead of herself.

"Did Jinhai deliberately leave those papers behind?" Ulricka asked. "What does Colonel Chiharu think?"

The lieutenant grimaced. "I have no idea. She didn't say anything about them to me, apart from telling me—"

"Where were they?"

"They were in his stove, Your Beatitude, smoldering, the way paper does. He must have left in a rush."

Jinhai may have moved swiftly from time to time, but he had never rushed. Chiharu's people must have tipped their hands, or perhaps Jinhai had spotted them. And, in all honesty, Jinhai could have left those remains behind in order to plant a false trail.

Again, Ulricka reined herself in. She was flying off in all directions at once. She was working herself into a lather, like an overheated horse.

She needed facts: deliberate, solid, cold facts. She did not need emotions, hopes, fears, or what-ifs.

"Thank you, Lieutenant," Ulricka said. "My complements to Colonel Chiharu. She is to make a full report to me by midday tomorrow, in person. She is to report orally. She is to write nothing down."

"Yes, Your Beatitude," the child said.

"Dismissed."

When the child had gone, Ulricka slumped against the bench's backrest. "Is Harakhty on the grounds?"

"No, Your Beatitude," Yingpei said. "Narmer's envoy has gone hunting."

"Again? The man's obsessed."

"Shall I send for him?"

Ulricka weighed her options. "No, on second thought, let's leave things as they are for a while longer.

SEVEN

Steam boiled into the January air gusting in through the broken workshop windows. The cold condensed the steam, and Vlod could feel the gritty droplets on his neck and face.

Lengths of pipe jutted grotesquely from the remains of the boiler, and jagged pieces of metal lay scattered across the floor.

The explosion had destroyed the flue, and smoke was boiling up into the rafters.

Here and there, several fires had started, and despite the quantity of water released, the boiler fire continued to burn in the remains of the firebox. It looked like a campfire built in the jaws of a bear trap.

Vlod picked his way forward.

A heavy-footed scrabbling came from behind the barricade.

"Are you all right?" Desmond asked.

"I'm fine," Vlod said, and looked around for Eakan. Where had his foreman ended up?

"Your voice is muzzy. Are you sure you're all right? Any sign of concussion?"

"No. Scalded here and there, but I'm fine," Vlod said.

Vlod spotted Eakan. He was halfway across the floor, on the opposite side from the door.

"I'll see to Eakan," Vlod said. "You tell the workmen to get the fires out!"

Desmond nodded and ran to the door, which was hanging on its hinges.

Eakan was on his back and unconscious. His face was scalded and lacerated, but he hadn't let go of the sledgehammer. Blisters had come up on his forehead and around his mouth, and his lips looked as though he'd been hit in the face with a red-hot frying pan.

Those injuries were bad enough, but there was more.

The real problem was the iron splinter protruding from the base of Eakan's his neck. The splinter was the size of a man's thumb, but it was covered with snags that looked like the barbs on a fishhook.

Blood flowed out around the splinter. It flowed. It didn't spurt or pulse. It wasn't arterial blood, then.

Thank the Gods and the Generations for that!

It meant that Eakan might live long enough to be treated.

"Bring a stretcher!" Vlod shouted, toward the door, which was standing open.

He ripped a strip of fabric from his shirt and pressed it carefully around the wound.

Eakan groaned.

"Planks," Vlod yelled. "Anything we can use to move him!"

"On the way!" one of the workmen answered.

Eakan came around and opened his eyes. "Shitty iron."

Vlod pressed on the cloth. The flow lessened.

"Too much heat," Vlod said.

"We fucked up."

"No, I'm the one who fucked up," Vlod said.

"No argument from me, your magus-ship," Eakan said, and passed out.

They took Eakan to the port infirmary. It was the nearest one.

The medics there were good with trauma cases, in part because they had plenty of practice. Stevedores, shipwrights, riggers, and carpenters smashed fingers, sprained ankles, broke bones, and burned hands at a mind-numbing rate.

After treating Eakan, the medic reported that the burns and gashes were painful but not deep. The splinter had come out with a minimum of fuss and nonsense.

A degree of infection and scarring were inevitable, but if he kept his bandages clean, he would avoid the worst of both.

"What about his collarbone?" Vlod asked.

"The splinter grazed it in a minor sort of way," the medic said. "It'll hurt like hell for a few days, but it ought to heal acceptably."

The medic was a tall, spare man with gray hair. The ring and little fingers were missing from his left hand. The stumps were white with age.

"What about his upper-body mobility?" Vlod asked.

"The muscles ought to heal as good as new." The medic added, "He ought to be able to return to work in four or five days."

That much inactivity would kill Eakan long before any infection ever did. "I don't care about that. We aren't working on anything that won't wait."

"Nothing strenuous for a few weeks."

"You're sure he'll be all right?"

The man grinned. "I learned my trade in the army, sir. Twenty years."

Vlod felt about a centimeter high. "Field medic?"

"Yes, sir. I've seen these sorts of wounds countless times." He held up his left hand. "Interesting scars are always welcome. They build character."

One of the workshop laborers met Vlod and Desmond outside the infirmary. Ash blackened the laborer's face.

"The fires are out, sir," he said.

"Good. Thanks," Vlod said.

"Sir? What about Eakan?"

After Vlod had answered the man's questions about the foreman, the man asked, "What's next?"

"Lock up. Come back tomorrow."

"Tomorrow it is," he said, and walked off.

A cold wind blew down the street. With the mouth of the Columbia River a scant twenty-three kilometers downstream from Fort George, the Iredale capital, the air was sharp with the tang of salt and nearby tide flats.

Vlod walked to the west. East would have taken him back toward the workshop. Out of a longstanding, field-born habit, he rested his left hand on the pommel of his sword. It wasn't a field weapon, but scaled for self-defense and ease of carry.

Desmond fell in beside him. "Where to?"

"No idea."

Desmond pulled the hood of his cloak over his head. "Damn cold for a hike."

"You don't have to come."

"Says you."

The street was neither empty nor crowded. People hurried from shop to shop. Some carried bundles and bags. Others went empty-handed. The raw weather had reddened their faces, and the drizzle had soaked their hats, capes, and boots. Their hands looked like the shells of boiled crabs.

Up on the hill above the flat, the cloud cover, low and gray, brooded over Olney Castle.

It was another glorious January, Vlod thought. Would the weather never clear? No, not for months yet, and then only for a day or two at a time, a week at most.

"You're lucky that splinter didn't slit his throat," Desmond said.

Vlod made an effort to forget the guttural whir those razor-sharp pieces had made as they'd spun through the air.

"We were both lucky," Vlod said, and sank into what he hoped Desmond would take for a companionable silence.

He wished he could say the same for his own thoughts. They were anything but companionable.

Pushing water uphill to the castle's cisterns was a fairy story. The real prize was steam-driven machinery.

True, the clan needed a better way to pump large volumes of water from one place to another—for drinking, bathing, cooking, fighting fires, washing clothes, and operating dry docks.

The clan also needed steam to propel its ships, to power its mills and yards, and to move its freight.

However, steam engines were the great heresy. It was steam that had powered the industrial revolution, and it was the industrial revolution that had led to the chaos and deprivation the Goddess had sent the Great Winter to expunge from Her creation.

Nevertheless, windmills and waterwheels were becoming inadequate. There weren't enough natural waterfalls to go around, dams were next to impossible to have approved, and the wind was patently unreliable.

Whenever the wind died away or blew too hard, whenever the streams ran dry or flooded, the lack of motive power threw whole crews out of work.

Steam.

As it had been countless centuries before, steam was the answer.

After Vlod had learned how to move large volumes of water at will and after he had solved scores of additional riddles, he could move on to building steam-operated pistons. Those pistols would be able to turn cranks and operate levers. He would then achieve the mechanical basis upon which to build machines, machines to perform the tasks now done by wind, water, animals, and people.

Power.

The clan's wellbeing, its very security, hinged on its access to motive power.

The tragedy was that the current lack of power was self-imposed. Rather, it was imposed by the Engineer's Guild and a slew of additional guilds and boards; by the Mother Metropolitan of the Inland Empire and the Holy Oregon; by her sister mothers metropolitan, who governed the continent's other provinces; and, at the very top of the hierarchy, by the Matriarch of All North America, the Holy Mother herself, Mayumi.

The use of animals and people to turn cranks, to spin saws, and to work pump handles was absurd. Since when did the Harmony require that people lead stunted lives of endless labor? Since when did the Harmony require the production of iron and steel that burst at the first application of pressure?

"You're glaring," Desmond said. His rotund face was lined with concern.

Since *never*!

"Sorry," Vlod said.

Desmond shook his head. "Do you intend to give it another try?"

"Yes!"

"My sympathies to the witless bastard who tries to stop you."

They skirted a deep puddle and hugged the buildings.

The drizzle thickened.

Vlod dodged into a doorway alcove and leaned against the wall.

The worst of the shower would pass soon enough.

"You look about done in," Desmond said. "Maybe we ought to find a place to sit down."

"It had to have been the metal," Vlod said. "We must have used the wrong type or the wrong gauge. The quality was subpar, but I thought I'd compensated for that."

"Shaping fatigues metal," Desmond said.

"True."

As suddenly as it had hardened, the rain let up.

They walked on.

In this section of Fort George, the shops clustered together like overgrown bushes, and the odors of horse dung, fish offal, boiled crab, and cooking grease hung between the structures.

Desmond said, "I hear you've applied to have your father's name added to the *Dirge*?"

Vlod missed a step but recovered.

Edmund was aware of the appeal, and the people at the Iredale manor henge, which had the honor of also being the châtellenie's principal henge, were aware of it. But how had Desmond heard about it?

"From whom?" Vlod asked.

"It's a small river."

"Too small."

"The rehabilitation of a heretic. That's heady stuff, that is." He let out a low whistle. "I'll say one thing for you: you've got balls. What do you think your chances are?"

"Nil, but it's worth a try."

"Let's hope, but you're attracting attention to yourself."

"One of the hazards."

Desmond shook his head. "Attention lights fires, my friend."

"I'll piss on them," Vlod said, doing his best to answer in kind.

Desmond paused in front of a tavern called The Undertow's Revenge. It had black, red, and gold awnings. The sign over the door showed a hand clutching up through a breaking wave.

"Speaking of piss, I could use a drink," Desmond said. "How's this place?"

"The owner distills his own brandy."

"Tell me, was it from this worthy proprietor that you learned your vast storehouse of boiler lore?"

Vlod felt his face burn.

"I guessed as much," Desmond said.

EIGHT

A log fire crackled in the tavern's fireplace. The chimney smoked, not badly, but enough to mute the odors of beer, spilled food, and the backroom distillery.

Vlod and Desmond sat at a table in the corner farthest from the door, which put them comfortably near the fireplace. Thanks to the rain and the late-afternoon lull, the tavern had an uninhabited feel, and thanks to the large tables and comfortable chairs, Desmond and Vlod were able to sit without their swords getting in the way.

Perhaps they were no longer incipient warriors. Perhaps they had become warriors without realizing it. For Vlod, his sword did not feel like an affectation; rather, it felt like a part of him. And were Wolfram ever to see him without it, bolts of lightning would rain down from the heavens and the very jaws of hell would rise up to devour him.

The ceilings were high and the floor was low, a good meter below street level. Rusty handsaws, ancient hammers with cracked plastic handles, glass jars, wooden oars, crab pots, nets, and an assortment of nautical miscellany decorated the walls.

The tavern's owner had pulled the items from the river, combed them from the beaches, or dug them out of several ancient garbage dumps.

An ancient headstone held pride of place above the mantelpiece. The stone was black with white flecks and gold lettering where the leaf had survived. The deep-chiseled message read:

Steadfast Father
Karl Raphael Orrfeldt
January 3, 1965 to June 18, 2050

Loving Mother
Flora Christina Orrfeldt
March 3, 1968 to July 28, 2060

Forever in Our Hearts!

Vlod assumed that the owners of those *Hearts* had been the ones to order the outline drawings of a sailboat, a kite, a cottage, and a pair of bicycles engraved into the headstone's corners.

Desmond pointed at the stone. "Whoever owns this place is a maudlin bastard."

"Not maudlin, only interested in the past," Vlod said.

A man arrived at their table. He was tall and skeletally thin. He wore an apron around his waist and bore a loaded tray. His smile carried a sarcastic note.

The man said, "The wonders of distillation and the dangers of the past: that's me in a nutshell." Both the smile and the sarcasm intensified. "My apologies, O noble magi. I have a big mouth and the ears to match."

Vlod said, "Gluth, meet Desmond. Desmond, meet Gluth. Gluth owns, runs, and mucks out this establishment."

Gluth made a good-natured joke of a bow, and Desmond responded with one of his own.

Gluth turned to Vlod. "Your usual order, but for two." Gluth transferred the brandies, the cups of coffee, and a pot of cream to the table.

Desmond said, "I'm told you taught my friend everything he knows about boilers."

"I tried, but I hear he was doping off in class." To Vlod, Gluth added, "Naughty, naughty. Anyone killed?"

"A few cuts and bruises," Vlod said.

"The news has wings," Desmond said.

Vlod said, "Around here it travels at—"

Desmond cut him off with a glance toward the doorway.

Vlod turned and looked. A magus stood there. It was Royden. He was of medium height, close to middle age, with shoulder-length brown hair. His robes were of the flowing, semiformal variety.

Vlod, by way of contrast, was in his work clothes. They were frayed and grimy and stained.

"Ah, the Iredales' engineer," Gluth said.

"Please, he's the *supervising* engineer," Vlod said. He sipped his coffee. "Notice the commendable speed of his arrival, the steely gaze, the oversize brain—"

"The gigantic ego," Desmond said.

"He is an example to us all."

Royden waved to them, less in greeting than in command for them to stay where they were.

"How'd he find us?" Desmond asked. "Spies?"

"Brute force. He traced our route away from the infirmary and checked every tavern and shop until he found us."

"Lucky guess, you mean," Desmond said.

To Vlod, Gluth said, "I like the way your colleague thinks."

"That makes one of us," Vlod said.

"Who says I can think?" Desmond asked.

Royden pulled a chair over and sat down. To Gluth, he said, "Five brandies. I'll drink one, and my friends here will each have two."

"Why would we be doing that?" Vlod asked.

"Because you're going to want them."

"A celebration, then."

"Not as such," Royden said. To Gluth, he added, "We'll have those brandies now, if you don't mind."

"Yes, sir, five brandies," Gluth said, and hurried away.

Vlod winced at the edge of fear in Gluth's voice. A magus, any magus, ought not to have that effect on people.

"Desmond had nothing to do with the boiler," Vlod said.

"Call it a gratuity, then," Royden said.

Neither Vlod nor Desmond laughed.

To Desmond, Royden said, "As I remember it, you're Aerian's new assistant, aren't you?"

Vlod felt his stomach tighten in an emotion akin to loathing.

Royden had to be perfectly well aware of who Desmond was. So why was the clan's supervising engineer throwing his weight around?

It was a good question, but since when did a member of one of the magi's four major guilds—engineers, geneticists, augurs, and agriculturalists—need a reason to act like an arrogant fool?

"That right," Desmond said. "I'm his new clean-and-polish man."

Royden smiled happily. "Oh, yes, I remember now. You've registered your arrival, haven't you?"

"When I arrived."

"Remind me, when was that?"

Royden's face had the innocence of leaves sprinkled across a deadfall.

The muscles in Desmond's neck tightened. It was a danger signal Vlod remembered from their days at the Academy of Archmagus Basil the Anchorite and Wonderworker. Flabby or not, Desmond was a skilled brawler, and Royden, supervising engineer or not, would do well to cherish his teeth.

"Hasn't the chapter secretary shown you my form?" Desmond asked.

"How long ago did you register?"

"Check the form."

"How long?"

This really was too much. Vlod set down his coffee. "I don't mean to lecture, but Aerian and I are attached directly to Edmund's staff. Desmond works for Aerian. Therefore, it was enough for him to report for work. He signed in at the chapter hall as a courtesy to the chapter."

"Aerian's work falls under my supervision."

"No, in point of fact, it does not. Their final product may, when and if a license to implement is required, but not the intermediate work product and *never* the men themselves. *We* work for Edmund. We are under *his* protection."

"I'll trade you lecture for lecture. You, Aerian, and Desmond *report* directly to Edmund as a *courtesy* extended to him by the College of Magi of the Inland Empire and the Holy Oregon. *The magi—*"

"Courtesy?" Vlod asked. "I'd like to see the college refuse it."

"*The magi* serve *the clans but are not of the clans.*"

"*A man cannot serve two masters,*" Vlod said.

The aphorism was a relic of one of the archaic patriarchal religions. As such, it was bound to touch one of Royden's many nerves.

It did.

Royden's face froze like a splash of molten lead hitting a cold floor.

Gluth appeared with the five brandies. He set them on the table and collected from Royden.

To Vlod, Royden said, "The odds are, you're going end up on a stake, just as your father did."

Vlod shifted his right hand from his coffee mug to the hilt of his sword.

"Have a care," Vlod said.

Desmond slipped his right hand onto the hilt of his own sword.

"What are you after?" Desmond asked Royden. "Why disturb the afternoon?"

Royden leaned back in his chair, and placed his hands in plain view. "I'm here to talk to Vlod."

"Then let's talk. Why are Desmond and I going to need the extra brandies?" Vlod asked.

Royden exposed his teeth. Only a fool would have mistaken it for a smile. "You're building a steam engine. People—"

"No, I'm attempting to push water up a hill."

"Then why aren't you using one of the approved pump designs?"

"I'm developing a new technique. If it works, I'll apply for an implementation license. Until then, it's none of your business what I'm doing."

As smoothly as ever, Royden said, "People have begun to worry."

"Which people?" Vlod asked.

"I could issue an order requiring you to cease work."

"You could try to enforce it, too," Vlod said.

The show of teeth made a second appearance. "You like to play on the edge, don't you?"

"Not particularly, but let's pretend that I do. What do you imagine would happen if I did build a rudimentary steam engine?"

"There's no such thing as a rudimentary steam engine," Royden said. "Pregnant is pregnant, heresy is heresy, and a steam engine is a steam engine."

Ignoring that line of reasoning, Vlod said, "Would the sun fall from the sky? I doubt it. The ancients had steam engines, and the sun continues to shine."

"They also had self-propelled wagons, steel that didn't rust, mechanical birds, and machines that played chess. And every one of them, including the steam engines, violated the Harmony."

"Where's your proof?"

"You sound like a heretic."

"Humor me. Maybe we can burn at the stake side by side."

The muscles along Royden's jaw flexed. "The fact that they don't exist in this age proves that they violated the Harmony." Royden finished his brandy and stood. "Give it up, Vlod. The Goddess consigned steam engines to oblivion. For all our sakes, have the intelligence to leave them there."

And then he was gone.

NINE

"Dramatic bastard," Desmond said.

"Entrances and exits, he loves making them."

"Must keep his women happy."

"Not a chance. I know for a fact he hangs doors to earn pocket money."

"What?" Desmond asked, befuddled.

"Doors? Entrances? Exits?"

The scowl on Desmond's face gave way to a grin. "Oh, I get it. It's another one of your idiotic puns."

"I do adore them," Vlod admitted.

Desmond sipped his first brandy. "I wonder if Royden has any idea how close he came."

"Close to what?"

"The next world."

"Never," Vlod said. "He's as safe as a babe in arms."

"The last time I saw that look on your face, someone died."

"I am a changed man."

Vlod raised his half-empty glass in a toast. "Academy days."

"You graduated four years ago, not four decades ago," Desmond said, but he picked up his glass.

They emptied them in one go.

Desmond sipped from the second glass. "You'd better not piss him off, though."

"He's a pipsqueak."

"All the same, you'd—"

Gluth joined them. He sat in the chair Royden had vacated.

Vlod pushed a brandy over to Gluth.

"Thanks," Gluth said. "Can he close down my distillery on his own say-so? The engineers have rules, don't they?"

"Why would he want to do that?" Vlod asked.

"I hate his guts and he knows it."

"Personalities don't enter into it."

"Maybe," Gluth said, "but I've heard stories."

Everyone had heard stories, but most of them were unbelievable. The magi could be as corrupt as anyone else could, but as Gluth had said, they had rules.

"Rumors," Vlod said.

"Yeah? Well, here's one for you. Rumor has it that a couple of years ago, a whiskey distillery up toward the cathedral sells a few more barrels of whiskey than it was licensed to. A little while later, along comes the local clan's supervising engineer. He takes a look around and asks the owner for a pile of money."

"As in extortion?" Desmond asked.

"He wasn't collecting for charity," Gluth said. "The owner refuses to pay, and in retaliation the engineer closes him down and charges him with violating the Harmony. A tribunal of engineers convicts him, and his chieftain hangs him. The chieftain then confiscates the dead guy's property, including his distillery, and auctions it off to none other than the supervising engineer. The engineer then dutifully kicks back a healthy portion of it to the chieftain."

"You're joking," Vlod said. He was certain he would have heard about a crime so egregious, and he hadn't. The story had to be a rumor, a tall tale to frighten the credulous.

But then Vlod remembered what they'd done to his father. They'd brought anonymous charges. They'd admitted hearsay and innuendo as evidence. They'd ignored established court procedures.

No one had had the courage to halt the farce.

"Would I joke about good booze?" Gluth asked.

"You must have gotten a garbled version," Vlod said. His father had to have been an exception, a once-in-a-century paroxysm.

"Maybe," Gluth said.

"What happened to the still?" Desmond asked.

"The bastard smashed it."

"That doesn't make any sense."

"It does if you're the supervising engineer's cousin and you can't make a go of your distillery," Gluth said. "Thinning the herd, you see? If you can't beat 'em face to face, stab 'em in the back."

It was the other shoe.

"What about the barrels set aside for aging?" Desmond asked. "Those ought to be coming onto the market, year by year. You ought to have seen them by now."

"I'd be a rich man if I had. My customers thought it was the next best thing to Spieden Blue."

At this mention of Spieden Blue, Desmond's eyes lost their focus. He seemed to have been transported to another world.

To Gluth, Vlod said, "You'll have to forgive him. At the Academy he was a famous drinker."

"Fine by me. My best customers are famous drinkers."

Recovering himself, Desmond asked, "This whiskey, what was it called?"

"Van Horn Butte Reserve," Gluth said.

"Came in a green bottle, like wine?" Desmond said.

"That it did," Gluth said. "Very unique for a whiskey."

"As I remember, it was a hell of a lot better than rotgut."

"It was, too," Gluth said. "Had of way of sneaking up on people."

Vlod slid the untouched brandies toward Gluth. "Pass those around, would you? And bring us a fresh pot of coffee."

Gluth left their table, and Vlod finished his brandy.

The coffee arrived.

The tide of customers ebbed and flowed. Gluth greeted and bade farewell. Pots and dishes clanged and banged. The aromas of bean soup, baking bread, and frying onions trailed from the kitchen.

"What do you think?" Vlod asked. "Is Royden out to shut him down?"

"Can't say, but the guy who made Van Horn Butte *was* hanged two years ago."

"What about the presiding engineer and his cousin?"

"What about them? It may be a small river, but it's big enough to hide whatever the right people want to keep hidden."

By common, unspoken consent, Vlod and Desmond let the subject drop.

They ordered dinner.

While they were waiting, guzzling enough coffee to dispel the lingering brandy fumes, Desmond said, "How'd you like a chance to burn at the stake? I'm talking about a real, solid chance."

TEN

Hours ago, the afternoon had darkened into night, but the weather was as cold and windy as it had been all the day. The one bright spot was that it had quit raining.

The on-again-off-again drizzle didn't count.

Driftwood ash and beach sand gritted between Vlod's teeth. He, Desmond, and Aerian, the same Aerian who'd been his roommate at the academy, had built a windbreak and a fire up in the dry sand, against the piles of driftwood to the south of the South Jetty. The older logs and stumps were white with age.

Aerian reminded Vlod of a wolfhound. His hair stood away from his scalp, rather than laying flat against it. Topping off the canine impression, Aerian had a long, thin face, a thin, prominent nose, and long, very white teeth. He tended to snap his head toward whatever he wanted to look at, as though he had suddenly scented an animal worth catching and devouring.

The three of them ate, drank, and reminisced about the Academy of Archmagus Basil the Anchorite and Wonderworker. They complained about their current jobs, and they grumbled about the way the clan's men-at-arms, the bar pilots, and the shipmasters invariably wound up with the prettiest women and the most money. Magi, especially junior magi, stood pretty far down on the social ladder.

They rated above dung-cart cleaners but not by very much. They ranked noticeably below slave breakers.

But those were, Desmond pointed out, comparatively useful and honest occupations. "We're nothing but whores."

Aerian passed the bottle of Gluth's brandy they were sharing. "Why are we whores?"

"Who says whores aren't honest and useful?" Vlod asked.

He sipped from the bottle and passed it to Desmond.

"We're whores because we'll come across for anybody who pays us," Desmond said. "Give us our toys and we'll hand over the results. What are they? What'll they do on down the road? Who cares? We'll deliver them!"

"Don't forget the money," Aerian said. "Toys and money."

"By the bagful," Desmond said, his sarcasm plainer than plain.

The truth was that the average magus considered himself wealthy if he owned the boots on his feet and the sword on his hip. More often than not, his sword was a graduation gift from his sponsoring chieftain.

"You make us sound like spoiled brats," Vlod said.

"We *are* an infantile bunch," Desmond said. "We ought to grow up and follow productive careers."

"You're hogging the bottle," Vlod said, and held out his hand. "Like what? Which productive careers?"

The bottle went to Aerian.

"Aren't all careers productive?" Aerian asked.

"I don't know which," Desmond said. "How about farming? That's productive. Most of the time, anyway. There's shipping. We could go into the merchant marine."

"I'm partial to dry land," Aerian said.

"How about the military, then?" Desmond asked.

"Would you want to be a soldier?" Aerian asked.

The bottle was making the appropriate rounds, but the level wasn't dropping very fast. They weren't so much drinking as sipping.

"I nearly was," Desmond said. "A soldier, that is. Not sure why it didn't work out. Funny, but I've never been sorry I went to the academy instead."

Vlod decided that Aerian and Desmond were trying to get him slightly drunk—so he'd be in a more receptive mood—while they were staying as sober as possible in order to control the conversation.

At the same time, Vlod was barely sipping so he could keep his wits about him. Whatever these two had in mind, it was bound to lead to a stake-and-bonfire party. Desmond's jokes about heresy hadn't been jokes at all.

Unless Vlod were savagely misreading the situation, which he doubted.

"I've never been sorry about the academy, either," Aerian said. "Vlod? Would you do it again?"

"*I* didn't do it the first time. I *wanted* to be a soldier."

"What happened?" Desmond asked. "Didn't meet the height requirement?"

Aerian's face went blank.

"Ha ha. Very droll," Vlod said. "No, Edmund pointed me at the Academy, and Wolfram kicked me in the ass." This was not the unalloyed truth, but it was convenient.

Aerian recorked the brandy bottle. "Well, lads, it's time to sober up." He twisted the bottle into the sand as though calling a halt to a legendary drinking bout, which he wasn't. "We have work to do."

"Dark and dangerous work, I gather," Vlod said.

"It's the best kind," Desmond said.

———

Wolfram's rooms in Olney Castle were not cramped, but neither were they remotely spacious. His sitting room faced south, and during the daylight hours it gave him a panoramic view of Youngs River and the hills beyond. But now, late at night, he could see nothing but the lights from a handful of freeholders' cottages and the fires on the watchtowers.

He turned away from the window.

His older brother, Edmund, Chieftain of Clan Iredale; Lord of the Columbia River; Guardian of the Western Approaches; Marshal of Clatsop, Willapa, and Rainier; Protector of Wauna, Mayger, and Oak Point; Champion of the Cathedral Henge of Eileen the Immortal; Priest-

Consort of the Mother Metropolitan; President of the Council of Chieftains; Defender of the Harmony; Legate of the Harmony; Beloved of the Sun, the Earth, the Moon, all the Gods, and the Great Goddess; and the Chosen of the Generations of His House, sat in a chair in front of the fire, his legs stretched toward the lowering flames.

He looked old.

He was a large man, broad and powerful through the shoulders, but he was also softening around his gut. It was the inevitable predation of too much deskwork, not enough time spent in the field, and four-and-a-half decades of life. His hair, which had once been reddish-brown, had darkened across the top of his head and had begun to gray at the temples.

With a start, it occurred to Wolfram that although he worked with his brother daily, he rarely, if ever, *saw* him.

How long had those new lines been in his face? When had the gray spread that far?

Had grief worked such abominations or was it the toll of the chieftaincy?

Time itself?

And why had he, Wolfram, rehearsed his brother's titles?

He had so many it was hard to remember them all.

Out of envy?

No, Wolfram would never accept the chieftaincy, not even if all the Gods had combined to force it upon him. Which in Their wisdom They weren't about to.

The chieftaincy was Edmund's lot, not Wolfram's.

For which he gave thanks daily.

It was Wolfram's lot to guard his brother's back, defend the clan, and tend the fires.

Speaking of which, another piece of wood was overdue.

Wolfram provided it.

He worked it in among the pieces already burning, and within a matter of seconds it was ablaze.

Fear.

Yes, fear was why he'd run through his brother's titles.

How much longer would Edmund own them? How much longer

would they have a clan—if the whisperings were to be believed—and the Iredales their chieftain?

"Will Vlod do it?" Edmund asked.

"He loves a puzzle," Wolfram said.

"Yes, but will he help them?"

"He might."

Wolfram moved away from the hearth and returned to the chair flanking his brother's.

"Can we protect them?" Edmund asked.

"We can try."

"We *tried* before, with his father."

Wolfram sipped his whiskey. "He's not stupid."

"Only a fool would agree."

"We don't need a fool," Wolfram said. "We need Vlod."

They made coffee. It was abysmal, tasting as it did of wood ash and a percolator that didn't so much percolate coffee as scorch it.

Aerian drank off a swallow, made a face, and asked Vlod, "Can you keep a secret?"

It was the perfect opening for a lame joke about the coffee, but Aerian looked as though he were about to deliver a death sentence.

Vlod said, "Depends on how energetically I'm being tortured."

Desmond looked positively sour—brows knit, mouth turned down, skin pale. He looked as though he were terror-ridden.

"You can't repeat any of this," Desmond said. "Word of honor."

Vlod nodded. "Word of honor."

"We need your help," Aerian said.

No kidding. "With what?" Vlod asked.

Aerian took a breath, then answered.

By the time Aerian had finished, Vlod understood why Desmond had made that crack about a chance to burn at the stake, why the pair of them had that haunted, hunted look about them.

Under Wolfram's direction, Aerian and Desmond had set out to improve the "reliability and utility" of the clan's marine and military signal rockets.

Reliability and utility: it was an innocent-enough sounding phrase, and it had an innocent-enough list of objectives to back it up. They wanted to make rockets that could tow a heaving line across a gully or between ships, or light up the night with flares that would drift down on parachutes, or deliver messages. They wanted to increase the distances at which their explosive signals could be seen and heard. According to Aerian, the new rockets were "bound to save countless lives."

Vlod didn't see any point in accepting what he'd been told at face value. "No, they won't," he said. "Just the opposite, in fact."

Aerian said, "What are you talking about? We're—"

Vlod cut him off. "You're out to make a new class of weapon. You're out to kill as many people as possible, as rapidly as possible, and as inexpensively as possible."

Desmond goggled at Vlod.

"Tell me I'm wrong," Vlod challenged.

"Signal rockets are already weapons," Aerian said.

"No, they're not," Vlod said.

Aerian smiled like a terrier that's sunk its teeth into a rat. "Well, tell me, then, what makes the anvil used to make a sword any less a weapon than the sword itself?"

Vlod understood his point. Maybe the steel, and the tools, and the skill that went into producing a sword *were* as much a weapon as the sword itself. From a distance, it was hard to argue they weren't. One thing was certain: Without them there would be no sword. Destroy the armories and the armies would vanish.

"What about Royden?" Vlod asked. "He could issue a ruling in principle tomorrow. You two can't be the first morons who've tried to shoot rockets higher and make them go *Bang!* louder."

"And flash brighter. Can't forget that part of it," Aerian said.

In full canine mode, Aerian drew his lips back.

Vlod couldn't tell whether his fellow magus was grinning at him or threatening to bite him.

"We'll apply for a license when we need to," Aerian said. "Until then, Wolfram will shield us."

Vlod scoffed at that notion. "Even Wolfram's power has its limits."

"Which is why we're working in secret."

The flames of their fire fluttered like dozens of orange and yellow flags, snapping in a fresh breeze.

"There are no secrets," Vlod said.

"Not perfect ones, no," Aerian said.

"The best we can do is the best we can do," Desmond said.

The three young magi sat in a semicircle with their backs to the windbreak. Around them the night was dark and cold.

Why hadn't Wolfram or Edmund asked him? So they could deny any awareness of the work?

That was unworthy.

The likely explanation was that they wanted the request to come from the two men who were heading up the project. They were the ones who could provide the details, magus to magus. And, too, it would be easier for Vlod to turn them down than to reject a request that had come directly from either Edmund or Wolfram.

"All right," Vlod said. "Why do you need me?"

"Because you're the best mechanic on the river." Aerian glanced at Desmond. "We can design, and we can tinker, but you can *build*."

"That's where you're wrong. I've never been much of a blacksmith." His failure with his boiler proved as much, but he left that to one side. "And I've never worked with rockets or with gunpowder. I've set it off, but I've never milled it."

"I'm sorry. I put things badly," Aerian said.

"Take another run at it," Desmond said.

Aerian nodded, then said, "Okay. Of the three of us, you're the one who's mechanically skilled. Every time Desmond and I have a failure, we have to wonder whether it was our design or our ham-fisted execution."

"At least you can find your way around a workshop," Desmond said.

"I wonder if my foreman would agree," Vlod said.

"I heard what he said," Desmond said. "'Shitty metal.' He doesn't blame you for what happened."

Aerian said, "We're about to move our operation up onto the Long Beach Peninsula."

With mock enthusiasm, Desmond said, "Just think of it! The idyllic shores of Grays Harbor: remote, isolated, and dismally alone."

"It's perfect for us. We'll have water on three sides for the rockets to fall into, and any fires we start won't have anywhere to go," Aerian said. "We'll be able to post guards to keep out the riffraff."

"What riffraff?" Vlod asked.

"Riffraff. You know. Hunters, trappers, lost travelers, gawkers."

"What about the guards? What keeps them from blabbing?"

"Wolfram's boot."

"There is that, I'll grant you," Vlod said. "Curious supervising engineers, then?"

"Royden won't be able to come within a dozen kilometers of the place," Aerian said. As though clenching the deal, he added, "In exchange, we could help you with your boilers and pumps."

The bribe was too heavy-handed, too obvious.

"Thanks for the offer," Vlod said, "but I have my own unpopular projects."

ELEVEN

Vernon, Chieftain of Clan Innes-Martin; Lord of the Six Rivers; Warden of the Seven Lakes; Guardian of the Northern March; Priest-Consort of the Mother Metropolitan; Beloved of the Sun, the Earth, the Moon, all the Gods, and the Great Goddess; and the Chosen of the Generations of His House, handed Jinhai's last report to Trevor, his battlemaster.

While Trevor read it, Vernon considered their guest. He was Ziellottes, and he had risked his life and more than his life to deliver Jinhai's final, hasty scribbles.

Two hundred and ten kilometers of the Columbia River lay between the Cathedral's and Vernon's lands. True, for Ziellottes, they were downstream kilometers, but they were also 210 kilometers of opportunity for Ulricka's people to have intercepted, tortured, and killed him.

Those kilometers were also 210 demonstrations that although Ziellottes would be highly paid, he did not work for money. Not this time. Perhaps not ever.

On the flip side, had those 210 kilometers provided a reason for him to lie? Had he delivered Jinhai's last report, or had he struck a deal with Ulricka and delivered a fabrication instead?

Fabrication was decidedly in vogue these days, from the headwaters right on down to the bar.

Vernon continued to study his hired agent. The man was built like a gravel barge, designed from the ground up for rough treatment. The Goddess had provided him with massive timbers, and had instilled in him the capacity to be out in all weathers.

He was also like a fishboat, built to seek out, to net, to hook, and to trap—to take advantage of any weather, and to deliver his catch at its maximum value.

Today, Ziellottes had dressed in gray and brown. He never dressed in white, red, yellow, orange, or blue. His boots were old but in good repair. His sword and dagger were rugged and plain, but their hilts and scabbards betrayed the care he lavished on them. Not loving care, not narcissistic care, for he was no sentimentalist. He took care of them because his life depended on them, because he respected them for what they were, and because he respected himself for what he was.

He was an enigma, and no one could say how dangerous a man he was. But he was also an honest one. His life depended on that too, at least as much as it depended on his weapons and his ability to use them.

Therefore, Vernon concluded, the document Ziellottes had handed over was without doubt the last report Jinhai had written. No, it was the last report Jinhai had *sent*. No, still not correct. It was the last of Jinhai's reports that had made it into Ziellottes' hands.

Vernon asked, "Who killed Jinhai?"

"I wasn't present," Ziellottes said.

The answer wasn't an evasion, but a warning that Ziellottes could do no better than speculate.

"What do your informants say?"

"Ulricka shot him," Ziellottes said, and related the details.

Trevor looked up and asked, "How did they find out about him?"

"My guess is that he gave himself away in one way or another. Ulricka's people are often maladroit, but they're not incompetent. She has her sources."

"I'd like the specifics," Vernon said.

"To what end?" Ziellottes asked. "Now is not the time for a vendetta."

"No, no, nothing of that sort," Vernon said. "Call it morbid curiosity.

Jinhai was Innes-Martin through and through. I recruited him, and Trevor trained him. I turned his running over to you, and now he's dead."

"I understand," Ziellottes said.

"If there's a problem, we need to fix it."

"Or use it."

"Well, that's a fix now, isn't it?"

"Indeed."

Vernon turned to Trevor. "Anything more you want to ask?"

"Not immediately."

To Ziellottes, Vernon said, "You'll be around for the next few days, won't you?"

"If you'd like," Ziellottes said, and took his leave.

Vernon poured fresh mugs of coffee.

Trevor grunted his thanks and looked back down at the report.

"How many times are you going to read it?" Vernon asked.

"Until the words change."

"They won't."

"Then we're at war," Trevor said.

"When?"

"Six months. A year at most." Trevor leaned back in his chair. "I'm afraid we've driven Ulricka into Narmer's arms."

"We couldn't stay fat, dumb, and happy."

"No, not in this world."

Vernon sipped his coffee. It had been in the pot too long.

"The sad thing is Narmer may be right. Unifying the basin under one ruler could be the best thing all around."

"Bite your tongue," Trevor said.

"No, we have to give him his due."

"Like the devil he is?"

They chuckled over the lame joke.

Vernon said, "We can't wait any longer."

"We aren't ready," Trevor warned.

"To hell with *ready*. I'm sending you to Edmund. I'd go myself, but it would create too much of a stir."

Trevor nodded his agreement. "The purpose of my visit to your brother chieftain?" Trevor asked, making no effort to hide his contempt for the Iredales in general and Edmund in particular.

"I want you to tell him what's happening at the Cathedral. Take copies of Jinhai's reports. He won't take our word for it, but he might believe Jinhai."

"Assuming he hasn't forgotten how to read."

TWELVE

Narmer, chieftain of Clan Pasco-BurbankS, enjoyed walking along the trail that hugged the edge of the Burbank Slough, over on the Burbank Island side. He had left his horse and his bodyguards on the mainland and had rowed across in a farmer's boat. It had been like old times, like the days before he had won the chieftaincy of the Pasco-Burbanks at the Battle of Little Goose Dam.

Hundreds of years ago, the Burbank Island Slough had been the remnant of the channel that had once separated the island from the mainland. Shortly after the Second Creation, however, one of the local tribes had dredged out the slough and occupied the newly re-formed Burbank Island. It had been a gigantic undertaking, but it had enabled them to survive in those blood-drenched decades.

Within two centuries of the feat, however, the Burbanks had quit the island and merged with the Pascos.

Of the village the Burbanks had left behind, nothing visible above ground remained. Hummocks dotted the island. Many considered them to be human-made structures, centuries old, but whenever the curious dug into one, they found nothing but dirt, sand, and rocks.

No, the melancholy truth was that the original Burbanks had vanished into the Pascos without leaving behind any *material* trace: no villages, no tombs, no temples, no statues, no monuments.

It didn't matter.

Their survival itself was a greater monument than most of the clans from that era had left behind.

They had, however, left behind their poetry.

That they had bequeathed in quantity, and it was their poetry that kept their history alive.

Narmer's happiest memories were of listening to their epic poems. None had given him as much pleasure, had touched him as profoundly, as "The Saga of Set and Igraine," which celebrated the dredging of the Burbank Island Slough and the completion of the first defensive wall around the island.

It was a dark tale, but it told of devout heroes and demanding but benevolent Gods who had joined forces, struggled, fought, and won against overwhelming odds and at a staggering cost.

Following the example of the Burbanks, Narmer was determined to lead today's cacophony of clans out of the darkness of ignorance and internecine war. He would lead them into the bright sunshine of unity and peace. He would lead them into the peace of Amun-Ra, the god of the sun and of creation!

Narmer's boots crunched on the sand.

The sun was high, and the weather was warm for the middle of winter. February. Winter? No, call it early spring.

It was time to prune the roses, and soon, soon enough, the early crocuses would be pushing up.

When Narmer came to the place where the slough, fed by the Snake River, joined the Columbia River, he sat down on a large rock. He wasn't tired, but he was alone, a rare pleasure, and he wished to savor the moment. Soon enough his duties and his plans would call him back to Pasco, *his* capital, back to the fortress within its walls, *his* fortress.

A falcon swooped near him. It climbed away, turned, and flew downriver.

The sight of it filled Narmer with an everyday variety of awe. It also filled him with a riddle. Had he seen the mundane flight of a bird, or had Amun-Ra sent him a sign of divine favor? Had the bird pointed out, once again, the path Narmer's future must take? Had it confirmed Narmer's faith in the Gods and in the foundation of his personal dynasty?

Narmer yearned to believe that the falcon was a sign, but he lacked that degree of sublime assurance. Paradoxically, he believed that the falcon *was* a sign.

Just as Ra showered the world with His rays, He also showered it with tokens—some dramatic, some so ordinary they went unnoticed—of His pleasure, His wrath, and His divine will.

Narmer watched the flow of the river.

Hundreds of kilometers downstream, the river flowed past the Cathedral, and hundreds of additional kilometers farther on it flowed through Edmund's lands and on out into the Pacific Ocean. It was one river, and it ought to flow through territories united and ruled by one clan. It was the manifest will of Ra.

Narmer, the chieftain of the Pasco-Burbanks, the self-styled Pharaoh of the Upper Land, the future Pharaoh of the Upper and Lower Kingdoms, watched the falcon as it shrank in the distance.

He wished it well, and again promised to obey.

THIRTEEN

Dagna, the second-born of Edmund's two daughters, had long hair. It was as thick as her sister Brenna's, but rather than raven black, it was sunshine blond.

Dagna's friends said that her hair was the color of daffodils, but she thought it was closer to the color of buckskin...or very old hay. Whatever the color, she pulled a wandering strand of it away from her face and drew her hunting bow.

She aimed at the stag. He was some forty meters distant. He had lowered his head to a clump of grass. His teeth and jaws worked methodically, without concern, as though he were not seconds away from death. His antlers rose from his skull like the branches of a winter oak.

She'd given the best part of a rainy February day to stalking him. Hour after hour, she'd tracked and circled and worked around until she could make her approach from downwind.

Her companions guarded the flanks.

Mavianna and Valentinian were to her left, while Orva and Sanjiv held down the right. Neither of the pairs were lovers. It would have turned Dagna's stomach if they had been.

She'd invited Halvard, but at the last minute Wolfram had sent him off on an errand.

None of the four would shoot until she did, and then only if she missed.

The honor was hers.

The shot was perfectly aligned.

The stag was hers!

She flexed a knee, turned a degree or two to one side, and then refused to compensate for her altered stance.

Her arrow made a sharp *thwurr*. The flight was true, and the shaft *thupppted* into the ground a few centimeters in front of the stag's nose.

That she could have bagged him was enough. Such an animal deserved to live.

The stag bolted and ran for the nearest line of trees.

Dagna's companions loosed, but none of the arrows hit.

Halvard would have chided her for missing such an easy shot, but none of those with her would dare.

Had they, too, missed deliberately.

She hoped that they hadn't. She would have been ashamed of them if they had.

For her sake as well as theirs, she prayed that they'd done their best.

A few hours later Dagna and her hunting companions said their goodbyes and went their separate ways. Alone, Dagna rode over to the Iredales' principal henge, the Manor Henge of Desdemona the Shipbreaker.

The earliest Iredales had sited it on the crown of a hill that offered a view that circled the compass, workable horizons all the way around. To the north, the hilltop overlooked Fort George, the Columbia River, and the lands beyond. To the east, south, and west, the hilltop provided views of the surrounding valleys and hills.

The henge's builders had used fired brick, hewn boulders, granite monoliths, shaped rock, and rough-hewn timbers. They were the materials of the manor, the materials of the earth.

Dagna went to the stalls and purchased a yearling stag. He was unblemished and had an intelligent, attractive face. The poor creature. His eyes were so dark a brown that they were almost black.

Rather than have the charge for the stag sent to the castle, Dagna counted the coins into the attendant's hand.

The Reverend Mother Charlotte, the mother superior of the Manor Henge of Desdemona the Shipbreaker, approached. She was dressed in heavy clothes and draped in a winter cloak. The hood was down, and the wind caught at her hair. Her hair was thick and as dark as the yearling stag's eyes.

Mother Charlotte said, "You're covered in mud and you smell like a horse! Or worse! Have you been out hunting?"

"Yes, Mother Charlotte," Dagna said.

"Any luck?"

Dagna felt like a child desperate to explain herself. "We had a good ride."

"What a shame."

"It was a beautiful day."

"I'm glad you enjoyed it," Mother Charlotte said. "I see you've bought a sacrifice. A good ride is worth acknowledging."

"Indeed it is. We've come back unharmed, too." Dagna's face burned. Would she never outgrow her adolescent piety?

"Then thanks are doubly appropriate," Mother Charlotte said, and took her leave.

Apparently, she was off for a stroll on one of the paths that crisscrossed the grounds of the manor henge.

The attendant led the yearling into the altar precincts.

Dagna followed.

After the priestess had sacrificed the animal and daubed Dagna's forehead with the blood, Dagna rode down from the promontory and then up the next hill to the east, up toward Olney Castle.

She was looking forward to a short, hard walk in the hills. There were no sedate, primly graveled trails there. A walk would loosen the muscles left kinked by a day spent riding and crawling through underbrush. Dinner and bed would follow.

Perhaps she'd dream of her stag, the one she hadn't killed.

Whether she dreamed of him or not, she would spend the night alone.

As Edmund's only fertile daughter, she could not afford to take a lover before her father had bargained her away to the highest bidder. Harsh words, but true. A harsh reality, but a necessary one. Her proven fertility was too powerful an advantage to be frittered away on sentiment or, worse still, on impulse.

From time to time, there were those who behaved in such a cavalier manner, but Dagna could not endure the prospect, the possibility, of a pregnancy that the Geneticists Guild had not approved. There could be only one ending for such a pregnancy, and no lover was worth as much as that.

Giving up her baby at the end of her Virgin's Year at the Cathedral, when she and the others in her cohort had served as *kedeshahes,* that is, as sacred prostitutes, had been agony enough.

To have a baby ripped from her womb, to be forced to cooperate in its murder, would kill her. Not physically perhaps—if she were lucky—but spiritually. Both her baby and she would be dead.

No, it was better for her to remain alone than to risk such a hideous chain of outcomes.

When it finally arrived, dinner would be another loathsome banquet. It would be an offering to the gods of politics and hysteria. Vernon's battlemaster was due to arrive on diplomatic business, and Dagna's father would feel compelled to display as many of the degrees of hospitality as prudent. He could not and would not allow himself to appear weak or in search of an ally.

He was, Dagna knew, both of those things, but he dared not advertise the fact. His suitors must come to him, not the other way around.

Which, it would appear, one was.

Ostensibly, Trevor wanted to discuss a disputed tract of land on the northern shore of the Columbia and the troop levels at Morven's Gate.

The tract of land was a trivial matter, but the troop levels were not. Morven's Gate was a fortified Iredale outpost on the southeastern side of the river, directly across from the Innes-Martin capital, Monticello. The troop levels there were, therefore, not a trivial matter. Rather, they were an inexhaustible bone of contention.

Be that as it may, Trevor had come with another purpose in mind.

What it was, she couldn't say, but whatever it was, it would be treated as though it were *important.* It wouldn't be, not really, but that's how they were to treat it.

Dinner would be a somber affair, and everyone would have to look their best.

Dagna would have to choose a gown. It would have to be colorful but sedate, serious but not dour.

Brenna, her elder sister, would be in uniform. Brenna, the barren Amazon, the major in her father's marines, the hero of the Skamokawa Salient, never *dressed* in anything but her dress uniform.

As Dagna rode on toward the castle, as she brooded over the evening ahead of her, she noticed three vessels maneuvering out on the river.

She opened her telescope and studied them. Each was running under a combination of sail and oar. Two were escorts. They were fast, shallow-draft vessels with catapults mounted in their bows.

The third was larger. She was not an armed scout, nor an armed merchantman, but a no-nonsense war galley. She had crenellated fighting platforms fore and aft, and both of them, together with her main deck, bristled with catapults and mounted crossbows. The Innes-Martin standard streamed from her masthead, while below it flew Trevor's personal flag.

Wolfram went down to the docks to greet Trevor, battlemaster to battlemaster. He took Brenna, Vlod, and a showy-but-not-lavish escort with him.

They arrived ahead of time, but the vessels were late, delayed by their own blunders in negotiating the final approach into the port.

Vlod huddled his shoulders deep into his cloak, and told himself not to grumble aloud about the snotty weather, the insanity of making firm schedules where travel by water was involved, or about the meager boat-handling skills of upriver clans.

Red buoys were okay. Clear enough. Most of the time. Green was also okay. Like red, only in reverse. But yellow? What the hell did yellow mean?

Could they tell the difference between a covered sandbar and a tide rip?

Maybe twenty-five percent of the time they could.

Would they listen to their own pilots?

They'd refused the pilots that Wolfram had sent out to them.

Edmund ought to have turned them around and sent them back upstream, but he hadn't.

Something was afoot.

Or maybe Edmund was merely being polite. He had his moments. But in this case, he was acting out of motives that were deeper than enforcing the correct protocol. Yes, sometimes it was better to smile and look the other way.

And Edmund, if anyone, was smart enough to know when to do just that.

The wind was gusting in off the river one minute and falling to a dead calm the next, only to gust again.

Vlod watched the gusts as they ruffled their way across the water, turning it dark, like a child blowing on a cup of hot tea, trying to cool it.

Rain was on the way. It promised to be heavy, driving, and cold. What else would it be?

Snotty weather.

Wolfram seemed to be pacing but without the benefit of movement, without the release of fidgeting.

He stood head and shoulders above Vlod and Brenna, who were of roughly equal height. The battlemaster was long-boned and tightly muscled, the sort of build developed by weapons training, riding, hunting, and decades in the field. His hair and beard were dark brown, tending toward his niece's raven black. His face, where his beard did not cover it, was tanned even in winter.

Vlod returned his attention to the tableau on the river. The sails of Vernon's vessels were large rectangles of medium-weight canvas, their working sails. They were strong enough and large enough for everyday use on the river, but they were difficult to handle in unsettled weather. The sails rolled and snapped.

Vlod cringed at the thought of the resulting shock loads on spars and rigging.

The net result was that the galley and her escorts crept over the water. Their sails were doing more harm than good, and ought to have been hauled down.

"How long are we supposed to stand out here on this damn dock?" Brenna asked.

"Until he lands," Wolfram said. "I suspect he's chosen to make a hash of it."

"Why?"

"To annoy us."

"That's a bad sign," Brenna said.

"He's out to reverse our expectations. By annoying us, he hopes to persuade us to give in to him."

"What?"

"He wants us to believe we have the advantage."

"We do," Vlod said.

"I say we slit his throat and be done with it," Brenna said. "Return his head to Vernon on a pike."

"I'm not sure a pike would be able to carry a load that heavy," Vlod said. "As fish go, pikes are pretty big, but they're not that big."

"Oh, shut up, you insufferable boor," she said, but her smile betrayed her.

"I hear and obey, O sharp-bladed one, whose merest displeasure causes the people to tremble," Vlod said.

He caught the half-hidden stare of one of the members of the escort detail and the unabashed effort of another to overhear their conversation.

How long would it be, Vlod wondered, before his exchange with Brenna had become gossip fodder?

He and Brenna were on-again-off-again lovers, comrades-in-arms when called, and variously opponents and allies in the court's power struggles.

Uncomplicated was the least of the many words the Iredales used to describe their relationship.

Brenna had joined her father's marines shortly after she'd failed to conceive during her Virgin's Year at the Cathedral. It wasn't unknown, of course, for women who hadn't conceived during their years to do so later on, but because those pregnancies took place outside the boundaries of a Guild-sanctioned union, the Guild aborted their products without hesitation and without mercy.

Brenna's hair hung in a thick braid down her back. She was in uniform. It was one of her older ones, complete with sewn-up tears and a permanent bloodstain.

Out on the river, one of the scouts had flubbed her turn and was now taken aback.

She held one bank of oars, powered forward with the other, put her helm over, and turned. Slowly, awkwardly, her crew braced her yard around. Her sail refilled, the oars gave way together, and she was off again, running at a right angle to her previous course.

"That ought to do it," Vlod said. "No teacher like the river."

"You're assuming it wasn't deliberate," Wolfram said.

As if the war galley's captain had read Vlod's thoughts, a signal raced up to the masthead. Moments later, the vessels brailed up, lowered their yards, furled their sails, manhandled the yards onto their crutches, and lashed them down.

One of the escorts lost a man overboard, but she backed her oars, tossed him a line, and retrieved him. That done, the squadron's hortators resumed the beat, and the vessels maneuvered into line-ahead formation. They steered for the docks.

Out of nowhere, Brenna said, "Maybe we ought to give them what they *really* want."

"Unlimited access to deep water?" Wolfram said. "You have to be joking."

"It would save us the trouble of drowning them ourselves," Brenna said.

Ever the stern uncle, Wolfram did his best not to laugh.

By the time Trevor's war galley was alongside, with her mooring lines over and her brow down, Wolfram's face had set.

Trevor and an aide came ashore, and the welcoming rituals began: greetings, introductions, inquiries about their trip down from Monticello, and matching inquiries about a buoy that might be off station.

A gust of wind ruffled the puddles of rainwater.

Embracing the business at hand, Wolfram said, "I'll escort you to Edmund."

FOURTEEN

Vlod sipped his whiskey and took in as much warmth from the log fire in Edmund's study as he could. The fire popped and snapped, and now and then a puff of smoke back-eddied into the room, due to the strength and direction of the wind. Mixed in with the fir was a goodly portion of scrap cedar. The combination created a bone-comforting, blood-calming aroma.

As soon as they'd begun the ride up from the docks, the rain had hardened, and by the time they'd reached the castle, Vlod's cloak was sodden and his clothes, despite the protection of his cloak, were damp and cold.

The study's north-facing windows didn't help. The cold flowed off of them as a river cascading over a sheer drop. Meanwhile, the wind howled around the castle. It rattled the shutters and banged the flag hoists.

All told, the weather made a fitting background for the storm that Trevor's revelations had set off inside the otherwise pleasant chamber.

The pages of Jinhai's reports—or what Trevor claimed were Jinhai's reports—lay scattered across the floor, on the nearest tables, and in people's laps.

Despite their lack of immediate order, the image those pages painted was absolutely clear, and Vernon's reasoning in the face of it was equally inescapable—austere, vile, manipulative, but inescapable.

A war was coming, and it would be with Narmer, that upriver megalomaniac.

Well, that much had been in the wind for months, if not years, but Jinhai's work had given the wind-borne rumors shape, substance, and schedule.

Vernon's response was to propose allying the two major downriver clans—the Iredales and the Innis-Martins—to stand against the onslaught. With the Iredales and the Innis-Martins united, they might be able to gather enough additional support to defeat Narmer's attack.

But how to ally the two feuding clans?

It was the same old problem, and Vernon was proposing to solve it in the same old way: by marriage.

The marriage was to be between Dagna, Edmund's fertile daughter, and Gregory, Vernon's eldest son and heir.

The happy couple's firstborn son would be Vernon's grandson and ultimately, through Gregory, his heir. At the same time, the child, through Dagna, would be Edmund's grandson and ultimate heir. Therefore, as chieftain of both the Iredales and the Innes-Martins, the child would permanently unite the two clans.

Vlod could recite a laundry list of counterexamples and objections, but he held his tongue. He was there to speak when spoken to, and to support his chieftain in all things. Which Vlod would have done in any case.

Wolfram said, "The lower Columbia makes one hell of a dowry. Why should we hand it over to you?"

"You're being childish," Trevor said.

"Humor me," Wolfram said. "Why should we?"

"Because we must stand together or grovel side by side, assuming Narmer doesn't feed us to his pet crocodiles."

"They're alligators in this hemisphere," Vlod said, unable to resist the quip.

"He'll make do," Trevor said in kind.

"He has deep-water ambitions," Edmund said, returning to that topic.

"He says he wants to unite the basin."

"He says a lot of things," Wolfram said. "A unified basin would give him a highway to the ocean trade routes."

"He doesn't know the difference between a spring line and a spring tide," Edmund said. "Why's he in such a lather for blue water?"

Trevor shrugged. "He knows the difference between poverty and wealth."

"I'm not stopping him," Edmund said.

"Aren't you? You control the bar."

"I provide pilotage across the bar," Edmund said. "I dredge the channel, and I inspect vessels for seaworthiness." He added, "And I transfer cargoes from the inland sailing barges to deep-water cargo carriers."

"Most of which you own," Trevor said, stating the fact.

"Narmer couldn't build a raft if his life depended on it."

"No, not one that could meet your specifications," Trevor said. "As we Innes-Martins have found out. Repeatedly."

After a long, brittle silence, to the room in general, Edmund said, "Trevor and I need to speak in private."

Wolfram, the aide, and Vlod got up to leave.

"Vlod, I want you to stay," Edmund said.

"Then my aide will also remain," Trevor said.

"No, he won't," Edmund said.

Trevor arched an eyebrow, but he nodded to his aide, and the man followed Wolfram out.

When they were alone, Edmund asked Trevor: "Who killed Morven? Which one of *you* killed my son?"

Trevor cocked his head to one side.

The gesture was so spontaneous that Vlod could *almost* believe that Vernon's battlemaster hadn't expected the question.

"My lord?" Trevor asked.

"It's a simple question. Who killed him?"

"Ah, I see," Trevor said. "Well, it wasn't Vernon, and it wasn't Gregory, and it wasn't me."

"Then who was it? Not that little shit Bevan?"

Bevan was Gregory's younger brother. Bevan was the sort of malevolent malcontent who made people thankful he wasn't the elder brother.

"No, it wasn't Bevan. He wasn't there," Trevor said.

"So Morven died by *accident*? Is that what you're saying?"

"He died in a skirmish," Trevor said. Verging on sarcasm, he added, "People die in skirmishes."

"It wasn't a skirmish. It was a cattle raid. A prank. They've been going on for centuries. Make a lot of noise. Steal a few head. Kiss a couple of girls. No one has to die."

Trevor made an openhanded gesture. "Nevertheless..."

"I'm entitled to an explanation."

Trevor's face set. "You could call in a necromancer and ask Morven himself who killed him."

Necromancy was a perilous practice. It was often suggested and often spoken of, but it was rarely practiced.

Due to the barriers, the abrasions, the opacity, between the temporal and eternal realms, the results were often, to put it charitably, erratic. The dead, it seemed, were no more reliable than the living.

Now and then, a flash of authentic communication would take place, an exchange of half-heard whispers between the worlds, but on the whole, the results were usually a stew of urges, guesswork, and hysteria.

The magi performed some of it, as an aspect of divination, but by and large, the basin's necromancers were drawn from the ranks of the basin's priestesses. Few of the manors were without one.

Moreover, there was no telling to whom a necromancer might repeat what they'd heard, accidently or deliberately.

Edmund said, "I'd rather *you* told me what happened."

Trevor's expression didn't change, not an iota. "I was fighting next to Vernon, and we were nowhere near Morven when he was killed. This I swear."

Edmund scoffed. "So and blessed let it be." He left a space, then said, "Tell my brother chieftain this. He had best pray I *never* learn that it was he who killed my son."

"I'm sure he understands the situation," Trevor said. He finished his whiskey. "What about the marriage? What shall I tell him?"

"I'll agree to the marriage in principle, but the final decision will be up to Dagna."

"Will she accept?"

Edmund scoffed. "I can't speak for her."

"Very good, my lord," Trevor said.

"I don't mean to be rude," Edmund said, "but would you excuse us?"

"Certainly, my lord," Trevor said, and left the room.

"Your opinion?" Edmund asked Vlod.

"Vernon is afraid."

"Tell me something that isn't obvious."

"No, my lord, he is *afraid*. The Iredales might be able to stand alone, but not the Innis-Martins."

"What about me? Should I be afraid?"

"Fear isn't in your nature, my lord, but the danger is greater than you may imagine."

"I haven't told you what I imagine."

"You've granted Trevor a private audience."

Edmund made a face. "I never should have sent you to the Academy."

"I tried to persuade you not to."

"Ingrate," Edmund said.

"Yes, my lord."

Edmund thought a moment, then said, "I want you to auger Vernon's proposal. Does it bode well or ill?"

FIFTEEN

Four days after her blunder-ridden arrival, Trevor's war galley eased away from her berth. She had moored portside-to, headed west. She needed to go east, upstream.

Once clear of the dock, rather than come around in a wide, comfortable turn, her captain put her rudder over to right full, backed her starboard bank of oars, and went ahead on her port bank. The vessel pivoted in roughly her own length.

As far as Vlod could tell, the maneuver was strictly a display intended to show that her captain, an overweight woman who resembled a constipated cocker spaniel, knew how to handle a ship as well as a knife and fork and that sneers about "lubbers with grand illusions" were unfair.

And it was nicely done.

The galley spun like a dancer. The wind, which was blowing from the northwest, held her back for a moment, but once her bow was through the eye, she continued on around smartly.

The rudder was brought amidships, and the two banks of oars gave way together.

Her escorts took up their positions, and the diminutive squadron quickly steadied onto its upriver course.

The skill of the evolution put the lie to the earlier display of ineptitude.

That display had been a waste of time, and, evidently, Trevor had decided to drop the pretense.

A cheer went up from those on the dock—Edmund and most of his inner circle.

From the galley's quarterdeck, Trevor smiled and waved. He had a right to. He was headed home with the agreement he'd come to negotiate.

Through the augury Vlod had performed, the Gods and the Generations had approved Vernon's proposal. Edmund had announced Their approval and his resulting approval to Trevor.

Dagna fell into line, adding her consent.

In principle had become *in fact*.

Dagna had remained glum but obedient to the good of the clan.

If she didn't marry Gregory, it would be another princeling just like him. Such marriages were the price the members of the nobility paid, men and women alike, for their high places in the machinery of necessity.

Edmund and most of his people drifted away from the dock.

Vlod turned to follow, but Wolfram touched his arm.

"A word," the battlemaster said.

Gulls wheeled overhead, crying. Their droppings left white-and-brown splotches on the planking.

"We'll be at war soon," Wolfram said.

"Which we'll win," Vlod said.

"Better signal rockets would help."

Vlod could only shake his head at the euphemism.

"You're not using me to light up the sky. If you want peace, build a stronger army."

A sarcastic grin played around the edges of Wolfram's mouth, as though a joke or a jab had occurred to him. Rather than make it, he said, "Any chance you'll change your mind?"

"Any chance they'll change the rules of heresy?"

Dagna folded the length of llama-wool fabric into a neat rectangle and wrapped it in two layers of a coarser sheep's-wool cloth to protect it. For this gift, paper would not do. She set the bundle into a cedarwood gift box. She wrapped the box with sailcloth and bound it with twine. She sealed it with wax.

The result was a stout package. Stout or not, it was too fragile—and too important—to be sent in any other method than by personal courier.

It would be a shameful expense, but she lived in a shameful time, an expensive time.

Was her business also shameful?

It might be.

She had woven the fabric herself. It was neither ornate nor conventionally pretty. She had woven no images into it. She had given the interplay of threads no hidden pattern.

No, there was none of that. Instead, this material was as elegant, as durable, and as beautiful as her own meager talents had allowed her to make it.

Meager.

No false humility in that regard. When it came to weaving, her talents were unquestionably meager.

Meagerly trained was nearer the mark.

She had intended to make the fabric into a suit of hunting clothes for herself, but now she would use it as a bribe.

Would her motive be understood? If it weren't, she would be truly lost.

That was why she would send the cloth to the Crone of the Cathedral and not to the Mother Metropolitan. Some people said Shabnan, the Crone, was the most perceptive person in the Mother Metropolitan's court. Others said she was the most powerful. Whatever the truth, Shabnan would understand.

Vlod ripped the last of the charred planks from what had been the top of the workbench in his workshop. He set down his crowbar and pitched the wood onto the growing pile of scrap.

The door opened and Wolfram entered. His face was grim.

"What's wrong?" Vlod asked.

"Eakan was your foreman, wasn't he?"

"He will be again as soon as I can get back to work on the boiler."

"Did he tell you he'd gone to work for Aerian?"

"On the rockets? Yes, why?"

"He's dead. He was mixing gunpowder and it blew up."

Sixteen

Vlod swung down from his horse.

They'd called it a horse, but was that what it really was? A horse? Really?

The ill-tempered, conniving beast was a foul-smelling nag.

He'd borrowed it from the garrison at the ferry landing on the north shore of the Columbia.

They'd called it a horse, but no one else would have.

To call that vile animal a horse was an insult to horse-ness.

Vlod tethered the creature with the other horses, hoping they wouldn't take too much offense, and approached the powder shack on foot.

Aerian, Desmond, and Wolfram were waiting for him. They looked like naughty schoolboys being born down on by the school's sternest teacher.

The wind surged across the peninsula as though determined to scour away each and every trace of human activity, as though it had condemned humanity out of hand.

"It isn't a pleasant sight," Aerian said.

"Wolfram told us you'd want to see everything," Desmond said.

Wolfram nodded. "I did."

Vlod felt numb and he felt angry. "Understood."

Vlod pulled the door open, and then he and Wolfram stepped inside.

Flies crawled and buzzed wherever Vlod looked, and the stench was like a blow to his stomach. It was as much as he could do not to vomit.

Aerian and Desmond had removed Eakan's body, but they had left his blood to soak into the floorboards.

The explosion hadn't been large, but it had blackened the walls and blown loose a number of the boards that made up the walls. A half-dozen mortars and pestles lay scattered around. Off to one side were the remains of a small hand-turned powder mill.

"He must have created a spark," Aerian said.

"How?" Vlod asked. "The mill doesn't have any steel or iron parts, does it?"

"No, of course not. We're not stupid," Aerian said.

Vlod glanced around the shop. Its condition said otherwise: bags of chemicals had been piled carelessly in a far corner, the heads of iron nails protruded from the floor, ordinary lanterns—not the reinforced double-shielded type—had been hung up for light.

Had they bothered to take them all the way outside to light them?

"What was he working on?" Vlod asked. Wolfram had already told him, but he wanted to hear it from Aerian.

"He was mixing a batch of propellant," Aerian said.

"Why make your own gunpowder?" Vlod asked. "Why not draw it from the mill?"

"An excellent question," Wolfram said. "I arranged an account for you."

One of the more daring—some would say reckless—Iredale families ran the powder mill. It was located up in the hills above Fort George. They brought in the sulfur from outside, but they obtained the saltpeter and charcoal locally. The mill supplied enough gunpowder for the Iredales to make their own flares, signal rockets, and celebratory fireworks.

"We've been experimenting with different mixtures and grain sizes, and with different grades of chemicals," Desmond said. "We've discovered—"

"It doesn't make sense for us to keep a lot of powder on hand," Aerian said, cutting Desmond off. "We mix up what we need when we need it."

"The gunpowder and the rocket bodies work as a unit," Desmond said. "Neither can be tested in isolation."

"Anything special about the batch Eakan was mixing?" Vlod asked.

"We'd obtained the saltpeter from a different source. We wanted to make sure it was as potent as what had come from the old source."

"By mixing a batch with the new saltpeter and comparing its performance to batches made with the old saltpeter?" Vlod asked.

"That's right."

It was the accepted procedure. Vlod decided to move on. "What about reserve supplies?"

"A couple of kegs of the mill's standard propellant for rockets, but they're stored well away from here."

If they hadn't been, there wouldn't have been a shack left for them to stand in.

Wolfram picked up a pestle. He turned it this way and that. "What were you two doing when the place blew up?"

Desmond said, "We were in the workshop."

"Eakan was alone," Aerian added.

"Who saw it happen?" Vlod asked.

"No one."

Wolfram dropped the pestle onto the ground. "Show us what you've accomplished so far."

Several minutes later, one of the modified signal rockets *zhuuffed* across the firing range. Its announced target was a square of canvas strung between two poles a good distance away.

The rocket followed a shallow trajectory and left behind a trail of white smoke.

The air smelled of burned sulfur. It wasn't an unfamiliar smell, but this time it had a malevolent edge to it.

The current round of modifications included three small wooden fins, like the fletching on an arrow, and an enlarged signal charge with a slow fuse.

The propellant charge burned out, and the rocket tipped through the top of its arc.

"Watch this!" Desmond said. He sounded like an excited child, eyes huge, mouth fixed in a contorted grin.

The rocket hit the ground and tumbled. It came to rest at a spot that was short and far to the left of the target.

"Here it comes!" Desmond said.

Aerian, Wolfram, and Vlod remained silent.

"Wait for it."

Vlod wondered if Desmond was going to wet his pants.

Desmond counted: "Three...two...one..." His expectant pause lengthened into an embarrassed silence. "Plus one...Damn that fuse! Plus three...Plus—"

A bucketful of sand sprayed up, and a fraction of a second later, a credible *Bang!* sounded.

The flat expanse of the northern tip of the Long Beach Peninsula, with Willapa Bay to the east and the Pacific Ocean to the west and the entrance to the bay to the north, swallowed the noise.

It was hard to say what effect such a weapon would have on an opposing army.

Aerian said, "The fletching didn't work, the fuse is crap, and the extra weight of the charge shortened the range."

"That explosion wasn't much," Wolfram commented dryly.

"True, true," Desmond said. "We have a long way to go. But with Vlod's help—" Desmond choked himself off. He was running ahead of the conversation, and he damn well knew it.

"Go on," Vlod said, rescuing him. "With my help...?

"We'd have the problems solved in no time," Desmond said.

"Ahead of schedule for the next war, I imagine," Vlod said.

"If we can make this work," Aerian said, "maybe there won't be a next war."

There spoke an irredeemable optimist, fresh from the very pit of hell. "What's to stop it?" Vlod asked. "Signal rockets that throw up a few shovelfuls of sand won't. Besides, whatever happened to delivering messenger lines?"

"I don't see the problem," Aerian said. "In essence, a rocket is an arrow that contains its own bow."

"Its own *gunpowder* bow," Vlod said. "You're dancing on the edge of a volcano."

"We are not," Aerian said.

Wolfram cut into the conversation. "Can you work out the design problems or not?"

"Maybe," Aerian said.

"Very well," Wolfram said, and walked off toward the horses. He called over his shoulder, "Vlod, you're with me."

SEVENTEEN

Mother Metropolitan Ulricka awoke with her heart pounding. That was the overwhelming sensation, but then she realized that she was sitting upright in her bed. Her throat felt raw, as if she had screamed.

She went to her window and opened the draperies. They smelled old and dusty, even though they were neither.

The Saraswati Palace did that to things, made them old and dusty. It did it to young women in particular. It dried them out.

The windowpanes were ancient, the glass sagging. It distorted everything it revealed.

Nevertheless, at the moment, it was preferable to being closed in, cut off entirely from the outside world.

The night was dark, far into its cycle.

The Sun sailed His shining golden barge through the Underworld, while the Moon, His consort, paced the sky in anticipation of His return. Their love held the cosmos in equilibrium. Their love held it in balance between a treacherous chaos and an overpowering order.

Their sexual union brought forth life.

For good and sacred reasons the Great Goddess had made Their disks the same size.

Ulricka dressed, wrapped herself in a blue cape, and left her palace. She crossed the Cathedral precincts.

She paused outside the entrance to her cathedral, the Cathedral Henge of Eileen the Immortal.

Several paces behind her, a boot rasped on a stray pebble.

Her guards had followed. They were protective creatures, those girls, but locked in the throes of adolescence. They needed training in the arts of silence.

Calmly Ulricka said, "Mind your feet, and in the morning, have the pavement swept."

No answer. Good. Her protectors weren't complete cretins.

She forced her mind back to her purpose.

The outer ring of monoliths, the Guardians—which were massive, towering pillars of granite—humbled her. Good. They were supposed to humble those who ventured near them.

She compelled herself to forget about her guards and to surrender herself into the Cathedral's sacred presence.

Her irritation faded, and her breathing slowed.

She said aloud, "You've come far enough. Do not follow." Clear, but she had to make sure. "Remain where you are until I return."

No response, neither complaint nor protest. They would obey.

She moved on.

Beyond the gate, she entered the concentric inner rings. They had been hewn from basalt, granite, marble, sandstone. Wood, too: cedar, maple, redwood, oak, fir, pine. These were the Cathedral's Heralds and Oracles. The masons and carpenters had rough-hewn some but had polished others. Lintels of equal girth, the Hands and Feet of Nut, connected them.

Although stone and wood predominated, there were also pillars of fired brick and interlocked rock. There were lintels of iron, copper, and aluminum, too.

These were the elemental materials, materials as they came from the earth.

Yes, they had been smelted, forged, and worked, but they were *of the earth*. They were in harmony with it. There was no bronze, no brass, and no white steel—no alloy of any kind. Here, even steel, an alloy of iron and carbon, was suspect.

Purity...

From deep within the Cathedral came a flicker of light.

Who could be in the Circle at this hour?

No one would dare to trespass, and less than a dozen people could be there as a matter of right.

Ulricka considered returning to her apartments, but then she allowed her curiosity to override her desire for solitude.

She worked her way forward.

She trailed her fingers across the surfaces of the monoliths. She absorbed the textures, the tactile joy and resonance of the stone, the brick, the wood, the metal.

Various features of the rings marked the cardinal directions, the solstices, and the equinoxes. At sunrise on the days of the equinoxes, *that* pair of granite uprights ushered a ray of light across the Circle to illuminate the Disk of the Sun suspended above and to the rear of the altar.

That other set of Heralds, the ones wrought in rose marble, did the same thing on the summer solstice.

The pair in white marble did so on the Winter Solstice.

Ulricka transited the inner ring and entered an impromptu halo of torchlight. She crossed the nave and stepped into the Circle itself, the architectural center and spiritual heart of the cathedral. Its black and white paving squares distinguished it from its surroundings. It had a border of inlaid gold traceries and inlaid silver compass points.

The altar stood in the center of the Circle. Torches burned at each of its four corners.

The torches were in their correct positions, but they ought not to have been there, ought not to have been lit.

Stretched out on the altar, as though she were an honored corpse or a sacrificial victim, lay the Crone of the Cathedral, Shabnan. She wore a white, gauzy dress with pleated skirts.

Whenever Ulricka thought of crones, she pictured wizened old women with tangled gray hair, claw-like fingers, and voices that etched glass.

Shabnan was none of those things. True, she was in her sixth decade, and true, her monthly flow had ceased years ago, and true, parts of her hair had turned gray; but she had neither run to fat nor had she withered to an animated bag of kindling.

She was wearing a gold circlet, complete with uraeus. The cobra's eyes were emeralds, and enameled lotus flowers in yellow, green, and purple decorated the band.

The circlet was very Egyptian, the sort of thing Narmer would have sent her to curry favor.

Ulricka suppressed an absurd flash of jealousy. Narmer had sent her greater trinkets than circlets, gold or not.

"What are you doing here?" Ulricka asked.

Shabnan kept her eyes closed. "I've sacrificed myself to the Goddess and now I'm lying in state."

"You're perfectly alive," Ulricka said.

"No, not really. If I were you instead of me, and if at the same time, I were equipped with my shriveled ovaries, then I'd be dead. They would have murdered me ages ago. Whoosh! Chop! It's off to the Gods and the Generations for you, old woman. Send us a sign when you've achieved eternal bliss." She smiled. "Or scream loud enough for us to hear you if you end up roasting in the fires of hell."

Heaven and hell: such old, old notions, such an enduring duality. It seemed that people and societies needed them to live, to thrive, to make it through one day and endure on into the next.

Suddenly a sharp sense of dread swept through Ulricka. These days it was like a constant but unwelcome companion. The moment she could no longer become pregnant, could no long conceive, her successor, at her own command, would strike her down, just as Ulricka had struck Thora down. A mother metropolitan cannot be barren. As an avatar of the Goddess, a mother metropolitan must bring forth life. Otherwise, she is a curse upon the Creation, an abomination.

"Aren't you bored?" Ulricka asked.

"No," Shabnan said. "I don't have time to be bored. I'm dead, remember?" She made a circular motion with her hand. "Besides, they sing to me."

"The torches?"

It was a logical question. Apart from the two women, the torches were the only sources of sound within the cathedral.

"No, silly, the Guardians. The Heralds and the Oracles, too," Shabnan said. The Oracles were obelisks that marked specific liturgical dates apart from the solstices and equinoxes. "Above all, I'm listening to the Hands and Feet of Nut, Goddess of the Sky, She who is Herself the heavens."

Ulricka knew better than to dismiss the Crone as a crank. She was no posturing religious hysteric.

Ulricka stepped closer. "What do they sing about?"

"Eternity."

"Do they sing to you personally?"

"When they feel like it. Mostly, they just sing."

"About what?"

"Their song reminds me that every day of my life brings me closer to the day of my death. It's very sad. That's why I'm practicing now. I don't want to be so overcome with surprise and grief that I won't be able to lie in state properly when the time comes. I'm determined to present the proper degree of elegance...before I begin to rot. Once I do, I suspect I'll lose my head."

"The Mistress of Sojourners will make sure you perform as required."

"She's an unctuous cow! I'd rather make sure of it myself," Shabnan said. She sighed. "I'm afraid I shall be utterly overcome with grief when I die. I shall mourn myself terribly."

"You won't rot."

"Not right away, no, but sooner or later I will. We all will. Even you. Our resident ghoul can't prevent it, and the Goddess won't. Rot is part of Her divine plan. You do understand that, don't you, Ricki?"

The torches rustled. Their light flared across the innermost ring of monoliths.

"Death is an inescapable part of life," Ulricka said.

"Oh, go peddle your bromides to the novices."

"Very well," Ulricka said. "Perhaps I shall."

With the sure, fluid movement of a dancer half her age, Shabnan swung up into a seated position. She tucked her legs beneath her. Her skirts spread around her like an elegant ground fog.

Why her teeth weren't chattering from cold, Ulricka couldn't tell. The woman was as good as naked.

Shabnan said, "Tell me, have you ever noticed that we worship the

Goddess in a forest of penises?" She gestured to take in the whole of the Cathedral. "Look at them! Gorgeous, aren't they? Honestly, I can't decide whether to feel threatened or aroused."

"The lintels aren't phalluses," Ulricka said.

"The Hands and Feet of Nut? Don't let those fool you. Our henge is a forest of erections. You stroked them on your way in, didn't you? I know I always do." She stretched herself out again, one knee raised. Her skirts fanned down the sides of the altar. The torches sent up tendrils of aromatic smoke.

If Ulricka hadn't known any better, she would have accused the Crone of trying to seduce her.

"Yes, I stroked them," Ulricka said. "I like the feel of the stone."

"Why? What about it gives you such a sense of pleasure?"

"I have no idea."

"I do. You love it because they're solid and hard," Shabnan said. "Well, stone is as solid and as hard as anything can be in a world that you intend to grind into a bloody pulp."

"That *I* intend? How do I—"

Shabnan cut her off. "Have you noticed the way the Circle forms a slight mound, with the altar at its apex. I think the Circle is really an areola and that the altar is really a teat. I think we ought to call it the Nipple of Isis. After all, it *is* where we draw our spiritual nourishment." She flashed a smile. "What do you think? The Nipple of Isis? Yes or no?"

"The altar isn't round."

"Pedantry doesn't suit you, Ricki."

Ulricka had had enough. "How dare you—"

Again the Crone silenced her. "How dare I talk to you as though you were a spoiled child? I dare because you *are* a spoiled child, and because in that herd of sycophants you call a court, I am the only person who isn't afraid of you."

Ulricka's hands trembled. Thora had told her that no matter what the Crone said or did, she ought to allow it. For one thing, it wasn't within any mother metropolitan's power to depose a crone. And for another, Thora had told her, "Shabnan's lack of awe will be your greatest asset. At times you'll want to murder her, but you mustn't."

"Why not?" Ulricka had asked.

"Because you'd be deposed and dead before sunset," Thora had said. "Remember, Shabnan will be the mirror you'll need."

The four torches flared again, as if on cue, and Ulricka said, "Make your point."

In another of Shabnan's fluid movements, she resumed her seated position. She reminded Ulricka of a female incarnation of Shiva, Lord of the Dance.

In the torchlight, the cobra's emerald eyes twinkled with mischief.

Shabnan said, "I've decided to feel aroused. It's a delicious way to feel, even at my age, especially at my age."

Where was she going with this?

"You're not yet sixty."

"Don't condescend. It's me you're talking to."

Shabnan stretched. She threw her arms above her head and arched her back. The bodice of her dress tightened across her breasts. Her nipples, which were dark and erect, showed through the gauzy fabric.

Penises and nipples. There was no end to the erections.

Shabnan hopped lightly down from the altar. "Well, I'm off to find a playmate. Priests can be such fun."

Shabnan could fuck every priest at the cathedral if she liked, but no amount of sex would restore her youth. She had dried up for good.

Ulricka had formed the words, had dressed them in their ranks for the attack, but she could not bring herself to fling them.

The mirror was beyond her power to shatter, but she was afraid to insult it.

Shabnan said, "I want to take full advantage before you murder the rest of them."

"Jinhai was a spy."

"Spies have information, and now he's dead. He might have been of help."

"He was."

"True. It must be hard for you to get in enough target practice."

Shabnan walked toward the innermost ring, toward the pathway that would lead her out toward the priests' rectory.

She turned back. "It's a pity you'll never know what it's like to feel aroused and free to have sex with whomever you choose. No fear of pregnancy and no duty to become pregnant. The orgasms can go on forever." She smiled tauntingly. "But then I suppose you have other interests to make you hot and wet."

The muscles across Ulricka's chest tightened. The Crone's purpose was clear, or at least a portion of it was: the playing with sacrifice and death, the phony emphasis on the pharaonic religion, and the jabs about Jinhai.

Shabnan had attacked Narmer, that dabbler in all things ancient Egyptian, and she had attacked Ulricka's steps toward a military alliance with him.

But how had Shabnan anticipated Ulricka's arrival in the Cathedral Henge in the middle of the night?

Ulricka set that question aside. Her movements were no secret and neither was the fact that she liked to find solitude late at night in the Circle.

Ulricka said, "You've seen the reports: Wolfram's work on a new weapon, Dagna's proposed engagement to Gregory, Narmer's preparations to attack downriver. The Cathedral will have to stand with one side or the other or be crushed between them."

"What loathsome drivel," the Crone said. She crossed back to Ulricka. "Really, you ought to listen to yourself. I don't mean to pry, but have you become infatuated with that beastly little toad?"

"Narmer?" Ulricka asked, incredulous.

"That's the one, the self-proclaimed Son of Amun-Ra." She added, in a tone that she alone could muster, "I'd have thought that such a declaration would have sent him to the stake."

"Amun-Ra was admitted to the pantheon centuries ago," Ulricka said. A flash of irritation colored her voice.

"A necessary sop to the boys, I supposed," Shabnan said. "What about Narmer, though? Are you infatuated?"

"I find him repellent."

"Fine, but do you see through him?"

"Of course I do."

"Then why play into his hands?"

"I can't fight on two fronts. I can be the hammer or the anvil, but I can't be both, and I don't want to be what ends up in between."

"Then don't be."

"You sound as though I have a choice."

"You do," Shabnan said. "Wars happen because large groups of people decide to kill one another."

"Narmer can't afford to leave us in his rear."

"Geography is destiny? You'll have to do better than that."

"In our case it's true," Ulricka said.

"Wherever did you learn such prattle?" Shabnan asked. "You could stop this saber-rattling right now."

Ulricka felt her mouth drop open. "How?"

"By refusing to cooperate, you silly bitch!"

Ulricka let the jibe slide by. "How do I refuse? It takes power to refuse. I have a palace guard, not an army."

Shabnan's eyes looked like two pots of molten iron. "Call down the wrath of the Gods and the Generations upon them. Drown them in the living fires of hell. Refuse to enter the names of their dead in the *Dirge*. Refuse to solemnize their marriages. Have their babies declared weaklings! Turn back their pilgrims. Curse them! Damn them! Cast them out! Burn them at the stake! Send their virgins home unbedded. Pitch their offerings onto the garbage heaps! Blot them out!" She moved in closer, so close that Ulricka could feel her breath on her face. "You are the avatar of the Great Goddess. You are *Her* living presence on earth. You *are* the Goddess! Act like it!"

Ulricka twisted her hands together. Her eyes and nose burned, but she refused to allow the tears. "I may as well declare jihad upon every clan in the basin."

Shabnan rolled her eyes in exasperation. "Then bring Dagna here. To hell with their plans. She wants to come. Let her. Ordain her to the priesthood. When her father dies, you'll be able to pick his successor, or as good as. In the meantime, foment dissention in Narmer's clan and among his allies. Try him for heresy. His devotion to the patriarchal gods of ancient Egypt gives you ample grounds. The man's a heretic. Treat him like one. Throw him off balance and keep him there until he implodes. You have no need to enlist in Narmer's war."

No need? Circumstances were forcing war upon her.

Ulricka paused, rethought, and reached the same wretched conclusion. It was join one side or the other or bring down destruction upon the Cathedral.

There was a balancing truth, however. A war *was* approaching, but it was not yet upon her. Killing Jinhai may have been a mortal blunder.

"I can't exploit Dagna," Ulricka said.

"Why not?"

"Her presence would hamstring us. She'd be a distraction. Edmund would badger us until we gave in and forced her to return to her clan. The whole place will be in an uproar for years if we accepted her."

After a pause, Shabnan said, "The cloth was a good touch."

"Yes, it was, and beautifully woven. But she must stay where she is. Am I understood?"

"I'm no fool."

An undercurrent in the Crone's voice touched a nerve. "Neither am I," Ulricka said, coming down hard on every word.

The Crone smiled that superior little smile of hers. "And yet, dear Ricki, you have so much to learn and so little time in which to learn it."

This time it was Ulricka who left a silence. Breaking it, she said, "Good night. I'll see to the torches for you."

EIGHTEEN

After spending a few days at the proving ground, Wolfram and Vlod rode back down the peninsula toward the ferry landing. A small guard trailed behind them.

"It'll never work the way Aerian imagines it will." Imitating Aerian, Wolfram added, *"Maybe there won't be a next war."* In a disgusted tone, he finished with, "And maybe pigs will grow wings."

"Then you ought to stop the project," Vlod said. "Why risk a charge of heresy?"

"Because weaponized rockets will give us an advantage," Wolfram said. "Tell me, was that explosion in the powder shack an accident?"

"Eakan was a careful man."

"Mistakes happen. That's why they're called mistakes. You're careful and your boiler blew up."

"Shitty iron," Vlod said, and felt the words claw at his throat. "Shittier than we'd thought it was." Vlod made a face. "That was our, no, *my* mistake." After a small gap, Vlod asked, "How skilled are Aerian and Desmond with gunpowder?"

"Self-taught."

"They'll need experts from the mill," Vlod said.

"Done," Wolfram said.

Vlod had deliberately skipped over his questions about why they hadn't had expert help to begin with.

It had been a matter of secrecy and initial scope, of course. And too they couldn't have anticipated that they'd drift into tinkering with mixtures and granularity. They would have thought that premade gunpowder would be sufficient. They'd been out to prove a point, not to produce a perfect weapon—as if that were possible in an imperfect world.

There was the door to heresy!

Continuing, Wolfram said, "I'll send a couple of people."

"Thank you," Vlod said.

"Will you help?" Wolfram asked.

The question had been inevitable from the moment Wolfram had entered Vlod's workshop. Without understanding why, Vlod said, "You promised those poor, dumb bastards you'd protect them."

"They understand the situation."

"I wonder how much my father understood," Vlod said, throwing the words down.

"Not enough to keep himself alive," Wolfram said. "Your father suffered from those popular twin psychoses that the truth is knowable and that it can make a difference."

Vlod's resentment flared. "Edmund could have—"

"Your father could have held his tongue!"

To that, Vlod had no answer. Yes, his father could have; and no, his father couldn't have. He had spoken out, he had jeopardized the clan, he had committed open heresy, he had defied the Cathedral, and it had cost him his life.

And for what?

A fit of pride?

No, it had hardly been about ego or pride or the truth.

What then?

What had driven him onto that stake?

"Well, what's it to be?" Wolfram asked. "Yes or no?"

"Yes. I need to find out what happened to Eakan."

"That's not good enough."

This response left Vlod a touch dumbfounded. "You're the one who asked."

"I'm also the one who's turning you down," Wolfram said. "I need your commitment, not your curiosity."

Anger twisted the muscles in the small of Vlod's back. "Look at it this way: if your fancy rockets are important enough to sabotage their development, then they're important enough to build."

A few hours later, as their ferry crossed the middle of the river, an ornate felucca turned in toward the docks at Fort George. Her lateen sails were massive triangular sprays of red, white, and orange. They gleamed in the light of the late-afternoon sun.

She was a Cathedral ship. No other manor on the river—for the Cathedral was, along with everything else, a manor—deployed vessels of that rig. Nor was she one of the Cathedral packets that plied the river.

"*The Wings of Nekhbet*," Vlod said, his voice nearly hushed. "She's a gorgeous ship."

"She's too gaudy," Wolfram said.

"She has style."

"If you say so, Little Magus," Wolfram said, using one of Vlod's recently acquired nicknames. It was one of those nicknames that no one outside the household would dare to use. "I wonder what the Mother Metropolitan has sent us this time."

By the time Wolfram and Vlod landed in Fort George, the felucca had snugged down, and the bulk of her crew had gone ashore.

Wolfram and Vlod invited themselves aboard.

The ship's captain was a woman of striking good looks, named Selene.

Wolfram asked her about her trip.

She told them that she had delivered several routine packages on her way downstream, had brought a diplomatic dispatch for Edmund—which she'd already sent up to the castle—and had landed a couple of passengers: a vision dancer and a seminarian.

"I have the paperwork in my cabin," Selene said, helpfully. Her smile would have lit up a dark night.

"No doubt," Wolfram said. By now he was playing the suspicious battlemaster rather than being the suspicious battlemaster. Could it also be that he was flirting with her? "Anyway, it sounds like packet work, to me. Why send *The Wings of Nekhbet* all the way down here?"

"That's what I asked," she said. The smile redoubled.

"What did they say?"

"They ordered me to assassinate Edmund."

Wolfram's face split into a wide grin. "I'll redouble his guard. In the meantime, what are you doing here?"

She couldn't say. No, honestly, she didn't have any idea. Her commanders had presented the trip as a reward for her crew's steadfast service. Any trip downriver made a welcome break from their usual back-and-forth between Maryhill and the upriver clans.

Without saying it directly, she left no doubt that she thought of the clans above the Cathedral as pigs. Rude. Overbearing. Filthy. Dishonest. Tourists, not pilgrims. *Humorless.*

Vlod had never met anyone who could say as much with as few spoken words or with a smile or a tilt of the head.

After he and Wolfram had gone ashore and were well away from the ship, the battlemaster asked, "Notice anything?"

"Are you going to bed her?"

"Not in this life," Wolfram said. "We were having a little fun with each other. Period." He sighed a regretful sigh. "Answer the question."

"She was too easy with her answers," Vlod said.

"That, too. But, no, it's the fact of the ship herself." He pointed at the ground, and said, "It's the fact that she's *here*. A reward for a hardworking crew? Not bloody likely."

"Why then?"

"Can't say, but that lovely smile hides a calculating heart."

Later that evening, one of the dancers from the manor henge presented herself at the door to Dagna's apartments and handed her a sealed letter.

The wrapper was plain and so was its origin: the Crone of the Cathedral Henge of Eileen the Immortal.

Dagna dismissed the dancer, closed and locked her door, and tore off the wrapper.

Mother Metropolitan Ulricka has asked me to...

After much prayerful consideration, Her Beatitude has concluded...

Dagna skimmed.

Your manifest vocation is to support your family and clan as your father directs...

Always remember that a life spent in obedience to a secular role is also, profoundly, a life of religious profession...

Please feel free to contact me with your concerns. Our sincerest prayers are with you.

A physical pain shot through Dagna's body.

She had made herself into a laughingstock.

Wolfram put a couple of his spies to work, but the captain's reward-for-loyal-service explanation held.

Sort of.

Had there been a warning lodged in the captain's sub-rosa gossip about the upriver clans, or had it been a plea for help? Wolfram couldn't say, and Edmund was in no mood for riddles.

"If Ulricka wants our help, she'll ask for it," Edmund said.

"Maybe she can't," Wolfram said.

"Why not? She can do whatever she wants."

"Can she?"

At the end of a brief search, Selene, the felucca's captain, found Malabar's House of Golden Trinkets. It was a few paces off Fort George's main street. The shopkeeper—Malabar himself, she presumed—led her into the workshop in the back.

Malabar was a small man, neither fat nor thin, with gray hair, rounded shoulders, and the beginnings of a hunch. Jeweler's polish stained his fingers.

Selene handed over the small leather wallet that *they* had instructed her to deliver. It was a dispatch case, the kind messengers used when they wished to avoid attention.

The identity of *they* remained unknown. Their power did not.

They'd come aboard her ship shortly before she was due to cast off from the Maryhill docks. They had used no names, but they had made their authority plain. They'd given her minimal instructions, and had answered none of her questions. They had demanded her signature on a receipt.

When they had it, they had told her that she may or may not be returning with a small package. The utmost secrecy was called for. Demanded. Did she understand?

Yes, she understood.

They had then told her how satisfied they were with her grasp of her assignment, they had smiled encouragingly—threateningly, now that she thought about it—and then they had returned ashore.

The instant they had disappeared into the warren of buildings fronting the dock, the port captain had raised the signal giving *The Wings of Nekhbet* permission to depart.

The encounter had proved two of the popular sayings about shit: It floated to the top, and it flowed downhill.

"Any trouble with Wolfram?" Malabar asked.

How had Malabar found out about Wolfram's visit aboard? Had he been watching her ship?

"No trouble," she said.

"Good. Let's hope he remains satisfied."

Malabar retrieved a tiny package from a drawer and set it on his workbench. "You'll be carrying this back upstream with you." He unfolded the wrapping.

Revealed was a small pile of parchment sheets. He gently lifted the corner of one. Between each pair was a square of gold leaf.

"You're to verify the contents of the package. It's gold leaf, so don't touch it. The leaves might fly to pieces. I can show you as many sheets as you care to see."

Her instructions had said nothing about inspecting the package, only that she was to convey it upriver to the Cathedral. No doubt the old man was hoping to protect himself.

"My job is to make the deliveries," the captain said.

Malabar closed the wrapping, tied it securely, and placed the bundle in a small wooden box. He closed it, carefully tacked it shut, and handed it to her.

The moment she was back aboard her felucca, she hid the box under the cabin-sole planking in the great cabin. It wasn't a notably inventive hiding place, but it would do. Searching for better would only attract attention, as in, "Say, what's the skipper doing crawling around in the bilges? Did we hit a deadhead or something?"

She poured herself a stiff gin and sat at her desk.

The gin helped.

She decided that she was lucky to have left Malabar's shop alive. She also decided that she would be far luckier to complete the delivery and walk away.

Nineteen

Three days later at the Cathedral, Shabnan accepted delivery of the gold leaf. She dismissed the captain—who looked, she thought, rather too pale for such an outdoorsy type—and presented the small wooden box to the Mother Metropolitan.

Ulricka held it as though it contained an enraged viper.

Her face had recently turned pasty, far beyond the powers of her makeup to hide. No matter how well her previous pregnancies had gone, this one was making her ill.

It would be, the Crone reflected, a full two years before Ulricka permitted herself to conceive again. Two Year Kings would die without holy issue. They would plow and plant, but their seed would never sprout.

Poor boys.

***

Outside the Saraswati Palace, Selene let out a sigh of relief. Her head was on her shoulders, her blood was in her veins, and her heart was still pumping. Fortune had smiled upon her.

So far.

She shook off her paranoia and made for the docks. She thanked the Gods and the Generations that she had a ship to go home to.

Her felucca was closer to a trumped-up riverboat than she was to a ship, but she had a hull, decks, masts, spars, sails, and oars. She was quick and agile, too. Above all else, *The Wings of Nekhbet* was a home and a feeder, and at the moment, she was a safer place for her captain than anywhere ashore.

Ulricka paged through the sheets of gold leaf until she found the dispatch.

Shabnan looked on silently, statue-still, as though breathing would impose too great a risk.

Ulricka eased apart the foil sheets and withdrew the message. The folded sheets of paper had been pressed and repressed together until they were no larger than a playing card. Ulricka teased apart the folds. She opened the pages one by one until the whole of the message was revealed.

She read aloud.

The negotiations for Dagna's betrothal to Gregory, Vernon's elder son and heir, were moving forward.

"The happy couple must be simply agog with joy and anticipation," Shabnan said.

"You're a cynical old woman," Ulricka said, and continued reading.

The last hurdle for the betrothal to clear was the Geneticists Guild's approval of the union.

"Is there any reason for them to disapprove?" Shabnan asked.

"Not that I'm aware of," Ulricka said.

"What about Dagna and Gregory themselves?" Shabnan asked. "Might either of them balk?"

"Not according to our source."

"Do you believe him?"

"On balance, yes," Ulricka said. "Dagna *is* a dutiful child, and Gregory *is* an ambitious son."

"Oh, to be young and in love again," Shabnan said, with mock enthusiasm.

"You were never young and in love."

"What do you mean? I was in love. Once."

"You may have been in love. Once. But you were born *old*."

"Oh, please. I was born no worse than middle-aged."

Ulricka chuckled and continued reading.

Desmond and Aerian were making progress. Wolfram had redoubled his support for their project.

"How's he done that?" Shabnan asked.

Ulricka continued with the message. Wolfram had recruited Vlod, Edmund's personal magus, to work on it. They had sufficient funds and adequate security. Sooner or later, they were bound to produce a viable weapon. In the agent's opinion, the project had to be stopped.

"Do tell," Shabnan said dryly.

"Do indeed," Ulricka said.

Her source informed her that the local engineers were unlikely to stumble onto the project. They were an arrogant, lazy bunch of dullards. They had grown fat on the routine of an established and wealthy clan. Their extortion schemes, for example, were, for the most part, half-hearted, clumsy failures that netted less than a quarter of what they ought to.

"Arrogance breeds laziness like a swamp breeds mosquitoes," Shabnan said.

"It's the other mosquitoes that do it, not the swamp," Ulricka said.

"You take my point."

Ulricka returned to the report.

Finally, and this was an important issue, a batch of gunpowder had exploded and killed one of the project's workmen. Had it been an accident or had Ulricka infiltrated other agents into the clan, with instructions to sabotage the project?

Ulricka looked at Shabnan. "It wasn't one of mine. Was it one of yours?"

Shabnan held them up and waved them. "My hands are clean. See?"

"An accident, then?"

"Maybe," Shabnan said. "Edmund has his share of enemies."

"True."

"I don't understand what's driving Wolfram," Shabnan said. "It's not entirely his devotion to discovering more efficient ways of killing people."

Ulricka frowned in concentration, then said, "Vernon has tipped his hand to Edmund. That much is self-evident. Why else would they have gone off chasing after an alliance?"

Shabnan nodded, accepting the argument.

Ulricka went on. "By this time, Edmund has copies of every single one of Jinhai's reports to Vernon." She grimaced. "No, that can't be it, not entirely."

"Why not?" Shabnan asked.

"Because Wolfram's fascination with rockets started earlier."

"He's the Iredales' battlemaster."

Ulricka's face brightened suddenly. "Exactly. Wolfram must have taken a good hard look at Narmer's actions and come to the same conclusion I did."

"Vernon, too, then," Shabnan said.

"Yes, Vernon, too," Ulricka said. "But they've embraced the opposite response. They intend to meet him in battle."

"They have full-fledged armies. You don't."

Ulricka fought away the urge to jump up and pace. She must hold herself in check.

Like a pack of wolves closing in on a wounded man, Narmer's ambitions were closing in on the clans, closing in on the Cathedral.

This time, the survivors would not lay out their dead in neat rows, but toss them into common pits.

"Narmer won't allow them to engage him; rather, he'll engage them. He'll chose the ground, and leave them no choice but to fight upon it."

"You're giving him too much credit," Shabnan said.

"No, I'm not. He has skill, that one."

"What are you going to do?" Shabnan asked.

Ulricka swallowed hard. "Make friends with the pharaoh."

"Meaning what?"

"Don't be obtuse."

Shabnan arched an eyebrow. "Answer the question."

"Up until now, my objective has been to maintain the Cathedral's neutrality. Therefore, I've tried to hold Narmer at arm's length by tying him up in negotiations. However, due to Jinhai's meddling, my tactic has backfired."

"It would appear so."

"Neutrality is no longer possible. If the Cathedral is to survive, I must forge the least odious, the most defensible alliance I can with Narmer. I must, like it or not, stand with him against Edmund and Vernon."

Shabnan smiled. It was not a happy smile.

Ulricka demanded, "Well, does my recitation pass muster?"

"I'm not the one you need to convince."

"Who is?"

"Now it's my turn, Ricki. Don't be obtuse."

Ulricka let the dramatic riddle go unanswered. "Tell me," she said, "who's Ziellottes working for?"

"As far as we can determine, he's working on contract for Vernon. It's an open matter, of course."

Ulricka made a dismissive gesture. "That's a smokescreen. Vernon paid for those reports, but who was reading them long before he ever saw them, eh?"

"Good question. I'm not sure it makes any difference on the ground, but it's a damn good question."

"It makes every difference in world."

"What do you want done?"

"I want you to produce results."

TWENTY

The knock on the door to Ulricka's sitting room came a second time, polite but firm.

"Come," Ulricka called.

The door swung open, and Yingpei—how beautiful he was this afternoon!—ushered in Harakhty, Narmer's flunky.

Showing a broad smile, Ulricka asked, "My lord Harakhty, how are you? Did you have a good hunt this morning?"

He bowed comically low.

"Thank you, Your Beatitude. We did tolerably well."

He had, in fact, slaughtered a greater share of the Cathedral's game than was entirely polite. Perhaps his mother had failed to teach him the virtue of moderation.

Ulricka maintained her welcoming expression and ignored the anger burning across her chest.

"Congratulations! I hope to go out after I've delivered."

She glanced down at her stomach and added a self-deprecating smile. It was nonsense like this bit of play acting that put men like Harakhty off their guard. No woman—no woman with a brain in her head—would put up with it for a split second, but it turned most men into gooey mush, the spineless fools.

Ulricka added, "I'm not far along, but hunting is out of the question, for the time being. A bad spill might prove disastrous." How she disgusted herself!

"Nothing would make me happier than to accompany Your Beatitude. You're due in the summer, are you not, Your Beatitude? Perhaps in the fall, you would be good enough to act as my guide."

Ulricka swallowed her anger, which by this time was verging on a blinding rage. "Few things would give me greater pleasure."

"Then I shall look forward to it, Your Beatitude."

"In the meantime, if Narmer would be willing to accept it, I would like to invite him to enjoy the hospitality of my court at his earliest convenience."

Twenty-One

Ten days later, Ulricka welcomed Narmer to the palace. The March weather was bright and cold.

Ulricka had to admit that in the three years since they'd last met, Narmer had changed for the better. The repulsive toad was gone. The toad had been short and hairy. He had smelled of garlic, onions, and cooking oil. His breath had been noxious, and his teeth had been dirty. He'd had little piggy eyes.

The Narmer of today bowed before her.

He was still short. His thick bones hadn't changed, nor had the melon shape of his skull. His little piggy eyes hadn't grown into the eyes of a chieftain, either, but the rest of him had.

He was washed, shaved, and his hair was clipped. His teeth were clean, and his breath no longer threatened to reduce the marble to lime.

About his eyes…Three years ago they'd been arrogant and hungry. They had been the eyes of an underling greedy for his next reward.

Now those eyes were sharp with pride, courage, and determination, but not in the common sense of those terms. Rather, his eyes were ablaze with *purpose*.

Ulricka had heard rumors of Narmer's transformation, and her own spies had told her a lot besides; but she'd been unprepared for the actuality. Yes, she had seen it gathering, year by year, success by success, the adjustments here and there, but the totality had only recently come together. It was like realizing one day that the toddler had become a child, that the adolescent had become an adult, that the adult had become spent.

What, she wondered, had happened to him?

Had his fascination with the Egyptian pantheon remained a bit of window dressing or had it become *belief*?

Before he had hoped to conquer the river basin. He had planned, plotted. Now, he meant to do it.

Later in the day, Ulricka sent for Shabnan.

When she arrived, Ulricka asked, "Do I have a confidential way to contact the Iredales' chief geneticist?"

Shabnan indulged herself in a suppressed chuckle. "Warrick is here, Your Beatitude, on the grounds of the Cathedral."

Warrick. The name sent a tremor through Ulricka. He wasn't repulsive, not physically, not like Narmer, no matter how much he'd cleaned himself up. No, that wasn't it. Warrick was far too old to be either attractive or repulsive.

The things that disturbed Ulricka about Warrick were his voice and his eyes. His merest whisper seized her attention by the throat and threatened to choke the life out of it.

As for his eyes, they were so pale a shade of blue that they unnerved her. His gaze left the impression that he was able to see things the Gods and the Generations had forbidden *Themselves* to see.

"A visit?" Ulricka asked. "Why is he here?"

"Ostensibly, to do research in the genealogical archive, but he's spending most of his time in the Virgins' Pavilion."

"Those poor girls," Ulricka said. The thought of Warrick fathering a child on one of them made her feel sick.

"That's the strange part," Shabnan said. "No fornication. He talks to them."

Now there was an old story. "About what?"

"Where they're from. Their families."

"Funny way to have sex," Ulricka said.

"Any idea what he might be up to?"

"I don't care. Find out where he is."

Shabnan left Ulricka's study.

She was back in ten minutes.

"He's in the genealogical archive."

———

As far as Selene, the captain of *The Wings of Nekhbet*, could tell, the thin, wiry man she'd noticed earlier hadn't followed her out of The Drowning Pilgrim.

He'd kept a discrete eye on her while she'd eaten. He'd never ogled her, had never so much as nodded to her, but something about him had sounded an alarm.

Maybe it was a false one. Like as not, he was lonely or too shy to approach her. Or he could be one of those men who liked to look at women but who rarely took it further than that. Admirers from afar.

Maybe.

And maybe the Pacific Ocean was a freshwater lake.

A cool wind off the river caressed her face.

She made an effort to stroll instead of stride, to relax, let the tension flow from her arms and legs. She refused to give in to the fear that she was being followed. It had to be the product of too much time spent cooped up aboard and not enough time ashore.

Or it was that reflexive caution that went with being female.

The street she was on came out between two warehouses. Ahead of her was the pier where her ship was moored.

She crossed and walked along the pier until she came to the top of a downward-sloping ramp. Below lay a large floating dock. Tied to it were two ships: *The Wings of Nekhbet* and *The Eyes of Wadjet*. They were as sleek, gaudy, and beautiful as only well-built, well-loved vessels can be. Together they were called the Nebti, after the two Egyptian Goddesses for which they'd been named, Nekhbet and Wadjet.

Therein lay the captain's only uneasiness about her ship. Narmer had raised a subscription to build the Nebti as a donation to the Mother

Metropolitan. They were to have been her personal vessels, but she had ordered them assigned to the Cathedral's fleet.

Nevertheless, the appearance that they had been a personal bribe instead of a religious donation lingered.

A boot crunched on the roughhewn planking of the pier behind her.

She started to turn, but an arm closed around her throat and hauled her backwards. The point of a dagger pressed into her back.

"Don't struggle," a voice said. It was a remarkably gentle voice.

<hr>

The genealogical archive occupied a dowdy mishmash of a building on an outcropping of rocky ground upslope from the cathedral.

Over the centuries, as the records had piled up, the Cathedral had added section after section to the archive. Each had a steep roof, thick stone walls, thick stone floors, and had been built on and surrounded by drain tiles and gravel. There were windows for air and light, but no flames, none of any kind. When the light failed at the end of the day, work stopped.

Ulricka walked up from the Saraswati Palace alone. She could have sent for Warrick, but this way she could claim a desire to look up something for herself.

She smiled her way through the welcoming flurry and went inside. In the reception area she signed in as required of everyone, lied to the attendant about what she wanted, declined a dozen offers of help, and dismissed the people buzzing around her. She was not a midden and they were not flies.

Alone again, finally, she headed into the maze of rooms, passages, and shelves. Signs gave directions, but from experience, she knew they were of no use to anyone but the archivists. She would have to rely on her hunter's instincts.

In due course, her instincts failed her. She switched tactics and began a systematic search. It succeeded. She found Warrick in the Checkerboard Room, so named for its red and black floor tiles, eight to a side.

The room was much the same as the others, although higher, brighter, and larger. The stacks were in the center. These were rows of shelves that held volume after volume of registry information: the vital statistics for the Columbia River Basin, or, more narrowly stated, for the Province of the Inland Empire and the Holy Oregon.

Here were the abstracts of the region's conceptions, both supposed and real; miscarriages; abortions; exposures; infanticides; successful births; survivals to puberty; proof of fecundity; marriages; divorces; illnesses; occupations; education and training; career milestones; deaths; and whatever else the statisticians could imagine would be of use. Worktables and chairs lined the outside walls.

The initial reports filled room after room, with two additional rooms under construction.

Currently, two rooms held the abstracts. The first was the White Room; its floors being paved with white marble. The second was the Checkerboard Room.

There were plans underway for a third such room. It would be twice as large as the other two combined. It would be called the Chess Room and would feature a floor of white and black tiles, eight to a side.

Warrick didn't look up until she sat down across from him. "Your Beatitude! What a pleasure it is to see you at last," he said. "I expected you days ago."

The captain was chilled and naked.

She wasn't aboard a ship, but confined in some sort of building. Not a warehouse. The smells were wrong for a warehouse. And the air was too dry, too dry to be right over the water, anyway. But not inland from it, either. There was the reek of animal dung. Not overpowering, but strong. And fodder. A farm, then? A barn?

They had politely asked her questions, and she had politely refused to answer them.

They had stridently asked her the same questions, and she had told them to go to hell.

One of them had said, "We don't have time for this."

Whereupon they had stripped her and strapped her into a heavy chair.

Then they had beaten her in turns, and somewhere along the line her bladder had let go. Her urine had gushed across the seat of the chair and spattered onto the floor. They'd had a good laugh and told her she'd have to clean it up when they were done with her.

The beating had resumed.

Then it had stopped.

And now she was sitting in a puddle of her own piss. *That's beer for you*, she thought. Her jaw hurt where one of them had struck her. They'd opened a gash over her left eye, and the blood from the gash oozed down the side of her face.

There were five of them: one who was wiry and four nasty-looking thugs. They were standing in a circle around her.

If she included the one she'd kicked in the groin, there were six of them.

Hooray for her, she could count *and* do elementary arithmetic.

Fine, but what were they after?

It wasn't rape. They'd have done it by now. Torture for the sake of torture? Were they perverts who got their jollies by beating up women?

No, they'd asked questions, actual questions and not the nonsense crap interrogators usually opened up with.

Like it or not, she was in this fix because of the gold leaf she'd delivered to the Crone.

One of the men came close and stood over her. He cocked his fist. "How about I break your jaw?"

She almost laughed. They had to be amateurs.

But she had a hunch that wasn't right.

Could it be that they were otherwise decent people *pretending* to be thugs? The beating could have been a lot worse, not that it hadn't been bad enough—worse than a bar fight but not as bad as that time she'd been interrogated by an enemy clan, way back when. Those bastards...

The fist flew down toward her face.

Then again, maybe they were just thugs, after all.

The door swung open, and without a word said by anyone, the fist froze in midair.

Was that a relieved sigh she'd heard?

An older man came in. He took his time, moving smoothly, slowly, as though he were bored with the whole wearisome business of inflicting pain and humiliation in order to extract information.

He was of medium height or a little shorter, but he was wide through the chest and heavily built in the arms and legs. Stocky. He would have made one hell of a boatswain.

"That will be all for now," he said. His voice was calm and businesslike, but with a trace of disgust.

The fist eased down and opened, becoming a hand again.

The four pretenders left the room.

That left the wiry one and the new guy.

Two against one. She'd faced worse odds, but always in honest brawls.

The new guy's face was lined, and his hair was gray. He carried a lot of years, but he wasn't old.

Stocky said to her, "I'll not offend you by offering an apology, nor will I attempt to make amends. The force was necessary. In the long game, it was an act of mercy."

That was a laugh! "What happened to the leather hoses?"

"Whether I torture you or not is up to you."

It was the standard line. Even in cases of routine shipboard discipline, it was always the ones being flogged who were said to have brought it upon themselves. Which in most cases they had.

Her situation, however, *was* different.

Still, from what she could tell, Stocky was offering her a deal. Well, sort of a deal.

"Why the softening up?" she asked.

"I need you to believe in my sincerity."

"To hell with what you need!"

He sighed. It was a curiously sad sound, especially heard against the patter that her urine made as it dripped down onto the floor.

"I've stated it badly," he said. "I need for you to walk out of here alive."

Ulricka leaned over the worktable. "What are you doing in the Virgins' Pavilion? You're not attending for the copulation."

"No, I'm not," Warrick said. "They're lovely girls, but I'd feel as though I were molesting a child, and they'd feel nothing but revulsion and hatred."

Ulricka chose not to dispute his assertion. "Why then?"

"To give you an excuse to approach me. As the Mother Metropolitan, you have a duty to investigate unexpected behavior in the temple. Anywhere, in fact."

"I came for my own reasons."

"Yours, mine. No matter. You see, I've bet the few remaining years of *our* lives that our reasons overlap."

Ziellottes shifted his weight from one foot to the other. The accumulated weariness of the last several days weighed him down like a cargo of boulders bound for one of Edmund's jetties or wing dams. Ziellottes wasn't complaining, but neither could he fail to acknowledge his condition, not if he hoped to be effective.

Captain Selene was a lovely young woman. The odors of sweat, blood, and urine, each her own, did nothing to enhance her allure, but she was undeniably attractive.

She was also fiery, marvelously defiant, not a trace of timidity. She could kick, too, as the fellow in the next room, the one with the cold compress between his legs, could attest.

Ziellottes said to her, "While you were on Edmund's lands, a spy gave you a message for the Mother Metropolitan. You delivered it to Shabnan. Is that correct?"

"Go pound sand," the captain said.

"Very loyal, very brave, but very hazardous," Ziellottes said.

"Do tell."

"It's time we concluded our business."

"I can't speak for you, but I've already done my business."

More sarcasm. More defiance.

Entertaining, but what it amounted to was more wasted time.

That wasn't the whole picture, though. Her every act of refusal drove her closer to her first act of compliance.

What was the shopkeeper's mantra: Every "no" leads you closer to the "yes." That wasn't quite it, but it was close enough.

Her impotent refusals also drove her closer to panic, to the place where she would tell him anything, true or not, to end her torment.

It was the old trap.

How to break out of it...this time?

Ziellottes possessed a range of options, but no matter which he chose, he ended up in the same place: His success depended on her choice to cooperate.

To Chang, Ziellottes said, "Clean her up and return her clothes."

"Yes, sir," Chang said.

Ziellottes nodded to her and left the room.

Outside, the night was dry, clear, and cold. From where they were, on a farm by the river, he was able to watch the reflections of the stars on the water. They glittered like shimmering drops of quicksilver.

The breeze, so faint that he had to strain to determine its direction, so faint that it left the water virtually unmoved, bathed him in the odors of dry-land vegetation, of horses, and of the farm's dung heap.

Chang came out. "She's ready for you," he said. "Clean and spitting sulfur."

"Sulfur. How appropriate." Chang's face betrayed his bewilderment, but Ziellottes chose not to explain the chemistry of gunpowder.

And then he had it: the key to her cooperation.

Ziellottes sat down in front of the captain. She was washed and combed, dressed in her own clothes, and seated on a clean chair, but, of necessity, his men had tied her tightly into it. Her breathing was close to normal, and she wasn't shivering. Her eyes were clear and steady.

Good signs. They meant she was unlikely to fly off into either an embarrassing heroism or a pointless cowardice.

Ziellottes said, "You went to work on the river because ships intrigued you and life on the water delighted you. However, that life has left you with no ties, except to the ship you command. They are inanimate objects that you love as though they were alive. When one is sunk, or burned, or broken up, you weep, inwardly if not outwardly. When you leave a ship, turn her over to another captain, you feel not just remorse but a form of grief."

Was that why he cared so deeply about what happened to her? Was it because they were two solitaries, caught up in professions that were obese with danger?

She glared at him.

Ziellottes said, "Unless the right people in the right places take the right actions at the right times—"

"That's a lot of *right*s," she said.

"—the Columbia River Basin will soon be awash in a general war, and *Nekhbet*, your current ship, will be used up like so many sticks of kindling on a cold morning."

"A ship's fate is a ship's fate."

"I can prevent the war if I can obtain the *right* information and present it to the *right* people."

"That's none of my business," she said.

She'd tried for another one of her sarcastic flings, but it had sounded too much like a plea for help.

"None of your business?" Ziellottes asked. "She's *your* ship. Her people are *your* crew. They are *your* responsibility."

"She's the Cathedral's ship."

"Does Ulricka sail her?"

"No, I sail her."

"My point to a fare-thee-well."

Ziellottes untied the captain, and she stood.

"What happens now?" she asked.

"You help me or you don't."

"I won't betray the Mother Metropolitan!"

"Spoken like a true zealot. When you've made up your mind, send word to Chang." Ziellottes handed her a folded slip of paper. "Here're the instructions on how to do that. By the way, Chang is the one who looks like he's made out of sinew and iron plates."

She looked at Chang, and he inclined his head. "Ma'am," he said.

She recognized his voice from the dock. "We've met," she said. Turning back to Ziellottes, she asked, "Now what?"

"You're free to leave," Ziellottes said. "Maryhill is upriver from here."

She bolted toward the door, but after a couple of steps, she slowed her pace.

Chang's knife thudded into the door a scant half meter ahead of her. She froze in place and snapped her head around.

"Not one word," Ziellottes said.

She nodded her understanding and left the room, but not before wrenching Chang's knife from the door and slipping it into her belt.

"That was my best knife!" Chang protested.

"I'll buy you another," Ziellottes said. A smile lit his face, banishing for a moment his worry and lingering grief. Jinhai had been a friend as well as an asset.

Twenty-Two

Suppressing his sense of dread, Vlod rapped on the door to Edmund's office.

His chieftain's "Enter!" sounded angry enough to splinter the ironbound door.

It was, Vlod thought, a miracle that it hadn't.

For the last several days, the political body language around Dagna's betrothal to Gregory had gone from guarded to dismal. At one point, Edmund and Wolfram had locked themselves away with Warrick, Clan Iredales' chief geneticist.

That meeting had lasted for several hours, and over the following few days, a flock of messengers had raced back and forth between Edmund and Vernon. With each exchange, the messengers' faces had become increasingly grim.

Finally, Warrick had made a trip upriver to conduct research in the Cathedral's genealogical archives. He had not returned as a picture of happiness.

Out on the peninsula, that much of the story had reached Vlod and his team via rumor. What affect it would have on their work was a matter of conjecture.

Edmund's summons had not been a matter of conjecture. It had been as clear as a cold, dry day in January.

He had sent Brenna with it, underlining its importance.

She looked around the workshop. "A better signaling rocket?" she asked. Her voice could have curdled milk.

Vlod strapped on his sword. "That's right."

"Next you'll build one that can land on the moon."

Aerian said, "Why not? Ultimately—"

"Spare me your enthusiasm," Brenna said.

Vlod pulled his cloak on over his shoulders. "He's right. I don't know about the moon, but we could use a rocket to emulate the flight of birds, at least for short distances."

Brenna's face contorted into an expression of utter disbelief.

"You've been out here too long," she said, "with no one for company but these two." She sniffed the air. "The fumes have pickled your brain."

Aerian said, "It's the sulfur, and the manufacture of saltpeter involves a lot of manure and animal urine."

"Not your own?" she asked.

"No, it's animal," Aerian said. "So is the manure. Mind you, we could use human urine and excrement."

Later, as Vlod and Brenna rode south toward the ferry, Vlod said, "I think you frightened him."

"Who? Aerian?

"Yes, Aerian."

"He deserves to be frightened." Automatically, she scanned their surroundings. "He'll see you burned for heresy before he's done."

"The work itself will protect us."

"Whistle in someone else's dark."

Vlod had done his best to whistle, but Edmund's "Enter!" had dampened his musical efforts. Their last happy traces died away completely when Vlod saw that Wolfram and Warrick were also present.

Edmund sat behind his desk. Wolfram and Warrick sat in straight-backed chairs in front of it. A third chair, empty, had been drawn up. At Edmund's invitation, Vlod sat in it.

To Warrick, Edmund said, "Show him the file."

"Yes, my lord," Warrick said.

Warrick handed Vlod a folder. It contained a pair of genealogical charts—one for Dagna and one for Gregory—plus accompanying analyses and several related documents.

"Am I to read these?" Vlod asked.

"We'll wait," Edmund said.

After the genealogical charts and the analyses came a copy of the guild's record of the birth of a malformed infant. It had been Gregory's child.

The clan's geneticist had exposed the infant as a matter of routine. The baby's death had been mercifully quick in coming, and the marriage had been automatically dissolved.

In and of itself, Gregory being the father of *one* weakling, as such infants were called, meant nothing, or very little. However, a second such child would raise questions, and a third would result in Gregory's immediate castration and disinheritance.

Despite the work of the Geneticists Guild, weaklings were not unusual. They resulted from the tenacious effects of the conditions that had led to the Second Creation.

Edmund's paternal grandfather had sired two, and a great uncle had sired one. On Edmund's mother's side, there was a sprinkling of clubbed feet and cleft lips.

The exposure of such infants and the castration of those who repeatedly sired them was one aspect of humanity's ordained part in the Goddess's rejuvenating work. The negative traces of the Discordant Time, as the Patriarchal Age was referred to in this and similar contexts, could not be allowed to imperil the living.

Vlod turned the page.

The next document was a copy of a Geneticists Guild internal memorandum. It stated that Gregory had fathered a *second* weakling.

The story was simple enough. A few years ago, Gregory had quietly married a young women named Phillomina. Her uncle had been the chieftain of one of the minor northern clans, the Skokomish-Sheltons.

In terms of the Columbia River, it hadn't been much of a match, but it had shown a degree of promise: a move north toward Hood Canal and through it, eventually, to the open sea.

True, it was the long way around the Iredales, but it was a way around.

The Columbia River was not the end all and be all of life, regardless of what the Iredales might think.

In any event, ten months after the joyous marriage, Phillomina gave birth to a baby boy.

The Skokomish-Shelton's geneticist performed his examination and declared the baby fit. He was not a weakling.

Happiness abounded!

For a time.

However, the baby died a scant twenty-four hours later.

The Skokomish-Shelton's geneticist opened the corpse and found that the infant's heart had, literally, a hole in it. He immediately ruled it to have been a weakling.

At Vernon and Gregory's insistence, the geneticist ran further tests, both on the corpse, on Phillomina, and on her family's genetic record.

Sadly for Gregory's future as Vernon's heir, the tests turned up nothing suspicious: no poisons, no untoward agents, no unusual medications, and no previously unsuspected genetic hazards.

Gregory immediately divorced Phillomina and returned home to the Land of the Five Rivers.

Phillomina's uncle quickly married her off to the first chieftain's son who would have her. The lucky groom was the second son of the chieftain of Clan Belfair.

Vernon had made no particular effort to hide the episode, but neither had he gone out of his way to mention or explain it.

Two weaklings.

Two *known* weaklings. Not all weaklings were discovered and exposed.

Two...

One to go...

The man was standing on a precipice.

Yes, but was he teetering on it?

To Vlod, Edmund's office felt as though it were closing in, as though the door and windows were being nailed shut. The problems of gunpowder, rockets, payloads, targeting, and security seemed trivial in comparison.

Vlod held up the papers. He raised his eyebrows in a silent question to his chieftain.

"You see the problem," Edmund said.

Vlod did.

"How did Phillomina's *next* pregnancy go?" Vlod asked.

The presumption was that men carried the defective genes, a legacy of the Discordant Time. However, some women tended to give birth to weaklings, just as some men tended to father them. Often after the second, if there were no healthy children to care for, such women joined a *celibate* religious order. The vows of such orders were *strictly* enforced, no exceptions and no second chances.

"Her next pregnancy had a similar result," Warrick said.

"Another damn case of Trotter's womb," Wolfram said. "Her clan ought to have had her locked away."

Gregory's score, then, was one for sure and one perhaps. It was better, but it was no prize.

Warrick stiffened as though he'd been personally insulted. "Trotter's womb is a specious syndrome," he said. "We have no proof of its existence."

"Except for all those needlessly castrated men," Wolfram said.

"We have *no* proof," Warrick said. He sounded as though he believed that repetition would make it so. "None."

"When it comes to Gregory, you have to admit that Phillomina's second weakling clouds the issue," Edmund said.

"Of course it does," Warrick said. "Nevertheless, given his record and the predispositions amongst your family, especially on your father's side, the guild will be disinclined to approve the application. The risks of Dagna giving birth to a weakling would be catastrophically high."

Vlod almost pointed out, needlessly, that as far as the Iredales were concerned, Warrick *was* the Geneticists Guild.

Edmund glanced at Wolfram, who nodded. The brothers had reached a decision.

Edmund said, "Thank you, Warrick."

Warrick reached to gather up his papers, but Edmund stopped him. "Leave those. I'll have them returned."

"As you wish," Warrick said, and left.

Wolfram locked the door.

"All right," Edmund said. "Let's hear it."

For the next hour, they talked.

When they had no more to say, Vlod asked, "What do you want done?"

Edmund said, "You're to augur the marriage between Dagna and Gregory."

"A second augury, my lord?" Vlod asked.

"Not a second augury, but a distinct augury," Edmund said. "We've augured the *proposal*. Now I want to ask about the *marriage*."

TWENTY-THREE

Ziellottes watched Ulricka pour two cups of strong black tea. The aroma hovered over the low table between them. If nothing else, her household staff had an enviable talent for the selection and preparation of tea. They had no understanding of coffee, but when it came to tea, their expertise stood unrivaled.

Ziellottes declined milk and sugar. Ulricka had not as yet palmed a poison into his cup, but he could think of no earthly—or heavenly!—reason why he ought to give her two additional opportunities to do so.

It wasn't as though he feared she would try. He didn't. But it could do no harm for him to be careful. His hostess was, at the end of the day, well-known for her fondness for sweeping gestures, for throwing caution, or what lesser minds would take for caution, to the winds.

Steam wafted from the cup she held out to him. "I ought to have had you arrested," she said, "but here we are, having tea like two old friends."

He smiled happily and accepted the cup. The tea's aroma continued to betray no telltale chemical traces, no hint of poison.

For the present, he was safe enough.

As for the future, who could say?

He had been Jinhai's handler, and by this time, Ulricka doubtless had ample proof that he had been.

She might change her mind about their "friendship" and its utility. It wouldn't surprise him.

Ulricka always had been a bundle of inconsistencies. Anxious in the morning, elated at noon, quietly content in the evening. Suspicious one instant, trusting the next. And yet, generally speaking, she governed with a consistent insight and a skill that her critics belittled at their peril.

Perhaps her genius lay in deciding with whom to surround herself, in deciding whom to trust, in deciding whom to believe. But in that case, how was Ziellottes to explain Narmer's presence among her allies?

Allies?

Did Ulricka have allies, or were they people of another nature altogether?

Sycophants.

Opportunists.

Parasites.

Enemies masquerading as friends.

Call them what you will. They each amounted to the same thing, reduced to the same pathology.

Sadly, now and then, Ulricka's abilities fell short of her own mark, assuming it was her own mark and not a pretense.

Ziellottes set the cup untouched on the low pink-granite trestle table between them. It wasn't that he was reluctant to drink his tea; rather, two alternatives confronted him. First, he could conclude his business as quickly as possible and leave, or, second, he could rip her throat out and then leave. The latter would offer acute satisfaction in the short term, but the former would yield vastly greater results in the long term.

Alas...

"I believe," Ziellottes said, "that someone has taken a hand in your affairs."

Ulricka's expression showed a flash of surprise. "I don't understand."

"Neither do I," Ziellottes said, nor did he.

Some days ago, he had questioned and released the captain of *The Wings of Nekhbet.*

Yesterday, he had chosen to eat breakfast at the Fowled Anchor, a waterfront establishment. The tavern's sign featured a ship's anchor with a length of line wrapped around its stock and shank, fouling it. However, sly cormorants, grinning seagulls, and smug pelicans perched on the stock and ring. Inland humor, but it had made him curious enough to try the place.

Chang came in and sat on the opposite side of the table. "Have you heard about your ship captain?"

Ziellottes' stomach lurched. "Heard what?"

"She's dead, murdered. Come on, I'll show you."

Outside the Fowled Anchor, two of Chang's men fell into step, and the four of them hurried down to the docks.

At the end of Pier 4, a knot of people had gathered around a policeman, a member of the Cathedral guard. At his feet lay a figure.

Ziellottes threaded his way into the center of the onlookers.

It wasn't hard to piece together what had happened. The captain's killer had slashed her throat. In fact, the cut was so deep that it had nearly taken her head off. It was definitely not the work of a professional assassin. A commando? A man-at-arms who'd hired himself out?

The captain's eyes stared vacantly into the vault.

It was shameful that no one had yet closed them.

Until her outer eyes were closed, she could not open her inner eyes and set out on her journey to the Gods and the Generations.

Ziellottes knelt down and pressed them closed. He sensed her presence in the space around him. She accused him. It was his fault that she was dead. His questions had penned the order for her death.

He had no way to deny it.

Ziellottes took his fingers away. The lids stayed down.

The policeman gaped at him, but said nothing.

Ziellottes led Chang a good distance away.

"Whoever did this must have been covered in blood," Ziellottes said.

"It's not our place," Chang said.

Ziellottes' forearms tightened until they hurt. He wanted to strike back at the captain's murderers, to avenge her murder, but Chang was right. It was not their job to punish the people who had murdered the captain. Nevertheless, such an ignorant waste of her life could not go unanswered.

Ziellottes already had the important names. He couldn't destroy the lot of them, but he *could* uproot the source of the cancer. He could rip it out and pitch it onto the nearest burn pile.

Not only had they taken a hand in Ulricka's affairs, but they had had the temerity to interfere in his.

Now, with Ulricka hanging on his every word and doing her best to appear not to, he finished the story of what had happened to the captain of *The Wings of Nekhbet* and fell silent, passing the conversation to her.

To underscore where matters stood, he retrieved his cup from the table and sipped his tea.

Ulricka said, "You don't think I'm responsible, do you?"

"Strangely, no, I don't, not in the *direct* sense. Your ultimate responsibility is another matter. Directly, though? You couldn't have escaped your narcissism long enough to set those wheels in motion."

Her face reddened in anger. "I am the—"

"You are an unimportant, frightened, superstitious adolescent! Your willingness to conjure phantoms has driven the basin to the brink of war, and it murdered that girl."

"I had no hand—"

"That's true, as far as it goes, but Narmer did."

"He wouldn't dare, not on Cathedral lands."

"You can't be that gullible," Ziellottes said.

Rather than deny that she had been, she asked, "Why would he do such a thing?"

"His people are incompetents. They questioned her for the same reasons I did, but then they bungled it, panicked, and killed her."

"Where's your evidence?"

It was of no small significance to Ziellottes that Ulricka had not asked why anyone should want to question a ship captain.

"Find your own damn evidence!" Ziellottes said. "It shouldn't be too hard. You're gagging on it!" Just as the captain of *The Wings of Nekhbet* had gagged on her own blood.

Twenty-Four

The Manor Henge of Desdemona the Shipbreaker was in a festive mood and dressed to show it. Bright bunting festooned the buildings, and the henge itself had been bedecked with torches. Their flames danced and leapt like vision dancers, while the smoke rose and flitted like the smoke from dozens of summer bonfires.

Brenna and a detachment of marines escorted Wolfram and Vlod to the place where the augury of Dagna's marriage to Gregory was to take place, where Vlod was to perform it. Deliberately absent from the affair were Edmund and, apart from Brenna, the members of his immediate household.

The party wore formal attire: dress uniforms for the military and the robes of a chieftain's personal magus for Vlod. The uniforms weren't bad. Brenna looked powerful and attractive in hers, but Vlod was painfully aware of the fact that his formal robes made him look like a spineless nincompoop. He was also aware that he was allowing his ego to undermine centuries of tradition and whatever credibility he might have.

Because the augury was to be a festive occasion, two white horses drew the victim, a large brown-and-white bull, in a brightly painted cart.

The priestesses from the Manor Henge of Desdemona the Shipbreaker had brushed and combed the horses, and they had braided ribbons into their tails and manes.

The priests had garlanded the bull with ribbons and floral finery. With so many flowers out of season, they'd had to make do with green-house blooms, ferns, and tree boughs.

The animal looked as though he'd been trapped in the sort of festive wreath that might be hung on an entryway door.

A troop of dancers and flute players, more naked than clothed, were bedecked with flowers and brightly colored gauze.

The mother abbess of the manor henge, Mother Charlotte, danced with them. Although she had no fewer ribbons in her hair than they did, and although she was no less joyous than they were, in a concession to the dignity of her office, she wore festive robes and gestured enthusiastically with her crosier.

To Vlod, Wolfram said, "I thought this was supposed to be a nice quiet augury. Private. Discreet. No fuss and feathers. That's what Edmund wanted."

Vlod laughed. "He also wanted public and traditional. Aboveboard. Nothing hidden. We're sending the bull to the Gods and the Generations, and in turn, they'll send us an answer to our question. It's supposed to be a joyous time, especially for the bull. Short of a human victim, this is as public and traditional as it gets."

"And as quiet?"

"Yes," Vlod said, his voice raised so he could be heard over the musical racket and jubilant shouts.

The procession entered a sandy clearing behind the dunes to the south of the South Jetty.

The music changed to a minor key. The separate voices fused into a choir, and the song deepened into a chant. The dance transformed into a sacred procession.

Mother Charlotte and two of her priestesses cast the Circle. Vlod took his place. The chant rose into the vault of the midday sky, and the bull's attendants led the animal to the exact center.

TWENTY-FIVE

Ziellottes and Chang waited. While they waited, they watched. They followed, and they traced, and they identified.

In due course, Narmer grew bored with his own magnificence and returned upriver. He traveled amidst waving greenhouse palms, billowing gauze, gilded lotus motifs, and naked girls playing flutes and harps.

Significantly, he did not take Harakhty, his envoy to the Mother Metropolitan's court, with him.

With Narmer out of the way, and the fear of embarrassing Ulricka contained, Ziellottes and Chang got down to their search for Selene's murderer.

They didn't have far to search. A blindfolded child could have followed the trails.

At the end of them, they found a man named Mulopatjuan, and he was, as Ziellottes had suspected he would be, one of Narmer's agents.

Not long after finding him, Ziellottes and Chang dumped Mulopatjuan's corpse at Harakhty's feet, more or less literally.

Mulopatjuan's face had frozen in a mask of horror.

His execution for murdering the captain had been much too much for him: the fear, the panic, the sense of impending doom. It had been the approach of inescapable annihilation, more than anything else, that had stopped his heart.

True, Ziellottes' stiletto hadn't helped, but Ziellottes was as sure as he could be that it had been the cascade of emotion, like water spilling down a wedding-cake waterfall, from surprise, to shock, to fear, to terror, that had done in Mulopatjuan.

He had drowned in his own blood.

Ziellottes had made sure of it.

Chang closed the door to Harakhty's office, sealing the three of them, not counting Mulopatjuan, in the room.

In the time it took for Harakhty to yell for his guards, Ziellottes darted around behind him and pressed the edge of Mulopatjuan's dagger to the envoy's throat. The man's cries stopped immediately.

In an abrupt but smooth combination of moves, Ziellottes threw Harakhty onto the floor.

The envoy yelped.

Ziellottes planted a boot in the center of the man's chest.

"Are you listening?" Ziellottes asked.

Harakhty nodded frantically.

"Good," Ziellottes said.

"Do you recognize the name Kerrderwynn?"

Additional frantic nodding.

"Good," Ziellottes said, and ground the heel of his boot into Harakhty's breastbone. "I want you to tell little Kerrychens that if he interferes in my business again, he will end up just as dead as poor old Mulopatjuan here. In case you don't recognize him, in case you were kept out of the loop, he's the one who's oozing blood, piss, and shit onto your carpet."

One of the guards forced his way through the cordon of Chang's men —who'd been given orders not to kill anyone unless their own lives were at stake—and burst into the envoy's office.

The guard ran at Ziellottes.

Chang stepped in, went low, and drove his shoulder into the guard's stomach. In an extension of the same action, Chang lifted and threw the hapless guard out through the nearest window. The man screamed as he fell toward the pavement far below. A splintering crash cut the sound off.

Chang's men regrouped and blocked the doorway.

Harakhty wormed his right hand around and drew his dagger.

More of his guards rushed at Chang's men.

Harakhty struck at Ziellottes, or tried to.

In a tight, rapid movement, Ziellottes pinned Harakhty's hand to the floor with the unfortunate Mulopatjuan's dagger. Harakhty shrieked in pain, but a second movement brought Ziellottes' own knife to Harakhty's throat.

Harakhty went as silent as his outrageous panting would allow.

Meanwhile, Chang's men threw the guards back and advanced.

Again, the door closed.

Quiet reigned supreme.

To Harakhty, Ziellottes said, "You're a slow learner, so I'll speak slowly. Here are the rules. Be sure to pay close attention. First, I do not hide my nature. I am a mercenary. Specifically, I'm a spy. Second, I work for whomever I choose, whenever I choose, however I choose. Third, I am an honest broker. I do not deliberately traffic falsehoods or hearsay. To the extent possible, I verify the information I sell. Fourth, I do not repeat things told to me in confidence. I do not gossip. I sell information. I do not prattle it away. Fifth. Listen carefully now. Here comes the most important part. Anyone who works for me is under my protection and is, therefore, beyond anyone else's reach. No one fucks with me or mine, and no one fucks with one of my operations. Anyone who does so invariably regrets it." Ziellottes twisted the knife pinning the hand, and Harakhty yelled in pain. It was the deep, sincere scream of a man in true agony. Sensitive structures, hands. "Five rules," Ziellottes said. "Can you remember them?"

Harakhty tried to repeat the rules.

Ziellottes had to help him untangle the third and fourth: no lies and no betrayal of confidences.

Ziellottes removed his boot from Harakhty's chest. "Give Kerry-boy my greetings. Tell him about Rule Five. Tell him that he's to stay away from me and mine. If he doesn't, I'll kill him."

Out on the street, Chang asked, "Who's Kerry?"

"Narmer. His name used to be Kerrderwynn."

Chang laughed. "No wonder he changed it. It's too close to *cur*."

"Not close enough."

Vlod sat in the chair Edmund indicated.

The chieftain said, "Tell me about the augury."

A memorable time was had by one and all, Vlod thought, except for the bull, but then only at the very last. Brave lad, but he did kick up one hell of a fuss. Anyone would've thought he'd wanted to live forever.

Vlod reined himself in. Where did such fits of sarcasm come from?

"The augury," Edmund said, prompting. "What did the Gods and Generations say?"

Vlod's embarrassment at his lack of response, at his adolescent inner rebellion, at his distraction, burned across his face.

"Well?" Edmund demanded.

"The question was unambiguous: 'Will Gregory and Dagna produce healthy children?'" Vlod said, falling into a detached, professional tone. "The victim died well, and through the splashes of his blood, the Gods and the Generations answered in the affirmative. An examination of the blood itself also spoke a positive answer. The entrails were healthy, and so they too must be considered positive." How Vlod loathed his official voice! It matched his formal robes. They were both hideous. "According to this *one* augury—and it is only *one* augury—the answer is an unqualified yes. The Gods and the Generations favor the union and will bless it with healthy children." Which was, Vlod observed to himself, not the same thing as saying their children would be happy little princes and princesses, children who would grow up bathed in love, devotion, and loyalty.

Vlod's stomach burned as badly as his face had. What was the matter with him? What had caused him to sink into such a foul mood?

Edmund said, "Good. That's what I was hoping to hear." He sat back. "Now tell me what I need to hear."

"It's the same on both counts," Vlod said. "The Gods and the Generations favor the marriage and will bless its children."

"But?"

"As I said, it was one augury. It was one question. The Gods and the Generations answered it at a specific time."

Edmund made a face. "You're hedging your bets."

"I don't want to lead you off a cliff."

"Very commendable," Edmund said. "I want you to write the application for Dagna and Gregory's marriage. Anticipate and counter. Cut off the escape routes."

A light, cool wind was blowing across the firing range. It carried the odors of trees and saltwater.

Today, the rocket's agreed target was a cow.

There was the rocket, positioned carefully on the rails of its launching stand, and there was the cow, grazing several dozen meters downrange.

Vlod thought that the rocket looked malignantly evil and that the cow looked morbidly oblivious.

In a way, they complemented each other.

He despised what they were doing. "We're not ready for a live target," Vlod said.

"We have to figure out how live targets will respond," Desmond said.

"I'm not stupid," Vlod said.

"Would you rather we stood a dozen guards out there?" Desmond asked.

Aerian chimed in, "Maybe we ought to be firing at a dozen or so deer."

"Horses," Desmond said. "We ought try our rockets against horses. Horses panic and they run wild. Think about it. Panic-stricken horses might be a bigger danger than the rockets themselves."

"We can't afford horses," Vlod said.

"We could borrow them. Old ones. We wouldn't kill many, and we might be able to pay for the ones we did."

"Men-at-arms wouldn't be standing still," Aerian said. "The moment we fire rockets at them, they'll react. If they scatter—"

"The cavalry will swoop in and lop off their heads," Desmond said.

Vlod clenched his teeth. They were like two children playing with toy soldiers.

"What about the cow?" Vlod asked. "How did you come by her?"

"I bought her from a butcher," Desmond said.

Butchers were seldom deliberately cruel, and their trade association expelled those who were. But how would the cow die if the rocket did in fact hit her? Would it blow her apart in an instant, painlessly or as good as, or would it rip her open, leaving her to die slowly and in agony, until they put her out of her misery?

"She's not to suffer," Vlod said.

"We have our swords. She won't suffer, and she won't go to waste."

"That's true," Aerian said. "We can have steak for dinner."

"It's settled, then," Desmond said. "By the way, what's happening on the Dagna-and-Gregory front?"

It was such an abrupt change of subject that Vlod stared at him. Desmond's chain of mental association must have snapped a few links. Or, to be fair, he could have jumped from steaks to sumptuous meals, to celebrations, to marriages, to Dagna and Gregory.

"I've submitted the application to the Geneticists Guild." In his best mock-pretentious voice, Vlod added, "It is a work of erudite genius and compelling argumentation. I've left them no choice but to approve with neither a qualm nor a detraction."

"Good for you."

"Steaks," Aerian said. "I haven't had a good steak in months."

"There's a thought," Desmond said. A contemplative look drifted into his eyes.

Desmond thought with his prick and his stomach, Vlod observed privately. Desmond's mind must have died of loneliness years ago.

"If word of what we're doing ever leaks out, we'll have stakes, all right," Vlod said, "complete with the bonfires to go with them."

Vlod went for a spear.

Obviously, Desmond and Aerian hadn't done much hunting, either. No one with half a brain would use a sword to finish off a wounded animal. An arrow fired from a safe distance was preferred, but for a dying cow, a spear, handled carefully, would do.

Vlod hoped it wouldn't come to that, but if it did, he didn't want the job botched.

Using a small torch, Aerian lit the rocket's fuse.

The fuse burned down, and then, in a rush, the rocket streaked into the air. It made a loud, guttural hiss, and left behind a conical trail of sulfurous smoke. It spread like the wake of a rapidly moving boat. The noise buzzed in Vlod's ears, like a cloud of yellow jackets, as though they were probing and questing into his skull. The sulfurous stench threatened to close off his sinuses and throat.

Abruptly the trail cut off, and the rocket, now a dark smudge against the low, gray clouds, arced over and angled down toward the munching cow. So far, she hadn't as much as looked up. Poor thing. Too domesticated, too dependent for her own good.

The rocket streaked down like a stooping hawk.

Desmond and Aerian grinned like idiots, and Vlod imagined he could see the faint sputter of the charge's fuse.

Another of Vlod's unwelcome thoughts formed: *If this works, it will mean the end of everything.*

The notion was absurd. Their purpose was to preserve, not to destroy. The clans lived and died by their crops, by their industry, and by their ability to defend themselves. In reality, war brought peace, and death enabled life. The old Year King died in order for the new Year King to reign. The new Year King slew the old in order to take his place.

Both the Goddess and the God were eternal, immortal. Female and male, They cycled endlessly through Their paired aspects, Their symmetrical identities.

The rocket exploded in midair, short of the cow—lucky girl!—and far to the right.

The concussion struck like a puff of air, and the *Bang!* sounded like the single bark of a wild dog. Truthfully, it had been closer to an anemic yip.

It was not the stuff of fleeing armies.

The cow looked up, glanced around, and went back to her grazing.

Or of fleeing cows.

So much for terror from the skies.

The remains of the rocket body fluttered down like dead leaves onto an old grave. The wind blew apart the trail of powder smoke.

One of the hot fragments must have hit the cow, because she bellowed and jerked at her tether, but only momentarily.

"Short fuse," Desmond said.

"Crooked fins," Aerian said.

"Bossy lives," Vlod said.

"An army would have run away in panic," Aerian said.

"The first time," Vlod said. "Maybe."

"He's right," Desmond said. "We have to be able to kill on command."

"I didn't say we don't," Aerian said. "Look, even if our aim isn't exact, we'll fire with effect if we load the charges with arrowheads."

"Are you kidding? Arrowheads?" Desmond asked.

"What's the problem with arrowheads?"

"Cost," Aerian retorted.

"All right. All right," Desmond said. "Sharp pieces of metal, then. The point is, archers don't shoot at individuals but at formations."

"Thank you for that insightful lecture in military tactics," Aerian said.

Vlod chuckled. Of the three of them, he was the only one who'd ever fought in battle. Win or lose; live or die. The stuff of epics: the stuff of bellicose delusion: the stuff of *necessity*.

Vlod walked over to the cow. He stood directly in front of her and made soft, low-pitched noises. The cow looked at him. He patted her head and her neck. He untied her, and she ambled off. Forage was where you found it, where you could eat it without interruption.

She wouldn't wander far, and at milking time she'd wander back into camp.

As Vlod returned to Desmond and Aerian, he noticed the workmen and men-at-arms. With the test concluded, the workmen waited for one of the magi to tell them what to do next, while the men-at-arms milled around. They were on guard, but they'd watched the test. Heads shook. Shoulders shrugged.

Who else had watched? Who else had heard the explosion? Who would come to investigate?

Security? What security?

To Aerian, Vlod said, "I have business at the manor."

"What business?" Desmond asked.

"Chieftain's business," Vlod said, and walked over to the stable.

Desmond and Aerian followed him.

"I don't like the sound of that," Desmond said. "Carrying tales?"

The taunt stung, but Vlod cast aside the urge to strike back. "Our security is a joke. It needs to be strengthened."

Desmond said, "I don't—"

Aerian cut him off. "Never mind. Vlod's right. We need patrols, not just guards."

Vlod went inside and saddled his horse. He led the gelding out into the open.

He looked at Aerian and Desmond in turn. "Leave the cow alone."

"Why?" Desmond asked. He'd shifted his tone from outrage to joking bewilderment. "I promise to be humane."

Vlod slipped his left foot into the left stirrup and rose into the saddle. "We'll need her for later."

"That's what I was thinking. For later."

"Alive, not on our plates."

TWENTY-SIX

The moment the latest courier from her spies on Edmund's lands left her office, Ulricka permitted herself to plummet into a well-deserved bout of self-pity.

Shabnan silently watched her. It was a didactic silence. It sniped and it badgered, but it also instructed.

Ulricka was sick of being lectured and scolded. She was the Mother Metropolitan, and Shabnan wasn't.

Anyway, to hell with Shabnan. Let the old bitch stew.

It was March. Ulricka was constantly cold, perpetually ravenous, and never far from vomiting. She always had to pee, and she had started to look like one of Narmer's mythical river horses. He might believe in their existence, but she did not. Never mind the "tooth" he'd shown her. Whatever it was, it wasn't a tooth.

Just then a muscle in her back locked up.

The cramp spiked, but then, luckily, it subsided.

In a few weeks, she'd begin to waddle. Where had her body gone?

She was exhausted with being the Mother Metropolitan. She wanted to quit. Where did it say she couldn't abdicate?

Nowhere. It didn't have to. The prohibition was implicit in six centuries of theology, tradition, and practice. Elevation to the metropolitanate was an indelible sacrament. Moreover, there could be only one mother metropolitan at any one time for any one province. The only way for Ulricka to cease being the Mother Metropolitan of the Inland Empire and the Holy Oregon was for her to die, either by accident, by disease, in childbirth, or at the hands of her successor. Childbed fever was a historic favorite.

Ulricka shuddered.

The baby had done this to her. The progress of the pregnancy. The prospect of giving birth. The risk, the pain, the joy. The grief. The unavoidable separation from the child: another child who would never know its mother, just as she was another mother who would never know her children. She shared that much with her sister alumnae of the Virgins' Pavilion.

Ulricka loved the Children of the Cathedral, but she could not pick out hers from among the others. That one? That one? The one over there? And try as she would to fashion it otherwise, it did make a difference! She yearned to know. She longed for that forbidden, indelible connection.

Shabnan asked, "What does the message say?"

"Edmund's runt—"

"Vlod?"

"The same. Edmund chose him to draft the application for Dagna and Gregory to marry. Warrick will be ruling on it in a day or two." Ulricka gestured with the message. "I'm told it's a work of art."

Shabnan tilted her head to one side. "Unless I'm wrong, Vlod has an appeal on his father's behalf pending, here at the Cathedral."

"Does he? An appeal for what?"

"His father, Shivananda, was—"

"That man was evil incarnate."

"The son wants him rehabilitated."

"Won't happen."

Shabnan tilted her head to the opposite side. "What are your plans?"

"To ignore Vlod's appeal until it goes away."

"I meant, what do you plan to do about the marriage application?"

Ulricka stood. Her feet hurt. It had to be the weight she'd packed on over the last few weeks.

"I plan to lie down," she said.

"You have appointments scheduled."

"Reschedule them."

"You have a decision to make," Shabnan said.

"For the love of heaven, I have time for a nap!"

TWENTY-SEVEN

When the courier from the Mother Metropolitan had gone, Warrick locked the door to his apartment. It wasn't a large space, and the furniture was mostly castoffs. They were the bulky secondhand detritus of people who had moved on, paint-blotched and scarred, the varnish either peeling or tissue-thin with age.

Warrick drew his curtains and sat down at his desk. His hands were trembling, and it irritated him. He was a senior magus, the presiding geneticist assigned to Clan Iredale. No one could touch him. He had nothing to fear. Nothing!

He broke the lead seals on the dispatch pouch and took out the enclosed sheet of buff-colored stationery. It was rag paper. Expensive. The scent of the Mother Metropolitan's perfume rose from it. Had she blessed it with a few drops? No, not likely. Like as not, she'd lain a curse on it. Or the Crone had, that vile woman. She was deadlier than a pit of vipers.

The paper was folded and had wax seals. He satisfied himself that no one had tampered with them, then he snapped them.

In her coarse, awkward hand, which was a genuine anomaly for a woman with her physical grace, Ulricka had written:

Young heroes must seek their destinies in far off lands.

Warrick frowned. The message made no sense.

He rethought.

She was an intelligent woman. She wouldn't have sent him gibberish.

He reread the words.

The fog cleared.

Their meaning emerged.

How could he have missed it?

Because he was preoccupied these days. Not sleeping as well as he should. Traveling too much. Determining too many infants to be weaklings. Had there always been that many weaklings born or was he imagining it? A case perhaps of a kingdom of flowers or a kingdom of weeds? Had he grown too strict? No, not likely. The standards were clear and he prided himself on following them consistently, without fear or favor.

He refolded the scented paper, returned it to the dispatch pouch, and tossed both into his stove.

As he watched, the pouch blackened and ignited. The flames flared up. They made him feel wistful, almost sad. Those *young heroes* were the focus of plot upon plot, ambition upon ambition, threat upon threat: towering, creaking edifices of greed, fear, and ego.

Ulricka was right, though. Their only chance to live their own lives would be for them to seek their destinies in lands beyond the reach of their clans.

Warrick scoffed at his own sentimentality.

The flames lowered as they consumed the last of the pouch, the last of the paper.

In an about-face, he scoffed at his cynicism.

The months ahead would be awash in an ironbound objectivity, far beyond the desires and fears of those caught up in them. The months, the years ahead would drown in an inescapable flood of events, and he, too, would succumb to that flood. He, too, would be lost in that maelstrom, in that freshet of Egyptophile hubris.

However, for the moment, while the flames died, he could afford to indulge in a miasma of brute sentimentality.

And why shouldn't he?

Not nearly enough of it was going around these days, in these somber, mewling days of bloodlust and heresy.

TWENTY-EIGHT

Vlod would have rather stayed out on the peninsula with his unpredictable rockets, the new detachment of surly guards, and the annoying, seemingly unstoppable trickle of curious teenagers.

Wolfram had sent the new detachment and they were patrolling, but they were like a fence without boards, rails, or wire between the posts.

But like it or not, Edmund had summoned Vlod to the castle, and so here he was once again, in Edmund's study. The floor was cold and a rainstorm was rattling against the windows.

Edmund had made one thing clear: Vlod was there to listen to Warrick repeat his *rejection* of the application for Dagna and Gregory to marry.

There wasn't much to say, but Warrick was saying it at length.

As he listened, Vlod felt as though he and the Iredales were being driven into a box canyon.

It wasn't a bad analogy, either.

But if they were being driven, then someone had to be doing the driving.

Who was it?

Ulricka? Narmer? Vernon himself, playing a double game?

It wasn't enough to blame *events*, or *circumstances*, or *chance*, or a handy enemy. Or the will of the Gods and the Generations, come to that.

When Warrick had finished, Edmund asked, "Do we have any basis for an appeal?"

"To whom?" Warrick asked. "The Geneticists' Guild itself?"

"We don't have that much time," Edmund said.

Warrick's eyebrows lifted ever so slightly. He was not used to having his rulings appealed, let alone to the highest authority. "To the Mother Metropolitan, you mean?"

"The protocols are in place, aren't they?" Edmund asked.

"I found no basis for an appeal," Warrick said. "I would have reported it if I had."

What glowing professionalism, Vlod thought.

Warrick was the faultless exemplar of his type.

Not only were the geneticists willing to hand down their rulings—making or destroying countless lives at will—but they were also willing to provide the bases upon which to appeal their dictates, assuming they could discern such bases. If so, then so; if not, then not. What could be fairer? What could possibly be better for humanity's genetic future than *that*?

———

Dagna wanted to storm out of the dining room, to make a show of it, but she chose instead to answer her father's question. "Because he's a little shit."

Her father chuckled as though she were joking.

She wasn't.

Brenna, her older sister and their father's favorite, glanced from one to the other. In front of her, a steak, so far untouched, sizzled on a cast-iron plate cradled in a wooden frame.

Edmund said, "I'm not asking you to marry Bevan. He's the *little shit* in that family."

"What's the difference?" Dagna asked.

"Gregory's the heir," Brenna commented. "Oh, and his prick works."

"Which is more than I can say for your cunt!"

"My vagina works perfectly. It's my uterus that doesn't, unlike yours, which does." Brenna smiled. "Heels up, sister dear."

Dagna hurled a wineglass at her, but Brenna casually batted it away with her steak knife.

The glass smashed onto the floor.

"Don't worry," Brenna said. "Once he's a part of the family, we'll keep him on a short leash. No more whoring for him!"

Edmund looked pained, as though he found it embarrassing for his daughters, who'd grown up among men-at-arms, to behave as though they had.

Dagna's mood sobered. "*Does* his prick work?"

"Why wouldn't it?" Edmund asked.

"He has a history," Dagna said. "I don't want my baby to be a lump of goo."

"That won't happen," Edmund said.

"Why not? He's fathered two already, hasn't he?"

"Vlod augured your marriage. Your *children* will be healthy."

Maybe. Or maybe Vlod's augury wasn't as accurate as her father believed it was. Or maybe the risks were outweighed by the rewards: the bloodless assimilation of a neighboring clan, the creation of a military force second-to-none throughout the basin.

It was reason enough, but her mood careened back. "They murdered Morven."

"Gregory wasn't involved," Edmund said.

"They told you he wasn't," Dagna said. "What else would they say?"

"He wasn't involved," Edmund said, snapping down the words as though he were laying down a winning run of cards.

Dagna threw her fork onto her plate. It bounced and skittered across the table. It left behind a brown smear. "To hell with it!" She bolted to her feet. "Make your fucking appeal. I'll marry the son of a bitch if it'll make you happy!" She stood rigid for a time. "The Gods and the Generations will burn us in hell for being cowards."

"No, not for being cowards," Brenna said, "but for being spineless fools."

When the martial tread of Dagna's boots had faded down the connecting hallway, Edmund asked, "Spineless fools?"

"Spineless fools."

"What would you do?"

"I'd lop heads," Brenna said, and started in on her steak. It would be a shame to let it get cold.

———

For the first time since the Engineers Guild had assigned him to Clan Iredale, Royden felt at ease in Edmund's study. Edmund and Vernon's formal appeal to the Mother Metropolitan, which Vlod had played no small part in drafting, sat nestled in Royden's document case. He placed the case across his knees and felt the rosy glow of professional and personal elation.

Edmund said, "By the time you land at Maryhill, Ulricka will have figured out why you've come."

"Yes, my lord," Royden said.

"There's no hope for it," Wolfram said. "She will."

"Yes, my lord," Royden said.

"Once you've placed our appeal *into her hand*, sooner or later, she must rule on it. She won't want to, and she'll do whatever she can to avoid it."

"Understood, my lord."

"She'll make you wait—could be days, could be weeks. Use the time to learn what you can about the political situation at the Cathedral. Anything you can pick up about the strength of the Cathedral guard would be helpful."

Wolfram said, "The main thing is to determine the strength of Narmer's faction within Ulricka's court. Work quietly. Watch. Listen. Do not ask direct questions. Do not draw attention to yourself. You're an engineer. Think like one. See how the gears fit."

"How the machine works," Royden said. His enthusiasm had overpowered his good sense, and he felt himself turn red.

"Don't underestimate them," Edmund said. "They'll have eyes on you long before you land."

"Yes, my lord."

TWENTY-NINE

Four days after his departure from Fort George, Royden arrived at Maryhill.

He'd come in on the third packet to arrive that day. None had departed, none were scheduled to depart before sunset, and a substantial caravan had arrived from the east. The stench of their camels filled the streets.

As a consequence, the inns near the docks were full.

The desk clerk at the Klickitat Arms told him, "The whole downtown's booked cellar to ceiling. You might try uptown, up toward the cathedral."

Royden thanked the man and trudged uphill. It was ridiculous to think the Cathedral guard had him under surveillance already. Surely, Edmund and Wolfram had to be being overcautious on that score, but Royden saw no harm in taking the appropriate precautions. Playing the travel-weary errand boy, he adopted an attitude of thorough-going disinterest and kept to the busier streets.

The town's animal and human stench threatened to overpower him. He expected it to lessen as he went farther up the slope, but it didn't. The smells changed, but not their foul intensity. It was, he thought, a far cry from the crisp, clean air of Fort George.

The innkeeper at the Jubilant Firewalker suggested: "The Cathedral maintains a travelers' hostel. You might try there."

"Thank you," Royden said, and continued his search.

The hostel would not do.

Why?

Because the Cathedral and its district made him feel *uncomfortable*.

This uneasiness was the common lot of magi. Their profession imbued them with a spirituality that was mystical rather than dogmatic or ceremonial. Where there were dogma and ceremony, there was constraint. Where there was constraint, there was betrayal and enforcement.

Mysticism was a matter of direct experience. Dogma was a matter of prescribed belief.

No, the hostel would not do.

After another hour, Royden found a vacancy at the Dancing Headsman.

Unfortunately, the Headsman was twenty meters from the cathedral's western garden wall. It was close enough for Royden to smell the incense and hear the chanting.

At the same time, the inn looked passably clean and the food smelled fairly edible. Whether either was true, only time would tell.

His room was a low, cramped gable on the top floor. The floor was rough boards covered with a much-worn canvas runner. The bed had a straw mattress and a thread-bare blanket.

At one stage in its life the blanket might have been green or blue. These days it was as much brown or tan as anything else.

A chamber pot, which could have used a scrubbing, sat in a corner.

Dead houseflies littered the tiny, dry-rotted windowsill, and a brownish-blackish grime littered the equally tiny window. No curtain.

The window overlooked the street, as opposed to the backyard, and therefore did not offer a sweeping view of the privies and the stables. On the other hand, the fact that his room faced the street meant that it would be a matter of little or no effort for Ulricka's people to keep tabs on him, a definite minus.

Back on the first hand again, the more they saw, the less they'd suspect, provided he never broke character. Within limits, he could lull them into a grudging acceptance of his *bona fides*. They would mistake him for the role he was playing. *That*, if he kept his head, he could work to his advantage. Without it, his mission was doomed…and him along with it.

He looked down into the street.

There was damn little to see: people, horses, carts, messengers, loiterers, and the human detritus typical of most towns.

The question that had nagged Royden from the moment he'd stepped aboard the packet in Fort George picked that moment, that very moment, to dance an encore. Why had Edmund and Wolfram sent *him*? Were they out to see him dead?

No. That was absurd. They'd not need to go to such lengths.

The answer was, Royden told himself, nearly as uncomplicated as anyone could wish.

They couldn't have sent Vlod. He was too junior.

They couldn't have sent Warrick. Warrick had an altogether obvious conflict of interest. Edmund and Vernon were appealing Warrick's ruling.

They couldn't have sent Brenna. Nice girl, but they weren't ready to launch a war against the Cathedral. In a year or two, maybe, but not right now.

That had left Royden. He was senior enough to be taken seriously. He had no obvious conflicts of interest. He wasn't about to start a war. He was capable of keeping his eyes and ears open. He would scrupulously report what he saw and heard.

Decision made.

Royden turned away from the window.

He had no reason to doubt his reasoning and several reasons to trust it.

Then why did he feel as though he would be damn lucky to return to Fort George alive?

Could it be because of the loiterer he'd spotted. She was a youngish woman on the other side of the street. She was watching his window without looking directly at it. She was looking at a pilgrim's pamphlet, but she wasn't turning the pages.

In the morning, after breakfast, Royden walked the block and a half to the Cathedral's offices.

A woman, a very different woman, dressed as though she might be a housemaid rather than a pilgrim, followed him.

He entered the reception area and introduced himself. He stated his business, and asked for an appointment to meet with the Mother Metropolitan.

They said he would have to see Her Beatitude's appointment secretary.

"Where might I find her?" he asked.

"You'll have to wait your turn."

Playing the humble-but-determined functionary, he said that he would be happy to wait his turn, but that the matter was urgent.

"Urgent?" the receptionist sneered.

"Urgent," he said, keeping his voice neutral, stating a fact that she might find useful. He added a professional smile.

The sneer hardened. The receptionist told him that he would have to sign in and wait until one of the appointment secretary's assistants called him. She directed him to an office that opened off the reception area.

He entered, signed in, and waited.

The bench was made out of stone, no cushions. The black marble floor was polished, no dust. The plants were green, no flowers. The walls were flat sandstone, no expression. The air was dry, no life.

The morning passed.

Others came and went, but none of the assistants called him.

He continued to wait.

He studied the patterns in the black marble floor tiles. He listened to the bits and pieces of conversation, of business, of gossip, that he was able to pick up without obviously listening.

He studied the sandstone walls, the arrangement of the blocks. They were like bricks, but much larger.

He yearned for a cup of coffee, but he did not go in search of one.

Late in the afternoon, they told him he was free to come back in the morning.

Which he did.

They told him that the appointment secretary was away on business.

They invited him to return early the following afternoon.

Which he did.

This time he noticed that the barest hint of dust had collected under one of the benches. The cleaners must have been otherwise occupied.

Late in the afternoon, one of the assistants to the appointment secretary informed him that "Her Beatitude is most anxious to speak with you. Hearing genetic appeals brings her true joy and fulfillment. However, an urgent priority has arisen." She touched the word *urgent* with an undercurrent of emphasis. The Cathedral staff, it said, decided which matters required attention and which did not, not the clans. There'd been another undercurrent glossing the word *clans*. "Her Beatitude is sure you understand."

The assistant appeared to be in her late teens, and based on her getup, Royden guessed her to be a second-year seminarian.

"The matter *is* urgent," Royden said. "Would it be possible to make an appointment to make an appointment?"

"I'm afraid not. You did sign in on today's waiting list, didn't you?"

"As instructed."

"Good. You do remember that we do not carry the lists forward from day to day, don't you? You have to sign in each day."

"The procedure has been explained," Royden said.

"Well, I'm sure you won't have to wait too much longer," she said, and smiled.

Smiling appeared to be very popular among the Cathedral's receptionists and assistants. This one's smile was a dazzling display of very white, very straight teeth. They were well-brushed, and they had no chips and no obvious cavities. Her gums were not discolored. She was the picture of dental health and beauty.

Royden didn't succumb to her smile. Although he'd never seen piranha, he'd read about them, and he imagined that if they ever did smile that their smiles would be strikingly similar to this assistant's smile.

Royden asked, "To whom does the appointment secretary report?"

The teeth disappeared from view, and the assistant's nostrils flared slightly.

If Royden didn't behave himself, she wouldn't show him her teeth again. Or maybe she would, but not in a good way.

The assistant said, "Her Beatitude will ask to see you as soon as her workload allows."

"When will that be? Tomorrow? Next week? Next month?"

"I cannot speak for Her Beatitude."

"Take a guess."

"The appointment secretary can do nothing until Her Beatitude's schedule allows." The assistant treated him to what had to be her stock concerned-and-sympathetic-but-powerless-subordinate expression. It was definitely a smile—or intended to be a smile—but it offered no dazzling display of perfect teeth.

Royden had blown it. Never again would the assistant allow him to bask in the carnivorous glow of official amity.

"I'm afraid you'll have to check back tomorrow," the assistant said.

That night, Royden composed a coded dispatch to Edmund, sending it on the morning downriver packet.

Several days later, by the return packet from Fort George, Edmund sent money for lodging, meals, incidentals, and bribes. Edmund repeated his instruction, but added a dollop of additional pressure. Royden wasn't to draw any unnecessary attention to himself, he was to keep himself out of trouble, but he was also to pulverize the rules if he had to in order to produce a timely result. Further delay was not acceptable. Edmund and Vernon had to have a decision.

With Edmund's money in his pocket and his murky instructions clear in his mind, Royden settled in for the long haul.

Whether Edmund liked it or not, further delay was inevitable.

The Cathedral settled in, too. They assigned additional people, his minders, to watch him.

Every morning, he walked from his inn to the Cathedral offices, trailed by his minders, and signed himself onto the waiting list to see the Mother Metropolitan's appointment secretary.

Others registered. Others were admitted. Assistants bustled in and out. Messengers came and went. The representatives of the upriver clans barely had time to write their names before they were called. The appointment secretary granted the representatives of the downriver clans a chance to sit and collect their thoughts before she called them.

She did not call Royden.

The floors gave off the scent of floor wax. The plants gave off the aromas typical of flowerless plants. The scents of a dozen different women's perfumes prosecuted countless campaigns back and forth in the dry, unmoving air.

Royden observed the staff. He arrived when they did. He made himself friendly and accessible. He flirted with them without flirting. He ate lunch where they did. He used the privies they did. He left for the day when they did.

None of it did the slightest good. No suggestion came his way that a "consideration" would speed him into the appointment secretary's exalted presence, and they rebuffed his hints that he was willing to pay for the privilege of making an appointment to see the appointment secretary.

He widened his scope. He spent less time waiting for an appointment and more time eating and drinking where the guards ate and drank. He frequented the places where those on the fringes of the court ate and drank. He also spent a lot of time strolling along the docks and popping into one or another of the waterfront taverns for a quick pint before returning uptown.

He consumed a lot of mediocre food and drink. He met dozens of people, some boring, some interesting, but he learned nothing important about the Cathedral guard or about the strength of Narmer's influence in Ulricka's court.

Royden did, however, carefully note the number of Narmer's ships in the port, their arrivals, the lengths of their stays, and their departures. As far as possible, he determined their inbound and outbound cargoes, their inbound and outbound passengers.

As the days passed, his frustration mounted. Bribery was common in most courts, but this set of flunkies seemed to take pride in toeing the ethical line.

At the end of his third week, after dinner, he sent off his report—treble coded—and went to bed.

Several hours later, a soft knock roused him from an unsettled sleep.

Two women in plain, dark cloaks stood in the hallway. One was in her twenties. Another seminarian? Doubtful, given her military posture. A bodyguard, then. The other was older, not ancient, but not less than fifty.

The two swept into his room, and the younger closed the door, threw the bolt, and stood off to one side. The older, then, was the one who'd come to see him.

Royden lit a candle. The light revealed the older woman to be Shabnan, the Crone of the Cathedral.

Royden pulled the room's only chair around for her to use.

"Your presence blesses me, Your Eminence," he said.

"I haven't come to bless you," Shabnan said. She left the chair empty. "I've come to send you packing."

"Why would you do that, Your Eminence?"

"Her Beatitude will not consider Edmund's appeal. She will not allow herself to be used to further an offensive alliance."

"The number of Narmer's ships in the harbor says otherwise." With what he hoped was a knowing smile, he added, "Their passenger manifests scream it from the rooftops."

"Go home, magus."

"Not until I've completed my assignment."

"I'm putting you on notice," Shabnan said.

"Notice is it? Very well then. Here's one for you: Her Beatitude's refusal to rule on Edmund's appeal is not the act of a neutral."

Rather than lash out at him, Shabnan opened the door and left.

Her escort dutifully followed at her heels.

<hr>

Halfway down the stairs, Shabnan said to her lieutenant, "Double the watch on him."

<hr>

Royden allowed himself to slump down onto the edge of his bed.

The rumble of the two women's boots faded.

Royden's hands and legs shook. The muscles across his stomach and in his low back trembled.

Sleep was, understandably, no closer than the hint of a fond wish.

This would never do.

He needed to tame his emotions and untangle his thoughts.

He dressed, blew out the candle, and went for yet another walk.

Would this assignment never end?

It would, but not tonight.

His minders trailed him, as they always did, but to their credit, they left him ample room. They did not crowd nor try to intimidate.

No sign of a potential attack.

Nevertheless, he could almost feel the crossbows trained on him.

He did his best not to believe that each breath would be his last. Although, in the course of things, he accepted that it might.

The night was crisp, and the stars made a radiant canopy: the body of Nut, the ancient Egyptian Goddess of the sky.

The quiet and the beauty, the act of walking, began to calm him.

He went downhill, down through the wealthier parts of the town. He came out on the now-familiar waterfront promenade. He turned and walked upstream.

The most fashionable part of Maryhill, apart from the cathedral itself, lay to his left. The mooring basin was to his right. Behind him, downstream, the promenade gave place to wharves and warehouses, workshops and tenements, to taverns, brothels, and shops.

Beneath the night-silence of the street, against the punctuated susurration of a town at sleep, or mostly so at this hour, he heard the rasp and rustle of his minders closing in.

For the kill?

No. He may have angered Shabnan, but he couldn't have angered her as far as murder.

He settled his mind and slowed his breathing. These techniques were the wellsprings of a magus's skill.

An array of unique silences surrounded him, silences that betrayed the locations of his minders. Now and then, the accidental brush of a weapon against wood or stone confirmed what he had *not* heard.

Royden counted. One. Two. Three. Too many to watch him; too few to kill him.

A *click* and a high-pitched moan cut the silence.

Royden dropped to the pavement and rolled toward the river.

The *shiif-fuut* of a crossbow dart streaked over him, less than a meter and a half above the ground.

THIRTY

Vlod and Brenna stood inside the work tent.

They stood quietly, not frozen in alarm, but as still as their levels of skill would allow them.

Together they listened to the man's approach.

He was behind the tent.

He moved low to the ground.

Advance and wait. Advance and wait.

The stealth of an assassin.

Vlod drew his dirk.

Perhaps Royden had thrown one too many rocks at the wasps' nest upriver. Perhaps one too many curious teenagers had bragged to the wrong spy.

Brenna, who'd come out to the peninsula to gather information for a report to Wolfram, drew her own battle knife.

But why would an assassin, if that's what the man was, pick this moment, the middle of a rare clear day, to strike? Assassins tended to be nocturnal. A kidnapping, then? No, not without at least three or four.

And what about the guards?

Where were they?

The man outside moved forward, then parallel to the south side of the tent, then around the southwest corner, then across the front in a pair of steps that ended in front of the closed flap.

"Knockity-knock," a middle-aged voice said.

Ziellottes!

He was in one of his rare humorous moods, too.

Vlod returned his dirk to his boot top, and Brenna sheathed her battle knife.

"Come in," Vlod said. "I've caged the temple cobras."

"What about your black-haired friend?"

"Who says I'm his friend?" Brenna said.

"I'm not allowed to endanger the snakes," Ziellottes said.

"I promise not to bite," Brenna said, the epitome of innocence.

"Too bad," Vlod said, in a private aside.

The tent flap whispered to one side, and Ziellottes entered.

"Your security is wretched," he said.

"We're working on it," Vlod said.

"Work harder, O reader of entrails," Ziellottes said, with elaborate courtesy. It was ironic on its surface but genuine below.

"Why are you here, O seller of secrets?"

"Take me to Wolfram, and I shall reveal all. But take me privately. I must not be seen."

***

Vlod, Brenna, and Ziellottes found Wolfram on the archery range. He was alone, with an arrow nocked and his bow drawn. He loosed. The arrow flew downrange and hit the bullseye.

The target bristled with arrows. A few had gone wide, or high, or low, but most had hit the center.

Wolfram lowered his bow and fixed Ziellottes with an arched eyebrow. "Buying or selling?"

"Delivering."

"What and from whom?"

"A message from the Most Reverend Shabnan."

"You ought to be talking to Edmund, then," Wolfram said.

"This needs a low profile," Ziellottes said. "Her Beatitude wants to leave Clan Iredale room to maneuver."

Wolfram arched an eyebrow. "She's learning."

"That she is."

"Very well. What's Shabnan's message?"

"I'm to tell you that Ulricka is fully aware of your activities out on the peninsula. They are unauthorized, and they violate the Harmony. Ulricka is confident that since she has brought the situation to your attention that you will bring said activities to an immediate halt."

"Shabnan wasted your time to tell us that?" Wolfram asked.

"No waste involved. I'm being compensated."

"I thought I heard the jingle-jingle of coins," Brenna said, good-naturedly.

"No, you didn't. Not a single clink," Ziellottes said. Continuing to Wolfram, he said, "Ulricka must have felt a confidential warning was important."

"No threats?"

"None so far."

"Any steps in that direction?"

"Not that I've seen. Narmer's people come and go, but not his troops."

"We're in luck, then," Wolfram said.

"You are."

"Why would she tip her hand if she weren't going to threaten us?" Wolfram asked.

"Come now," Ziellottes said. "You can't expect to hide that much smoke and noise. Edmund may turn a blind eye, but no one else can."

"I've posted guards."

"Not very good ones. I was onsite for a good twenty-four hours before I contacted Vlod. I saw two sets of gawkers and one spy in that time."

"A spy? Who was he?" Wolfram asked.

"She. Promising girl. Very quiet on her feet. Moves as though she studies crane style."

"Tall, thin, hair down to her waist, wears it in a queue?"

"Not much of a chest, but enormous blue eyes?" Ziellottes asked.

"Madeline," Wolfram said. "She's one of Vernon's people."

"No reprisals, now. That wouldn't be sporting."

Wolfram laughed. "No, no reprisals, but tell her I'll shave her head if I catch her."

"If I see her," Ziellottes said. "Any reply for Ulricka?"

"Tell her we'll play nice if she'll play nice. No paranoid rockets in exchange for no explosive chieftains."

"Very good," Ziellottes said.

Vlod said, "With Wolfram's permission...?"

"For what?" the battlemaster asked.

"Our overdue messenger."

Wolfram nodded his assent.

To Ziellottes, Vlod said, "A magus named Royden, an engineer, may have gone missing at the Cathedral."

"Missing as in *missing*, or missing as in off on a lark?"

"Missing as in *missing*."

"I see."

"Her Beatitude may have him in custody. Please tell Shabnan that Edmund would consider the return of his engineer an important act of good faith."

***

A few minutes later, after the exchange of thank-yous and goodbyes, Ziellottes took his leave.

When Vlod, Brenna, and Wolfram were alone, Vlod asked, "Who's our spy?"

"So you caught that taunt. Ulricka is 'fully aware.'"

"Hard to miss," Vlod said. "Blustering?"

"No, not this time. Ziellottes is right. Our security *is* rotten."

"Any guesses about the spy?" Brenna asked.

"Guesses are worthless. I'll put a few people on it," Wolfram said. "In the meantime, work faster."

Wolfram nocked, drew, and loosed.

His shot was low and to the left.

The rocket hit several meters to the right and twice as far to the rear of the target. This time the target was not a cow, but a wooden framework two meters on a side. The rocket exploded with a dull report. The detonation threw up sand and left behind a charred depression.

"The fins don't work," Vlod said.

"Why not? Fletching works on arrows," Aerian said.

"Rockets aren't arrows."

"Forget about the rockets," Desmond said. "Maybe we ought to throw the charges with catapults."

Vlod mulled that over. "Good thought, but—"

"But what?" Aerian asked, his emotions flashing into open anger. "So far we've tried every fucking thing that makes any fucking sense."

"Then it's time we tried every fucking thing that doesn't make any fucking sense," Vlod said.

"Any ideas?" Desmond asked.

"Yeah, one of yours," Vlod said. "Remember the launching tube?"

"You said it was a stupid idea," Desmond said.

"I've changed my mind."

* * *

Eventually, Ulricka responded to Vlod's query by sending word that she had no idea what had happened to Royden. As far as she could discover, he'd hung around the appointment secretary's office for several days, and then he'd wandered around Maryhill for a few more days. Since then, none of the staff had seen him. Hadn't he returned downriver to Fort George?

Edmund and Vernon decided to resend their appeal and to try to find out what had happened to Royden.

Vlod volunteered to go upriver.

Edmund and Wolfram squawked about how much they needed him up on the peninsula, but in the end they agreed to let him go. They had, frankly, no one else to send.

Wolfram ordered a fast medium trireme, *Morning Victor*, to carry Vlod upriver to the Cathedral. He also assigned Brenna and a company of marines to keep him alive.

"It's no show of force, but they might come in handy," Wolfram told him.

Delays sprang up like morning glory in the spring.

The shipyards couldn't make *Morning Victor* ready for a hard run upriver for at least three or four days. They needed to clean her bottom and offload her excess gear. They had to load provisions and water.

Three days. Or four. Maybe five.

"We could ride," Vlod said.

Wolfram rattled off the reasons why they couldn't. Even with the delay, it would be quicker for them to take the ship. The ship would run twenty-four hours a day, whereas they could ride for perhaps eight or ten at most. And, too, they'd need a secure base once they were at Maryhill.

"I could go alone," Vlod said.

"The hell you can," Brenna said.

"You'll wait for the ship, Little Magus," Wolfram said. "We can't afford for Royden *and* you to disappear."

"Yes, sir," Vlod said. "Speaking of Royden, how long will they—"

"He'll keep," Wolfram said. "Go play with our rockets."

Vlod found Aerian alone in the work tent.

"Where's Desmond?" Vlod asked.

"He needed to take a break from sobriety," Aerian said.

"We need him here."

"I agree."

"Then let's send a detail to roust him out of whatever gutter he's crawled into."

The cow, Bossy, grazed on the test range. The guards had taken a liking to her. They fed her, and milked her, and made sure no one turned her into sides of meat, and built her a shelter, which she seemed to like.

Two days later, the detail found Desmond in the nearest fishing village. He was drunk, bruised, and stinking of his own vomit. They dunked him in a watering trough and returned him to the proving ground.

Over the next day and a half, while Desmond slept off his drunk, Vlod and Aerian launched two finless rockets from a section of water pipe. Neither hit the target.

After the second shot, Aerian said, "They're corkscrewing. It has to be the nozzles."

Vlod agreed. The lathe they were using was inaccurate, and thus the gunpowder burned away the nozzles, but not evenly. This caused the nozzle to skew the direction of thrust.

Why wood?

Because iron and steel had proven too difficult to work with the tools available.

With a signal rocket, erratic flight didn't amount to much. The objective was to gain height, make noise, and show a burst of light or a puff of colored smoke.

But their objective was to deliver an explosive charge to a specific place. Thus their rockets had to fly true.

"I'm running out of time," Vlod said.

"What do you want me to do?"

"Keep Desmond sober."

"Besides that."

"Forget about the nozzles," Vlod said. "We'll have to do without them."

"It'll reduce the rocket's range."

"We can increase the size of the propellant charge to compensate."

"Will that work?"

"We have to hit what we're aiming at. Otherwise, we're shooting off fireworks."

The afternoon was slipping on, and Vlod was due at the docks in Fort George by midnight. "Sorry, but I have to leave. Don't forget to record your numbers."

"Yes, Mother," Aerian said.

After clearing Fort George, *Morning Victor* settled into her run. Oars only, owing to the lack of wind.

The night was dark, no moon, but the handful of stars that were shining glittered on the water.

A scouting launch verified the channel ahead. The calls of the launch's leadsman drifted back like the calls of a plaintive bird.

Elsewhere, a heavier version of the scouting launch kept station between the ship and the nearer riverbank. The calls of that vessel's leadsman were plainly aggressive, as though he were daring the river to shoal unexpectedly.

The trireme's crew had arranged a cabin for Vlod. It was below the weather deck and abaft the rowing space. It had a hanging cot, space to turn around in, minimal headroom, and precious little else.

Vlod had tried to hand the space over to Brenna, but she insisted on sleeping with her marines, as she did in the field. Instead of the cold, hard ground, she was determined to sleep on a nice soft deck. Ha, ha, ha!

Military humor.

THIRTY-ONE

Vernon, the chieftain of Clan Innes-Martin, watched the flight of the missile. It was a large, spherical rock. Vernon watched its flight, with no small amount of interest. And why wouldn't he?

Seldon, the chieftain of Clan Sauvie, had chosen to show off his newest experimental throwing engine, and he was doing so in a grand style.

Both the engine itself and the overall display were masterful works of art: lots of color, lots of machinery doing complicated mechanical things, lots of men-at-arms rushing here and there, and lots of underlings licking boots and kissing asses.

Xenia, Seldon's sister, had chosen to create a display of her own. It was of an entirely different sort. It seemed that bare breasts had come into vogue, especially hers.

Vernon had heard she'd taken to exposing them. It was the latest fashion among vision dancers and henge dancers, and she did dance regularly at the Sauvies' manor henge, but he'd discounted the rumors.

He now saw that he shouldn't have.

She was prancing around in an open-front outfit that displayed her breasts to their best advantage. They were nice breasts, too; well worth the effort to show them off. Some would say that the April weather was too cold for such a display, but considering what the chill did for her nipples, Vernon had to disagree.

What was her game?

Her brother's embarrassment and her own exhibitionism, certainly, but what else?

Earlier in the day, she'd gone out of her way to flirt with Vernon, but when he'd made a polite suggestion, she'd responded with a polite refusal. Very friendly, and no surprise. Her preference—but it was only that, a preference—for women was notorious.

What was her game?

Seldon's target was a full-scale mockup of a section of the Sauvies' curtain wall. The replica was remarkably detailed and included the wall's normal complement of hoardings, those wooden structures that surmounted the battlements and were intended to shield archers and men-at-arms from the enemy's missiles and arrows.

Seldon had explained that the hoardings were the specific target. The wall could withstand a determined battering by any of the licensed throwing engines. The hoardings were another matter.

Seldon was hoping to design structures that could survive a prolonged attack, or, conversely, to develop a throwing engine that could obliterate the strongest defenses.

"What about licenses?" Vernon asked. It was a naïve question, a silly question, but he thought he'd risk playing the dullard and ask it.

Seldon rubbed his thumb and first two fingers together. "Money can exchange hands. Arrangements can be made."

Vernon doubted that. The engineers were sticklers and the Cathedral had a way of coming down hard on those who imagined they were free to follow their own paths in such matters.

Sheep and cows had been secured inside the hoardings, and their bleating and mooing added an anxiety-laden counter to Seldon's exuberance. Their purpose was to act as analogues for the men-at-arms who would man an actual wall during an actual battle.

Altogether it wasn't many animals. There were certainly fewer than were slaughtered on an average day to supply Seldon's kitchens. However, for some reason or other, Vernon couldn't escape the impression of the pointless extravagance that their use left bouncing around in his mind.

Still, Seldon was nothing if not extravagant. Like brother like sister. Extravagant. Showy. Determined. Exhibitionistic. But not, Vernon felt sure, half as clever as they imagined themselves to be. No, not by a long chalk.

As the first missile arced toward the wall, the mooing and bleating rose to a frenzy.

The missile smashed home. It made a sharp, splintering sound. It was like the sound a tree makes when a storm topples it. The impact opened a gaping wound in the hoardings. Planks shattered and ripped. Razor-sharp splinters flew and spun through the air like runaway sawblades. They cut and they pierced. Animals bellowed and screeched.

The second throwing engine, which had a marginally different design, launched its boulder. Its shot had a similar effect: more splintered wood, more dead animals, more whooping and cheering from the crews.

The officers in charge restored order, and the two engines fell into a rough alternating rhythm.

Additional gaps opened as the projectiles struck, mangling timber, hide, bone, and muscle. Blood flowed over the makeshift walls.

By the time the two engines ceased firing, they had swept the hoardings from the battlements. The projectiles had left nothing but crushed sections of wall, twisted pieces of wood, dead and dying animals, and blood-smeared stone.

One of the sheep had come through unscathed. Dumbly, it stared down from a section of flooring.

Others, not so lucky, hung down against the wall, suspended by their tethers. They had strangled, and their eyes and tongues bulged from their faces. Along the base of the wall, dismembered animals formed a grisly berm of legs, hooves, heads, bodies, and entrails.

Off to one side, having fallen unaccountably far from the base of the wall, a steer lay dying. A splinter the size of a man's arm had lodged in its side. The animal kicked and thrashed and bellowed in agony.

"Stew tonight, I think," Xenia said. "Yes, definitely stew."

THIRTY-TWO

And stew it was.

Much of the beef and mutton came in shapes other than perfect cubes, and Vernon surmised that not much cutting had been necessary in the kitchens.

The food was plain, but it was about the only thing in the banquet room of Seldon's Hall that was. Vernon couldn't remember a time when he'd seen so many nipples on display.

Seldon, the grandson of the Seldon for whom the Hall had been renamed, said to him, "I'm a strict neutral. My walls are high. My wells are deep. My throwing engines are powerful."

Vernon quelled his disgust with the man's arrogance. No army could win a war by hiding behind its walls. It might turn away an assault, it might stave off an immediate defeat, it might allow time for reinforcements to arrive, it might persuade a halfhearted attacker to withdraw, but it could never *win*. Victory was the reward of attack.

"Narmer's armies are large. His wealth is considerable. His siege engines are formidable," Vernon said, turning Seldon's recitation inside out. "His people are fanatics, and I fear you overvalue your walls."

"Time will tell, but my army defends my ground."

"As it should. While the ground is yours."

Vernon's assigned rooms were high in Seldon's keep. They were drafty and minimally furnished. According to the calendar, the month was indeed April, but the weather felt like January. The hour didn't help. What was it? Before midnight? Past midnight? He'd lost track.

Past. Had to be.

He dismissed his servant and threw three pieces of pitch-heavy wood, which was fir, onto the fire. The room would soon be warm enough. It was a waste of wood, but it would have been uncivil of Vernon to ignore the comfort of his uninvited guest, his uninvited *female* guest. He lit a second oil lamp and set it on the mantelpiece, next to the Clan Sauvie chronicle he'd been reading.

Xenia moved deeper into the chamber, closer to the light, closer to the flickering fire. She glided as though she had no need to walk in order to advance from place to place. She had renewed her perfume, and its aroma extended around her like an aura.

"I've changed my mind," she said. Like a dancer, she glided down until she was sitting on the floor in front of the fireplace, her skirts spread around her. "I want to have sex with you."

That she'd given either option a moment's thought was news to him. Oh, she'd pointed her nipples at him a few times, but he'd dismissed that as mere flirting.

Jumping to the core of the inevitable issue, he asked, "Hedging your bets, are you?"

"You can't save me."

"Assuming I could, why would I?"

"We haven't had sex yet."

He pulled over a footstool and sat on it. "You're that good?"

"I'm magnificent."

"The chance of a lifetime, no doubt," he said.

"No doubt."

"Sorry, but I do doubt."

"Well, you shouldn't," she said. "I changed my mind in my apartments, after that detestable banquet. The threat of impending death must be a powerful aphrodisiac."

Impending death? Narmer's attack was months away. What was she trying to do, trying to tell him?

Vernon asked, "What do you want?"

"You between my legs."

Vernon's abdominal muscles tightened. He felt a pulse, strong and insistent. He was fully erect, so erect that it was like a physical and insatiable pain.

If he had been twenty years younger, he might have believed her. For women, power may heighten interest, but power worked best on women who had none of their own. Xenia was not one of those. It would be a cold day in hell before a uniform or a title or a tract of land turned her head.

She did not, however, rule through her brother, and despite the power she wielded, in many ways she was no better off than a luckless, though well-placed, pawn. Which brought him back to the basic question: Why had she come to his rooms in the middle of the night? Was the pawn seeking to become a queen?

"Let me try again," he said. "Why seduce me?"

"For the fun of it."

In another one of her fluid, effortless movements, she stood up. He remained seated. She took his hands lightly in hers. The firelight danced across her body. It challenged, taunted, and promised. His erection throbbed.

He wasn't alone in his arousal. Her nipples had contracted into two dark mounds. She pressed herself into his arms, both shyly and provocatively. "What's it to be? Yes or no?"

"No."

THIRTY-THREE

Ulricka dismissed the courier and handed the message to Shabnan. "Edmund is sending us his pet runt." Edmund was also sending a trireme, two scout vessels, and a company of marines, with his Amazon daughter to command them—all in an effort to find Royden and to secure Ulricka's approval for the marriage between Dagna and Gregory.

Ulricka paced the room.

"What sort of a man is Vlod?" she asked. "Is he another leg-pumping Chihuahua, or is he the savant he's reported to be?"

It was an odd question for a woman who had a thick file on the man, who'd been watching him for years. Shabnan set the message on Ulricka's desk. "I'd have said terrier."

"A terrier?"

"Small, bright, quick, deadly against vermin."

Ulricka made a face. "Whatever he is, he's a magus."

"And so...?"

"In other words, he's a whore with a fancy robe and a taste for luxury."

"I wouldn't underestimate him. His father was a magus, remember. He did interesting work, until he was executed."

"His work was blatant heresy."

"Some heresies are more interesting than others."

Ulricka made a face. "True." She leaned back against her desk, clasped her hands on its edge.

"Where does the appeal on his father's behalf fit in? Is he using Edmund and Vernon's appeal as a blind?"

"Unlikely, I'd imagine," Shabnan said. "He'll want you to rule on their appeal, and he'll insist that you return Royden. Edmund didn't send him up here aboard a warship because they're a comfortable mode of travel. They aren't."

"Edmund's people can't attack the Cathedral with *one* trireme."

"Think of it as a down payment, waiting to make trouble if you don't behave."

Trireme. Ulricka pondered the word. Although she'd lived on the river all her life, she was grossly ignorant of the different types of vessels. Bireme. Trireme. Galley. War galley. Barge. Felucca. Yacht. Boat. Threes. Fours. Twos. Fives. Was a three the same as a trireme? No, she didn't think so, but she wasn't positive that it wasn't. Something about three oarsmen working one oar as opposed to a group of three oars, each worked by one or more oarsmen, and there was something about *stations*, too, wasn't there?

She couldn't remember.

Once upon a time, she'd worked through it with one of Thora's military advisers, but that had been years ago, and since then, the terms had blurred.

Whatever the specifics, Edmund sent a warship upriver, and he hadn't sent her a submissive token of his desire for a rapprochement.

Ulricka asked, "Have you found Royden?"

"Please don't play the dullard. Narmer's people have him and you know it."

"Yes, but where is he?"

"Does it matter?"

"Stop manipulating me! I'm not a child. Of course it matters."

Measured out as calmly as if she were separating eggs into yolks and whites, Shabnan asked, "Does...it...matter?"

Ulricka seized a coffee cup and threw it across the room. It shattered on the wall next to the window. The remains of her midmorning coffee dribbled down and puddled on the floor.

"No, it doesn't," Ulricka said, "not the *where*."

She called for a runner.

—————

The afternoon was cold and clear, and a fire burned in the fireplace in Ulricka's office. To help ward off the chill, she had chosen a gown with long, flowing sleeves. A silver coffee service sat on the edge of her desk.

There was a knock at her door. She glanced at Shabnan, and said, "Come!"

The door opened, and Harakhty, Narmer's envoy, functionally his ambassador, to the Cathedral, entered. Harakhty bowed, doubling over so far it appeared he might kowtow. He didn't.

Harakhty had brought an officer with him. The man had broad shoulders. His eyes revealed the intelligence of a lamprey eel. The eel went down on all fours and thumped his forehead on the floor. He rose and took a position beside the door. He was a bodyguard, not an aide.

The presence of such a man was a deliberate insult, but Ulricka was loath to give Harakhty a lesson in what was and what was not permissible behavior in her court. She smiled benignly from behind her desk.

Shabnan rose and stood behind and to one side of Ulricka's chair.

Harakhty bowed again. "Your Beatitude," he intoned. With a head bob to Shabnan, he added, "Your Eminence." He refocused his attention on Ulricka. "To what do I owe the honor—and the blessing!—of an invitation into Your Beatitude's presence?"

His voice sounded as though it had been marinated in sweetened chicken fat. What had Narmer done to his people? The Pasco-Burbanks had once been independent, stubborn, and proud, not arrogant snivelers.

"You have kidnapped one of Edmund's magi. The man's name is Royden," Ulricka said. "He was in Maryhill on Cathedral business. You will transfer him to our custody within twenty-four hours."

"I'm unfamiliar with the case, Your Beatitude. I beg permission to withdraw and enquire into the situation."

"You believe we are mistaken?"

"In all things, Your Beatitude is the essence of accuracy. However, I am unaware of the case. I must consult with my subordinates and my superiors, Your Beatitude."

"Consult as much as you wish, but you will hand him over within eighteen hours."

Harakhty's left eyebrow twitched.

Had it been a nervous tick, or the beginning of an arch?

"Do you accuse me of falsehood?" he asked.

Ulricka noted with no small satisfaction that he'd dropped his courtly pretenses.

"You will hand him over to me within *sixteen* hours."

"An ultimatum?"

"No, it's a blatant threat," she said.

Harakhty drew himself up.

He was, she observed, about to treat her to a display of diplomatic outrage.

She slipped her hands into their opposite sleeves, right into left, left into right, just as she'd learned to do years ago. How thoroughly Thora had trained her! The metal objects she found there were warm from her body heat.

Harakhty showed no cognizance, let alone understanding, of her new posture. "Narmer, the Son of Ra, the Chosen of the Goddess, the Gods, and the Generations of His House, is not to be threatened!"

"It is you whom I am threatening.

"In threatening me, you threaten him."

"*Fourteen* hours."

Harakhty turned his back on Ulricka and walked toward the door.

Ulricka flashed her hands from her sleeves and made simultaneous flicking movements. Her throwing daggers buried like crossbow bolts in the back of Harakhty's shoulders.

He shrieked and dropped to his knees. He vainly clawed toward the hilts of the weapons.

The eel drew his sword and rushed forward.

He went down with Shabnan's shuriken sunk in the center of his neck. If it had been much larger, it would have taken his head off. Blood spurted, pumping and spraying. It soaked into his clothes and spattered onto the floor. He made terrified strangling noises.

It was just as well, Ulricka thought. Gagging on his own blood would keep him occupied while he bled out.

Harakhty struggled to his feet. His face was the color of sunbaked mud, and he dribbled blood onto the floor.

The door banged open and six of Ulricka's guards ran in.

"Stay where you are," Ulricka said.

They halted.

Ulricka yanked the knives from Harakhty's shoulders. He screamed as they came out.

"Ah," she said. "The truth at last."

"You're insane," he said, his teeth beginning to chatter.

"*Twelve* hours," she said. "One, two: twelve."

"What kind of maniac are you?"

"The kind Narmer shouldn't fuck with," she said. To the sergeant of the guard, she said, "See to his wounds."

The guards divided. One group went to Harakhty. The other went toward the eel.

"Leave that one," Ulricka said.

The second group, their faces lined with bewilderment and fear, went to aid in helping the envoy.

Ulricka's guards were carrying Harakhty out when the eel began to pound his heels on the floor. He made wet rasping noises as he tried frantically to breathe.

The heel pounding stopped.

His neck was bubbling less furiously now. His eyes were huge. He tried to speak, but was unable to do so. A bloody froth covered his chin, his jaw. He tried again, but with an equal lack of success.

He shook his head back and forth violently, as though he were trying to clear his mind, as though he were trying to bring his thoughts to bear, as though he were hoping to ward off the end for a little while longer.

He was making his third attempt to speak when he finally died.

Morning Victor, one of Edmund's medium triremes, entered the Maryhill Channel at midday and picked up the harbormaster's agent.

"Where do you want us?" the trireme's captain asked.

The agent handed over a written order. "Pier Three, berth four." He pointed to the position on the chart and then pointed to it in the harbor. "It's on the west side of Pier Three."

An hour later, with the ship tied up and snugged down, Brenna and Vlod met at the taffrail. She was in field uniform.

"We're here," she said. "Now what?"

"Can any of your marines pass for ordinary people?"

"Handpicked."

When he'd told her what he wanted them to do, she said, "It'll take time."

"And money, but let's start with time."

THIRTY-FOUR

Ulricka struggled awake. Based on the angle of the light in her bedroom, she judged that she'd overslept her afternoon nap. She was groggy and her head was pounding. The pain seemed to pulse across her forehead and down into her eyes.

A headache?

Now?

Why?

No reason.

Who she was.

What she was.

The ship that had been due to arrive by this time no doubt had. Edmund's ship. A trireme. The terrier magus. Edmund's Amazon daughter.

She forced her mind away from the maelstrom.

She made a pot of tea and swallowed a double dose of willow bark. She sat in a rocking chair, spread a blanket across her legs, and felt old.

Shabnan slipped in and sat down in the chair opposite. She had the sense to remain silent.

Ulricka had the most absurd urge to curl up on the older woman's lap and be held. Thora had held her—not on her lap but in her bed. Thora had hushed her fears and her disappointments, her endless frustrations.

Those memories soothed Ulricka's terrors.

After half an hour, thanks to the tea, the bark, and the quiet, Ulricka could move her head without setting off a jab of pain.

The two of them moved into Ulricka's office.

The maids had cleaned away the blood, urine, and excrement hours ago, but the floor had not entirely dried. The room smelled of disinfectant.

A dull splotch marked the spot where the eel had died.

Shabnan said, "You ought to have the stone relayed."

"No, I think I'll leave it. Narmer, Edmund, and Vernon—the whole pack of them—need a reminder, and that will do nicely." A cat's paw of fatigue batted at her. "I'd like it to be one I don't have to point out. A brown patch on the slate. They'll see it and understand." She considered the stain anew. The maids had scrubbed away most of it. Maybe too much. "I'm tempted to work in a cup of pig's blood. Darken the stain. Eliminate any possible doubt."

Shabnan nodded. "Doubt leaves the hope of evasion."

"I need to make an example."

"Why not Aerian? He's the magus in charge of Wolfram's rockets. We could arrest him and bring him here."

"I want to make an example, not start a war," Ulricka said. "Don't we have anyone in custody?"

Shabnan rattle off a list of names and crimes.

"The heretic. He'll do nicely."

"Which one?" Shabnan asked.

"The one who tried to improve freight wagons."

Shabnan smiled. "An excellent choice, Your Beatitude."

"Have him prepared in secret. I want him to be a surprise for our uninvited guest."

"For the runt, you mean?"

"Exactly. But only when the time comes."

Shabnan smiled. "Yes, Your Beatitude."

The headache had begun to slacken. It was a dull echo of its former self. In an hour or two, she'd feel quasi-human. Another pot of tea might help.

"Before you go," Ulricka said. "Why didn't you pull your shuriken out of the bodyguard's neck? He would have died in a quarter of the time if you had."

"I had a job to do," Shabnan said. "Mercy is your line of country."

Royden leaned his head back against one of the supports holding up the freight wagon's canvas covering.

He had expected to be beaten, right there in the wagon, but no beating had come. No one had snarled at him in hours, either. No one had kicked him. No one had taunted him. No one had demanded that he confess his sins and crimes.

He was almost disappointed that his activities had elicited such a benign response on the part of his current captors.

He relaxed a fraction.

They had yet to remove his blindfold, but they were leaving him alone. For now. They were taking him someplace, but other than that, they were ignoring him.

He let his neck and shoulders relax, let the tension and the cramps ease. He directed his breath down and up the chakras. His heart slowed. His breathing slowed. His capillaries opened. He could feel his pulse beating in the tissues of his face. He felt warm, as though he'd emerged from a hot bath.

It felt wonderful.

Admittedly, it didn't smell wonderful. It smelled like a wagon that had endured rough use, and the men in it with him, his guards, smelled as though they ate nothing but highly spiced, overcooked sausage and hadn't had a good wash in weeks.

One thing was apparent, however, and had been for several hours: Narmer's people were out of the picture.

No formal handover had taken place, but nevertheless, these people were absolutely of a different sort.

Yes, a new set of captors were now in charge of him.

This change raised its own set of questions. Why the change? Who were the new guys? What did they want, and what would they do to lay their hands on it? Come to that, what would they do with it once they had it?

The answers were not to be had, not from the back of a freight wagon.

The attitude of this bunch was better, though. It was too soon to think about survival, but Royden was beginning to feel the catlike approach of a glimmer of hope.

Royden had expected Ulricka's people to take a run at him, but he hadn't expected Narmer's agents to push them aside and kidnap him. And it *was* Narmer's people who had done it. Their upriver accents had given them away.

They had interrogated him in shifts. They asked him about Edmund and Vernon's appeal to Ulricka, about Edmund's military, about Aerian's work with rockets, about the strength of Vernon and Edmund's alliance, about Dagna's health, about the factions within Edmund's court, and about scores of other topics.

It had been as though Narmer didn't have his own network of spies, which he did. Confirmation, then? Handy to have, but was it worth the fuss and feathers? On the whole, the magi didn't take kindly to such goings-on, nor did they ignore them.

Question: "Are Dagna and Gregory in love?"

Answer: "Hardly. She's been my mistress for the last five years."

That answer had earned him a beating.

Question: "What is the condition of Edmund's transport galleys?"

Answer: "They sank last winter."

Which had earned him a beating on the soles of his feet.

Question: "How many men-at-arms does Edmund command?"

Answer: "About fifty. The rest have gone on strike."

They had shown their appreciation by seizing him up between two posts and whipping him.

Then one day his old jailers marched out, and his new jailers marched in. They wore civilian clothes, but they acted military. They didn't stink of cheddar cheese, bacon grease, and spilled wine, which meant they didn't smell like civilians. They stank of leather, horses, and oiled steel, which meant they smelled like men-at-arms.

"Who are you?" Royden asked.

"Snow White and the seven dwarves," their officer said.

He had the pale complexion and the black hair of Snow White, but he was overweight and sported a beard, thin as it was. His lips looked as though someone had sewn two banana slugs around his mouth and then painted them an unhealthy pink.

Were those the sort of lips that any self-respecting handsome prince would kiss?

One of the seven dwarves tied Royden's hands behind his back, another blindfolded him, and together they shoved him into the back of a freight wagon. They climbed in, closed the tailgate, and the wagon started out.

Four guards, three men and a woman, rode with him. Snow White was riding up front with the driver. The guards were armed. One of the men had a heavy crossbow. As weapons went, it was too large for close work. He must have grabbed it in a hurry, not thinking about how he was going to use it in the back of a freight wagon. The obvious conclusion from this was that the exchange had been made on short notice.

And so, now, here Royden was, jostling along in the hands of a second team of kidnappers. Despite Snow White's posturing, maybe they could be persuaded to tell him what was going on.

He couldn't ask them outright, so he started small.

"Are we in for a long trip?" he asked.

"Wait and see."

The voice had an upriver twang. Another of Narmer's men? Maybe, but men-at-arms from upriver often drifted the length and breadth of the basin. It was the consistency of their accents, one to another, that had given the first bunch away.

"Are you from around here?" he asked.

"Shut the fuck up," the woman said. She had a downriver accent.

"Gladly," Royden said.

Two hours later, they entered Maryhill.

That much was evident from the street noise, the city stench, and the different sort of jostling and crunching as the wagon's wheels rolled over paving stones, as opposed to over the ruts of a dirt track.

They followed a confused route, but after a few minutes, the smells of river mud, creosote, and draft animals grew distinct. They were in the warehousing district, then. The wagon made two additional turns, and then pulled to a stop.

Here the air reeked of garbage, horse dung, cooking, and rats. A stable yard behind an inn?

His guards hustled him out of the wagon and yanked off his blindfold.

A stable yard it was, behind an inn near the waterfront. The surrounding buildings were no greater than three stories high, made out of brick, with a buildup of grime and filth that had to have been centuries in the making.

His guards rushed him through the inn's back door, which was suffering from an advanced case of dry rot, down a flight of stairs, and into the basement.

The air was dank and heavy with the odors of stored food, barrels of beer and wine, and the seepage from a leaking sewage pipe. The floor was packed dirt, damp and slick.

The space that served as *Morning Victor*'s great cabin was about the size of a large dog kennel. It was narrow due to the shape of the hull, and it was low due to the ship's shallow draft and minimal freeboard.

Vlod sat on a locker with his back to the stern windows. They were twice as wide as they were tall. The light they admitted was sufficient but muted, no need to light the lamps and no need to squint.

Shabnan sat in a chair across the worktable from Vlod, on the subordinate's side.

Vlod had wondered whether or not he should have arranged a neutral seating arrangement, but given the size of the cabin and the size of the table and the general lack of furnishings, he was stuck with things the way they were. Shabnan would just have to lump it.

They were alone, and at Shabnan's request Vlod bolted the door against intrusion. Two of the Crone's guards, two of Brenna's marines, and Brenna herself stood guard outside.

Shabnan repeated Ulricka's refusal to hear Edmund and Vernon's appeal. "Go back and tell Edmund that he's made too many enemies. Her Beatitude must remain neutral."

Was this the same bullshit she'd used on Royden?

"She's not acting like a neutral," Vlod said. He picked up two pages copied from Jinhai's final report. "You might want to read these," he said, and handed them across to her.

Shabnan skimmed the sheets and stuffed them into a pocket. "Lies."

"Then why didn't Her Beatitude put him on trial for treason, or heresy, or pissing in the koi pond? When it comes to show trials, the Cathedral has few equals."

"Go home."

"Not until Edmund has his ruling and Royden is aboard this ship, alive."

"You're in over your head, runt."

"Well, being a runt, I'm used to it."

Thirty-Five

Ulricka sat down on a bench in her garden. The sun was bright and warm, not the usual fare for April. The walls blocked out the breeze, but allowed a south-facing view of the Sacred Grove, Maryhill, and the Columbia River. She did not invite Shabnan to join her, and the older woman remained standing.

Ulricka listened to the birds. She ought to have turned Royden into fertilizer for the Sacred Grove. Few fell so far from grace that they were unable to contribute, each in his own way.

Sooner or later, that meddler in motive power was bound to prove as much.

What sort of contribution might she arrange for Edmund's magus to make? She could soak him in pitch and use him to light a midnight procession around the Cathedral. What a lovely sight that would be!

It had been decades since a procession of that sort had been done. Maybe it was high time that the *boys* were reminded of who held the power and who did not.

Shabnan handed her the two sheets of paper that Vlod had provided. "They're from Jinhai's dispatch, the one we couldn't intercept. Copies."

Ulricka scanned the pages. "Is Edmund making threats?"

"Nothing explicit. The *implicit* one is clear enough, though. If we don't turn over Royden and if you don't agree to rule—"

"To approve," Ulricka said.

"—*to approve* Edmund and Vernon's appeal, they'll circulate the full text."

A chill gust of wind blew over the garden wall. Ulricka shivered.

The prospect of death at a comparatively young age at the hands of her successor didn't appeal to Ulricka. As far as she could tell, it hadn't appealed to any of her predecessors, either.

Unless she could convince the provincial sobor to allow her to take the veil as an alternative, which necessitated her recognition as a living saint, she had only one way to avoid death at the hands of her successor: to be elected to the matriarchate of All North America.

Heretofore she'd given elevation to the matriarchate next to no attention.

Given the situation, it could be time for her to reconsider.

The Matriarch of All North America, the Holy Mother, was the one woman on the continent to whom the provincial mothers metropolitan were absolutely responsible. She was the one woman to whom all theological and organizational disputes were ultimately referred. She judged. She decided. She reigned *and* she ruled.

She was also the one woman of jurisdictional rank whom dogma did not require to pop out babies year after year.

The matriarchate was heady stuff indeed, but it also meant that a matriarch remained above ground until she died a natural death.

For any given mother metropolitan, election to the matriarchate was no better than a remote possibility. The politics were bad enough, but the main impediment was *time*. The vast majority of mothers metropolitan took office and left it well within the reign of one holy mother. *One*. Most matriarchs lasted in office for twenty, thirty, forty, or even fifty years. Svetlana the Areopagite had died at the age of eighty-seven, Yvette the Scribe had lived to be ninety-six, and Matilda the Theologian had lived to the age of a hundred and ten.

In contrast, on the whole, mothers metropolitan reigned for less than twenty years, often for less than ten. Most died in their early forties. Some much earlier. Gretchen, who had presided over one of the arid provinces to the south, had been thirty-seven when she'd dried up.

Ulricka was thirty-five. She sprouted new gray hairs as fast as she could pull out the old ones, her breasts were sagging, and her hips would never again see the inside of her pre-mother metropolitan trousers. Time and her office were killing her. At most, she had another ten years.

Ten years: It was a good long time, and the end of it was too far off to call for the Mistress of Sojourners to make plans.

The current matriarch, Mayumi, was in her late eighties. Her mind hadn't failed, but it had dulled. She was nearly blind and nearly deaf. Her hands trembled so badly she couldn't hold a spoon. Her voice was a disjointed croak. It was said, through the subtlest of back channels, that she had lost a shocking amount of weight and that her stools were bloody.

Within a matter of months, at most a year, Mayumi would make her journey to the Gods and the Generations, and when she did, the mothers metropolitan and the curia of the North American Communion would meet to mourn her death and to choose her successor.

For Ulricka, even though she headed a remote province, elevation to the status of matriarch was a possibility. She had friends who would nominate her, and she stood a reasonable chance of winning election as a come-from-behind compromise candidate, if not as the majority's first choice.

If Ulricka was reading the tealeaves correctly, the curia as a whole had grown impatient with East Coast dominance, with its manner of assumed, unquestioned suzerainty, with its smug, touch-me-not, oh-so-fashionable condescension, with its assumption of theological and liturgical preeminence. Thus the moment could well be right for a matriarch from the West Coast, for a matriarch with honest dirt under her fingernails.

Nevertheless, any possibility Ulricka could muster would vanish the instant Edmund published Jinhai's material. The calls for her replacement would echo throughout the province. Throughout the Communion? The calls would grow into a chorus, and she would be dead within the year.

Burned for heresy. Burned for treason. Burned for rank stupidity.

Never mind her motives.

Never mind her lofty intentions.

She fought away the rising fear, the terror, her own second-guessing.

She could not allow herself to be caught up in boxing with shadows, with chimeras of her own imagining.

First things first.

Narmer's underlings had turned Royden over to her people days ago. Through Harakhty, Narmer had offered no believable explanations or apologies. He had shifted the blame to overzealous subordinates.

Did he think she was a moron?

No doubt he did.

As for the captain of the *Wings of Nekhbet*, Ulricka had not as yet raised the issue. She hadn't forgotten—nor forgiven—the captain's murder, but some issues, like some soups, were better left to simmer.

Ulricka's people had not left Royden to enjoy his surroundings. They'd allowed him to rest in his new basement home for a few hours, but then they had gone to work on him. So far, their reports hadn't told her much worth hearing.

It was time for her to buckle down. It was time for them to buckle down.

Ulricka began with the basics. She said to Shabnan, "Tell me about Royden."

"His injuries have begun to heal. No broken bones. No dangerous infections. His interrogators are making progress."

"Not from what I've read."

"Early days."

"Do they have any idea what they're looking for?"

"They have questions. How much does Edmund know? What was in Jinhai's reports? What did Royden learn while he was snooping around? From whom did he learn it? What did Narmer's people ask him? What did he tell them? I could go on..."

Ulricka nodded.

Shabnan said, "You wouldn't think one kidnapping could spark so many questions."

"Not the kidnapping, but the dullards who staged it."

A seagull cried as it circled overhead. The volleys echoed across the palace grounds. Why did it seem so strange that seagulls lived this far inland? They were scavengers. They were not romantically attached to the sea, not like the Iredales; nor to the idea of the sea, like the Innes-Martins;

nor to the power that control of the mouth of the Columbia River conferred, like Narmer and his Pasco-Burbanks. Seagulls were realists. They went where the food was.

Ulricka sighed. She could also argue that Narmer was every bit as realistic as the seagulls. He was going where the trade was, where the power was.

Where the future was.

He was headed toward the mouth of the Columbia River.

Ulricka said, "Tell them to finish up. We need to turn him over. In the meantime, keep him well fed."

"You make him sound like a prize horse."

Ulricka smiled. "That's exactly what he is."

Over dinner in the cabin, Vlod told Brenna and the captain of *Morning Victor* about his time ashore. He'd visited the inn where Royden had stayed. He'd collected Royden's belongings and had settled his bill, but he'd learned nothing of value.

He said, "I had a nice walk. Maryhill's growing. Shops opening. New larger buildings taking the places of old smaller ones."

A knock sounded, and the door opened. Brenna's sergeant came in, his movements quick, efficient. He was an older man, massive through the chest, neck, and shoulders. He was dressed in civilian clothes. They were tattered and filthy. He grinned. "We found him!"

THIRTY-SIX

It was the dark before sunrise, the classic time for an attack.

Brenna had deployed her forces around the decayed waterfront inn where elements of the Cathedral guard were holding Royden prisoner. The sign over the door announced it to be the Mace and Labrys. The building fronted the Plaza de Armas, onto which several streets converged. The topography was ideal for what Brenna and the trireme's captain had planned.

The final ready report came in. The units covering the rear of the building were in place. The reserves, well out of sight, were in place and spoiling for a fight.

Brenna gave the order, and with a minimum of noise her mixed force of marines and sailors rushed the building. The leading unit burst through the door and overpowered the inn's fire watch—an overweight, middle-aged man who doubled as the inn's jack-of-all-trades.

The sailors spread through the common room and kitchen, while Brenna and her marines tackled the hallways on the main floor.

At the same time, an assault group made up of sailors, under the command of the ship's captain, broke in through the inn's rear door. They secured the main-floor storerooms and the rear of the building.

Brenna couldn't believe her good luck. So far they'd met with no material opposition. Indeed, the fire watch was already sitting off to one side, content to sit with his back to the fire and watch the show.

The captain appeared. "Nothing," he said.

"Marines, follow me!" Brenna said, and raced toward the stairs.

Her group surged up onto the second and third floors, along the hallways, and into the guest rooms.

Brenna and her force advanced with a power as irresistible as a river that has burst its dikes. They shattered locks and flung open doors. They searched closets and attics. They overpowered the proprietor and his guests. Swords dimpled nightclothes. Shouts and screams of alarm filled the night. The glint of sharpened steel choked off the pathetic, ineffectual noise.

Royden was on neither of the aboveground floors.

"Basement!" Brenna said.

Again taking the lead, she held a newly lighted torch aloft and raced down the stairs.

Vlod snatched the torch from her hand and pushed past her, taking the lead. "Sorry. My favor," he said, and raced down the stairs.

"How do you figure?"

"We are of the magi, Royden and I."

Without another word, Brenna plunged after him.

Their boots thundered on the stair steps.

One good shove did for the door leading into the basement.

A wash of dim light rose up the stairwell. A single lamp.

The sound of panicked breathing, too.

The rasp of boots.

Brenna and her marines crowded close behind Vlod. This was his show.

Near the bottom of the steps, Vlod halted and said, "You're overmatched. Throw down your weapons!"

Swords and guarding daggers thudded onto the dirt floor.

Vlod strode the rest of the way into the basement, not trusting for a moment that the people waiting there had completely surrendered. Still, any last-ditch effort on their part would be both fruitless and mortally absurd.

Brenna followed, less than two paces behind. She'd shifted her sword to her left hand and was holding her battle knife in her right, ready to throw it.

The basement was dim, dank, low-ceilinged, and reeked of spilled beer, black mold—up in the floor joists and along the mudsills—the smoke of a poorly trimmed lamp, and rats. Surprisingly, the dirt floor was powder dry.

The marines rushed down behind Vlod and Brenna.

"I'm over here!" Royden called from a corner.

The marines fanned out. They subdued Royden's jailers—four sour-looking men-at-arms in civilian clothes—and took control of the now-crowded space. They encountered no resistance and no reluctance to comply with their orders.

"This was too easy," the sergeant of marines commented.

The idea was so hackneyed that Vlod dismissed it. Royden's jailers had faced an impossible situation and they'd done the only thing open to them: they'd surrendered without a fight.

To everyone in the basement, Vlod said, "Vacate the area."

Brenna glared at him. "What are you talking about?"

"Vacate the area. Please," Vlod said. "I need to talk to Royden in private. I'll call you when we've finished."

Brenna's glare intensified. "What's going on?"

"Boy talk," Vlod said.

"Fuck this for a lark," she said.

"No lark," Vlod said.

"Have it your way, then." To her marines, she went on, reverting to officer-in-charge mode. "You heard him. Let's go!" There were four of the Mother Metropolitan's men-at-arms in the basement. Brenna pointed at them. "Bring them along, too. Can't very well leave them behind to tell tales."

When the two magi were alone, Vlod pulled a stool over and sat down in front of Royden. The engineer's hands were tied behind his back. Vlod made no move to release him.

"What's going on?" Royden asked.

"Do you want to get out of here?" Vlod asked, as brightly as he could.

"Of course I do!"

"I could leave you behind if you'd rather."

"Quit fucking around and untie me."

"We need to talk."

"About what?"

"Your plans to shake down a friend of mine."

"You're crazy," Royden said.

"My friend's a tavern keeper named Gluth. You know him. I watched you play with him a few months ago."

"I was—"

"He distills brandy. Not a lot, but it's pretty good. You've threatened to shut down his still if he doesn't pay you a percentage. I want his still to stay in operation. I don't want him to pay you a bribe. I want you to leave him alone."

Royden's face contorted into an expression that was a mixture of disbelief and raw fear. "Their morning relief will be here any minute. We have to leave."

"*I* have to leave," Vlod said. "*You* don't."

"Look, Gluth is in violation," Royden said. "It's a trivial matter."

"No attempted shake down?"

"No. He's in violation. That's all."

"I'm glad to hear it. I want you to fix it so he's no longer in violation."

"Fine. Consider it done. I'll draft the exemptions the moment we land at Fort George."

"Another thing," Vlod said.

"Now what?" Royden wailed.

"I don't think there's enough enjoyment in the world. What do you think? Is there enough enjoyment in the world?"

"I agree with you," Royden said. "There isn't nearly enough. But what am I supposed to do about it? I can't wave a magic wand and make everybody happy."

"I don't expect you to," Vlod said. "I just want you to fix it with your buddies in the Engineers Guild so that Van Horn Butte Reserve—that's a type of whiskey, by the way—"

"I know what it is," Royden said. "I used to drink it."

"Good. Then you know what I'm talking about. I want you to arrange for it to come back onto the market and for the Van Horn Butte distillery to go back into production."

"I didn't put them *out* of production," Royden said. His fear turned into anger. "Their stock was probably emptied into the nearest ditch."

"I doubt that very much," Vlod said. "Those barrels are locked away in a nice dry warehouse. I want them back in the proper hands." Vlod leaned in very close. "I want everything put back the way it was. I want whatever's left—plant, still, stock, records, formulas—returned to the original owner's family. I want what can't be returned to be replaced."

Royden looked as though he had fallen into the hands of a madman. "I'm an engineer, not a miracle worker!"

Vlod stood up. "Goodbye." He turned to leave.

"All right, all right," Royden said. "I'll do what I can, but I can't promise anything. The people responsible are out of my league."

"Try hard."

"All right. I'll try. I swear it." He swiveled his arms around for Vlod to untie them. "It may not be enough, though. The still itself may have been scrapped."

"Rumor has it that it was smashed, but I don't believe that. Rumors have a way of turning out to be wrong."

"What are you talking about?"

"Good distilling equipment is much too valuable to destroy."

"But it *might* have been," Royden said. "That's all I'm saying. *Might* have been. I can't be held responsible for something someone else did."

"Understood," Vlod said. "By the way, this little agreement of ours is strictly between us."

"I wouldn't have it any other way."

"Good." Vlod smiled. "Now, aren't you glad we had this little chat?"

"Yes, yes, I am," Royden said, fervently.

Vlod called up the stairwell: "We're through down here."

He untied Royden.

The door banged open, and Brenna and several of her marines hurried down the stairs. Their weapons rattled and jangled.

Royden tried to stand. He tottered and wobbled. Vlod steadied him.

"Sorry," Royden said.

Two of the marines partly supported and partly carried Royden up the stairs.

"We've got visitors!" one of the corporals called down.

Brenna and her marines ran from the basement and took up positions on the ground floor.

Vlod joined them.

Out in the square, the corporal's visitors, several dozen of them, had formed a skirmish line. They'd backed it up with men-at-arms positioned in doorways and sheltered behind the corners of buildings.

A crowd of gawkers had gathered.

"Make the signal!" *Morning Victor's* captain ordered.

His coxswain went to a side window, opened it a crack, and blew "All Hands" on his boatswain's pipe.

From the side streets beyond the ring of the Mother Metropolitan's men-at-arms, a cheer answered the call.

Brenna grabbed the door handle, but the captain said, "Let them engage first."

The functional chain of command was worse than muddled. Brenna and her marines were not part of the ship's crew, but they were responsible to act in concert with it. The captain was not her subordinate, but he was under explicit orders to cooperate with her and support her mission "to the best of his ability and as circumstances dictate."

Brenna replied with a nod of agreement. They'd wait.

Vlod moved to a place where he could look out through a front window without making himself into a target.

Roaring at the top of their lungs, screaming like enraged devils loosed from the pits of Hades, a handpicked detachment of *Morning Victor's* crew dashed into the street. There were a dozen and a half of them, but what they lacked in numbers, they made up for in ferocity.

The two forces met like an avalanche colliding with a cliff face. Swords and shields slammed into one another, sending up a deafening clash. Arrows hissed through the air and struck their targets with a sound that was not unlike a carpenter's hammer hitting a slab of meat.

The shouts and screams and yells reverberated back and forth across the plaza.

At first, the Mother Metropolitan's soldiers fell like saplings. As a body, they staggered and gave ground.

Others ran from place to place, vainly hoping to shore up the gaps forming in their line. They dropped in their tracks, impaled by boarding pikes, brought down by arrows, cut down by swords and knives, or because their skulls had been opened by tomahawks.

Their line wavered, and the melee showed every sign of descending into a rout.

Unbelievably, however, their three officers and four sergeants bullied the Cathedral's forces back into formation.

The fact that they were sandwiched between two enemy forces, one attacking them and the other one yet to attack, helped. The Cathedral's men-at-arms had no way to survive but to close ranks and fight their way out.

"To the rear!"

"Hold your ground there!"

"To me, to me!"

"Rally! Rally!"

"Stand!"

Brenna pulled again at the door, and again, the captain restrained her.

"We need to be out there!" Brenna said.

"Patience," the captain said, and gave her a smile that would have frozen boiling water.

A long, high-pitched scream filled the night.

From which side had it come?

Royden gave Vlod an apologetic smile. "See if I ever go for another walk at night."

"To me! To me!" a youngish voice on the street called.

Evidently, among the Mother Metropolitan's people, the instinct to flee had regained the upper hand.

"Hold your line! Form up! Form up!"

"To me! Rally to me!"

Vlod heard a note of desperation.

"Rally!"

It was unbelievable that a mere eighteen sailors could wreak such destruction!

"Now!" the captain yelled, and pulled open the door.

The captain, Brenna, and Vlod, followed by her marines and the ship's sailors among her party, poured out into the plaza.

The handful of archers they'd brought with them deployed, but they had no way to fire without the risk of sending their arrows into the ship's sailors. They put down their bows, drew their swords, and joined the fight.

Brenna's marines threw their weight against the enemy line.

They weren't an overwhelming force, and under different circumstances, the Mother Metropolitan's forces would have held.

But these weren't different circumstances, and they did not hold. At first, the enemy line sagged back on itself, but then it wavered, and then, as a line, it vanished, as though it had disappeared in a conjurer's puff of smoke.

Vlod had no other way to describe it. One moment he had faced a disciplined body of fighting men, and the next he was enmeshed in a rapidly disintegrating melee. Steel flashed, blood sprayed, men screamed, and the pavement grew slick underfoot.

All the while, in the back of his mind lurked the fear that additional units of the Cathedral guard would rush in to reinforce the engaged and disintegrating unit.

Had Shabnan decided to allow them their petty victory? Had Ulricka realized that the loss of this skirmish was the key to a much greater political victory? Had she managed to paint herself as the defenseless neutral and to paint Edmund as a blood-drenched thug, as a rogue chieftain who would stop at nothing to achieve his ends?

It would seem so.

Why hadn't they seen the trap and avoided it?

Because they'd had no viable choice other than to engage. Edmund could not drop the marriage. Edmund could not abandon one of his magi. Edmund could not let all Ulricka's pretense of neutrality go unexposed for what it was—a callus bit of political theater.

Without warning or visible cause, the melee itself convulsed and dissolved. The two forces stood away from each other.

The Mother Metropolitan's men-at-arms threw down their weapons and fled in whatever direction they could. They fell to their knees in surrender. They begged for their lives.

Brenna stood face-to-face with the enemy commander. She held the bloody point of her sword to his throat. "Yield!"

The man's sword clattered onto the blood-stained street.

Morning Victor's crew and Brenna's marines cheered.

The cheering echoed from building to building and along the streets.

THIRTY-SEVEN

Vernon leaned back against the headboard of his bed. It was his own bed, in his own keep, and it was both familiar and comfortable. Here he was not a guest. Here it was he who ruled, he who was responsible for his own security. Here he had no need to cooperate with self-indulgent dolts like Seldon.

Seldon's sister, however, was no one's dolt.

At the moment, Xenia was struggling with her emotions, fighting to calm them, fighting, Vernon was certain, to define them.

Anxiety? Fear? Excitement? Loathing? Ambition? Curiosity? Pleasure?

In the immediate sense, the specifics were of no consequence. She was losing her inner war against them.

Surrendering to her inner uproar, she swung her feet onto the floor and grabbed the top blanket.

It was clear to Vernon that she needed to pace, needed to stare out the window, needed to *move*.

She wrapped the blanket around her naked body.

As far as Vernon was concerned, the blanket was no great loss to him. It was one of three, and besides, Vernon still had Lyrisette to keep him warm. Xenia had brought her along as a traveling companion, and tonight she had insisted that the henge dancer, who was petite and lithe, share their bed.

Xenia went behind the screen, used the commode, and then sat on the widow seat. The only light in the room came from the fire, and it made her face, now in profile, appear to have been cast in copper. Her hair spilled past her shoulders. Her hair ranged from blond to auburn, no two strands were the same color.

Vernon joined her.

"Blanket?" she asked.

"I'm fine," he said.

He twined his fingers in her hair. She was an impossible riddle.

Four days ago, she had arrived unannounced at Vernon's gates. With her were Lyrisette and two men-at-arms. It was a dangerously small party.

"We went out after wild pig," Xenia explained. "That was two days ago."

One thing had led to another, and they'd decided to stay out. They'd slept in the open. The men-at-arms had taken wonderful care of them. The hunt had taken them northward from Sauvie's Island, also called the Manor Island. They hadn't found much to shoot at, and, well, here they were. They'd managed a couple of deer, though. Xenia hoped they were worth the effort to cook.

Vernon ordered rooms for Xenia and Lyrisette. He sent their horses to the stables, their men-at-arms to the barracks, and the deer to the kitchens.

"Fresh meat is always welcome," he said, "as are you and your companions."

The two women looked the parts Xenia had described for them: wool shirts, leather boots, and leather jerkins. Their riding cloaks were dark wool. They had plaited their hair into tight, single braids. They needed to bathe.

Vernon offered hot baths and clean clothes, and they accepted them gratefully.

Vernon did not stage a welcoming banquet. Instead, he invited them to dinner in his dayroom. It was a pleasant chamber, and it served a variety of purposes, off and on: office, workspace, council chamber, and, on at least one occasion, torture chamber.

Xenia arrived for dinner in a long, belted dress, complete with flowing sleeves. Her feet were bare. A jeweled ring glittered on one of her toes.

Lyrisette wore a short, sleeveless tunic that left her legs bare.

Over coffee and brandy, Vernon asked Xenia, "Time to come clean. Why are you here?"

"As I said, we were out hunting—"

"I can see that," Vernon said, cutting her off. He nodded toward the dancer. "The bait has been in view for some time."

Xenia smiled. "She is a lovely creature, isn't she?"

Lyrisette had the decency to blush.

"She's a diversion," Vernon said.

Lyrisette giggled. "I told you he'd figure it out."

Later that night, Xenia slipped into Vernon's bedroom.

He put aside the book he was reading.

Wordlessly she undressed and climbed into bed beside him.

"I told you no," he said.

She snuggled next to him. "I didn't believe you."

"Whore."

"I want to have your baby," she said.

"Not on your life. You might sacrifice him in one of your secret cultic rituals."

She hit him playfully on the arm. "How can you say such a terrible thing?"

"I'm told a terra-cotta furnace is involved."

"It's not true," she said. "We don't *sacrifice* babies. We send them *home*."

She pressed herself against his chest.

"You could have tried an original approach," he said.

"Why? Seduction works."

"Maybe with me it won't," he said.

"I fuck in hope."

The next morning, they went for a ride, and in the afternoon, they went for a sail on the river, back and forth in front of the Monticello docks. They played with the current and whatever wind they could find.

That night, Vernon went to her room.

The next day they hunted in the hills above the manor. Luck and the

Gods of the Forest were with them. They came back with two pigs and a wild llama. They saw elephant dung and the wolf-gnawed carcass of a camel.

Centuries ago such exotics as elephants and camels were kept for public amusement. In these enlightened times, however, they either roamed free or had been domesticated. Camels were the backbone of transcontinental caravans and without elephants, logging in the more hilly regions would slow to an abrupt end.

That night, Xenia and Lyrisette came to Vernon's room.

Xenia told him, "She's in love with one of my brother's magi, poor dear. Not the magus, her." In an aside to Lyrisette, she said, "Aren't you?"

The dancer blushed.

To Vernon, Xenia said, "See? What did I tell you? Pink ears. Personally, I can't fathom it. Magi are such rotten lovers. She misses him, though. After you and I are done, I suspect she'll want to cuddle."

Later, after Xenia and Vernon had brought each other to gasping, grunting, thoroughgoing climaxes, Lyrisette hadn't wanted to cuddle. She'd wanted sex: athletic, violent, bucking, screaming sex. And when it was over, she had kissed Vernon on the forehead and had gone to sleep.

Now, as Vernon and Xenia sat on the window seat, she leaned back against him. He let go of her hair and put his arms around her.

"First me, then her," she said. "I'm surprised you can walk."

"So am I. She's quite—"

"*Inventive* is the polite term."

"That too, but I was thinking of *eager*. Pick a word of your own. That magus is a lucky man."

"It's the dancing. When I'm in one of my dancing phases, I get unbearably *hungry*. No one's safe."

"Old men included?"

"You're not old."

"I'm not young."

"Oh. Well. That's true."

"Kind of you to say," he said, "but I do wonder what you'll want in return."

"That again?"

"That again."

"I'm not a prostitute."

"I didn't say you were, not seriously, but I must insist."

She smiled at him. Her attitude was ironic, playful. "It's one of my devilish tricks to make my brother's life a living hell. I have several of them. Right now my favorite is to parade my tits every chance I get. His formal banquets are especially fun."

And then the answer to his question blossomed.

"You *are* a whore," Vernon said. He laughed. "I can't make you chieftain in your brother's place."

"No, you can't, and I wouldn't want you to, even if you could. Seldon's life is a tedious bore."

How young she sounded!

"Fear, worry, and boredom," she said. "That's what being the ruler of a clan buys you."

Vernon had no counter list of goodies to offer. She was right about the boredom and the rest of it. There was a limit to the number of disputes over which farmer owned which pig that Vernon could settle before his brain went soggy.

Over the last few weeks, he'd often wondered what he could do to keep his brain alert after he and Edmund had become bosom allies. He'd have to give up weaving serious plots against him, and he'd have to quit raiding his lands, too. It was the brotherly thing to do, boring but brotherly.

Their alliance, however, did not mean an end to jockeying, nor did it mean an end to ambition. Perhaps life would not end up completely bereft of ambition, an interminable round of effete boredom.

The legal ownership of that pig *was* important, however. And without breaking a sweat he could list dozens of administrative and economic reforms that were sadly overdue. There were docks, canals, and bridges to be built. Gregory had no head for such things. It would be a blessing for them to be in place when Gregory ascended.

Be that as it may...

Without Edmund to contend with, how would Vernon fill the hours? How would he banish the tedium? Debauch young women? Play chess? Garden? Harass a different chieftain? Invent card games? Hunt? Join a religious cult? Learn to paint pretty pictures of lakes and trees, their fall foliage a poignant panoply of red, orange, yellow, green, and brown? Hunting? Cooking? Fishing? Fencing?

Meditation?

His brain would ooze out through his ears!

Maybe Xenia *was* the answer.

"Last chance," he said. "What *do* you want?"

She wormed around to face him. "I want you to be the ace up my sleeve."

Vernon chuckled. She had not caught him flatfooted. "What? Not down your cleavage?"

She gave him a look. "Be serious. Our lives may depend on it."

Suitably chastened, he asked, "To be used how?"

"I haven't made up my mind yet."

"What's the trade? I'm your sleeve-dwelling ace and you're my...what?"

"I promise to ride over and fuck you silly from time to time. I could bring Lyrisette, if you like."

"She is fun," Vernon said.

"She is, isn't she?"

"I love to watch you kiss each other."

"Voyeur!" Xenia said.

"Exhibitionist!"

"It's settled, then," Xenia said. "Will you be my hidden ace?"

He ought to have thrown her out, but instead he said, "The question is, will you return the favor? With your brother dodging this way and that, I could use an ace of my own. Will you be mine?"

"Of course I will," she said. "Pals forever."

"Or until one of us ends up on a stake."

"Or on the Mother Metropolitan's knife."

"Fair enough," Vernon said.

"Until death do us part. It's almost like a marriage vow."

"That's what marriage is, isn't it? A conspiracy of two against the world."

"I'll have to trust you on that score. I've never been married," she said, and leaned her back against his chest. After a moment, she said, "I've never wanted to be."

"I didn't think so."

"The Mother Metropolitan," Xenia said as though a new thought had just occurred to her. "I want her deposed."

That made sense. Ulricka had two dominant and contradictory traits. First, she was a resolute schemer, *and* second, she was an indifferent thinker.

Xenia, however, was a champion schemer and a first-class thinker. She could work calculus problems in her head.

"What's going on? Do you want to sit on her throne?" Vernon asked.

"Not necessarily. She spies on me."

"She spies on a lot of people."

"Well, I'm tired of it. It makes me break out in spots."

———

Ulricka poured herself a cup of hot, strong tea. She gestured with the pot toward Shabnan, but the Crone shook her head. Ulricka sweetened the tea with honey and drank it in a short series of quick gulps.

Shabnan was seated at one end of a couch. Ulricka refilled her cup and took the other end.

The ambush, which Colonel Chiharu had promised them couldn't fail, had failed. The debacle had demonstrated the incompetence of the Cathedral guard, and it had done so in front of the whole town. Therefore, it had done so in front of the entire province.

As things stood, a coverup was possible. The truth could be covered with layer upon layer of conflicting and colorful lies. A ring of smugglers had been overwhelmed and brought to justice. Yes, it had been a terrible fight, but the Cathedral guard had prevailed. A cabal of insurrectionists had been rooted out. A secret congregation of patriarchist fanatics had been arrested.

To launch an attack on Edmund's trireme at this point would shatter the pretense. The façade would collapse, and the result of that debacle would be unpredictable.

No, the pretense, whatever that turned out to be—Shabnan would think of something effective—had to stand. It had to become the reality of what had happened.

She was now faced with the manipulation of yet another improvised political drama, a set piece for those without the stomach to digest the truth.

Infinitely worse, Vlod and his people had rescued Royden and had taken him aboard their trireme, *Morning Victor*.

It was, Ulricka mused, an appropriate name!

Strangely, however, the ship had remained in port, and because she had, Ulricka had not yet lost control of the situation irretrievably.

Irretrievably. Not the sort of word normally associated with hope, but in this case it would have to do. Hanging on by one's fingernails was better than plummeting to the rocks below.

As the situation now stood, Ulricka was facing timings that were paralytically fluid. Nonetheless, within a matter of hours, she ought to be able to send Edmund's daughter, her marines, her ship, and her sailors back down the Columbia River, under a cloud of charges, disgraced and humiliated, but without Royden and without Vlod.

As for those two, Ulricka would be able to dispose of them as she saw fit.

She would have to pretend to bargain. But that presupposed she had something to trade, something either Edmund or Vlod wanted, something in addition to her judgment on Edmund's appeal. Royden was an errand boy, and Brenna and her ship were window dressing, but Vlod was the key.

"What does he want?" Ulricka asked.

"Who? The runt?"

"Yes, the runt."

Shabnan let the question hang for a moment. Finally, she asked, "What's the one thing that everybody wants?"

"Wealth, power, sex?"

"What's your stock in trade?"

"The presence of the Goddess," Ulricka said.

"Less mystically, less subject to personal hysteria."

Ulricka arched an eyebrow. "Answers to otherwise unanswerable questions."

"Besides answers. What makes the answers important?"

Ulricka's temper snapped. "Out with it!"

"That would spoil the effect," Shabnan said. "What do *you* absolutely want? At three o'clock in the morning, when no amount of sex or prayer or alcohol or religious ecstasy can extinguish the terror."

"Immortality," Ulricka whispered.

Shabnan smiled. "Close, but not quite."

———

Vlod and Brenna waited while Royden ate.

His assigned cabin aboard *Morning Victor* was cramped and dim despite the whale-oil lamp. Indeed, the space was so small that the hammock, when it was slung, had to be slung diagonally across it.

The afternoon air was sluggish, and although the port was open, no breeze came in.

At last, the older magus set his plate on the deck next to his chair and wiped his mouth on his sleeve. The fish-and-onion smell of what he'd been eating hung in the air, competing with the fumes from the lamp.

The lamp wasn't smoking, but close enough. *Morning Victor* had not brought aboard the best grade of whale oil, and Vlod had a hunch that the chandlers had cut what they'd supplied with a mixture of fish oil and alcohol. Rendered harbor seal or sea lion blubber were also perennial favorites.

"What can you tell us about what happened to you?" Brenna asked.

"Not much," Royden said. "I went for a walk, and Narmer's people kidnapped me. Several days later, they turned me over to a group of Cathedral guards. You rescued me a day or two later."

"Did they question you?"

"Incessantly," Royden said.

"What about?"

"Trivialities," Royden said.

A knock sounded at the door.

"Come," Brenna said.

A marine ducked his head in. "The Crone has come aboard. She's asking to see Vlod."

Vlod hurried up on deck.

Shabnan handed him a wax-sealed envelope. "Her Beatitude is pleased to grant you a private audience."

THIRTY-EIGHT

Vlod followed Shabnan into the Saraswati Palace's Blue Solarium. It was a large room, situated high in the palace. Floor-to-ceiling windows comprised the south and west walls, and the ceiling was a matrix of skylights. The air was warm without being oppressive.

Murals decorated the north and east walls. They showed the Goddess in Her various aspects: maiden, bride, mother, and crone. The God was nowhere to be seen, except by inference in the sheaves of wheat depicted in the plaster moldings.

Before the Second Creation, The Goddess had revealed Herself in three aspects: maiden, mother, and crone. However, after granting the mercy of her Second Creation, She had revealed Herself as maiden, bride, mother, and crone, to match the four seasons.

Oversize potted plants filled the corners of the room, and armed guards—all women—stood at intervals along the inside walls. Members of Ulricka's court milled about in twos and threes. Ulricka herself was at the center of a group of four.

The solarium was aggressively a woman's room, designed to impress and intimidate, to preach the ultimate subservience, if not the outright irrelevance, of the masculine, to marginalize, at the very least, all things male.

No images were to be seen of the God's cycles: the youth to match the virgin, the bridegroom to match the bride, the father to match the mother, and the sage to match the crone.

According to the Blue Solarium, men had no vital role other than to produce sperm, seed, as symbolized by the stalks of wheat, which were in turn to be planted in the earth and, if the Goddess were to grant it, bring forth an abundance.

The room, the cathedral itself, directly and forcefully dictated the place of men, their *acceptable* place. The Cathedral commanded them to live out their lives in silence and obedience, as manual laborers, as servants, as warriors, as hunters, as *lesser*.

Shabnan presented Vlod to Ulricka, and after she had acknowledged him, she ordered the room cleared and dismissed the guards. Shabnan, too, made her exit.

Dark matters, then.

No surprise there.

Vlod had been a fool to come onto her ground. He ought to have insisted on an open space. A barge in the middle of the river, perhaps. That, too, was foolishness. The whole of the province was her ground, and although that might not be rigidly true, the cathedral and Maryhill were.

"Come with me," Ulricka said.

She led Vlod into the rear of the solarium, through a door, and into a small office. She sat behind a delicately carved table. On it sat pens, ink, a box of stationery, and a document folder.

She did not invite Vlod to sit.

"Did you bring Edmund's appeal?" Ulricka asked.

"It's here," Vlod said, and reached into his cloak.

"Keep it for now," she said.

He withdrew his hand, empty.

"Warrick's ruling must stand," Ulricka said. "I want you to convince Edmund to withdraw his appeal."

"He won't."

"He must."

"His duty is to protect Clan Iredale, just as your duty is to rule on his appeal."

"You dare to instruct me?"

"You dare to evade your responsibility?" Vlod said.

Her eyes narrowed, then relaxed. "You're no coward. I'll grant you that." She smiled a little smile. "I wonder if I can bribe you." She opened the folder and took out a document. She placed it on the table so Vlod could read it.

It was Vlod's petition to have his father exonerated, to have his name added to the *Dirge*. Try as he might, he couldn't look away from the pages he had drafted months ago.

"I see you understand," Ulricka said.

"I'm not one of your sycophants."

Ulricka let a silence draw out, then snapped it. "A fierce loyalty binds the magi. Your rescue of Royden demonstrates it. You detest the man. Nevertheless, you hacked your way through a superior force to free him from my vile, brutish, superstitious clutches. The question is, will you rescue a second magus? Will you rescue your father from nonexistence?"

"State your terms."

"You know my terms."

"Clarity is golden."

"Very well, then. Clarity. The moment Edmund and Vernon withdraw their appeal, I'll pardon your father. I'll declare that he was the victim of false accusations and that he was delirious when he confessed."

"You'd never do it. It would mean picking a fight with the magi. It would mean censuring your predecessor. Above all, it would mean bringing the integrity of the metropolitanate into question."

Ulricka shrugged. "New evidence could come to light. One of your father's accusers could make a deathbed confession. The prosecutor, assuming he's still alive, could be discovered to have used his office for corrupt purposes. Incompetence. Malfeasance. Espionage. Jealousy. Judicial assassination. The possibilities are endless. You father would be rehabilitated, Thora would be exonerated of any wrong-doing, and I and the Cathedral would be hailed as heroes of righteousness and justice." She leaned back in her chair. "It would be as simple as brewing a fresh pot of tea—out with the old leaves, a quick rinse, and in with the new."

She was deadly serious, no hint that she was not.

Vlod could envision the steps playing out. First this, then this, then this: all the ducks in a well-ordered row.

Vlod's emotions froze. Since his departure from Fort George, he had dreaded this moment, aware that it was inevitable. He had denied that it would happen. He had told himself that Ulricka would never dare to abuse the metropolitanate in this manner, but here it was.

She was offering his father's salvation in exchange for Vlod's betrayal of Edmund and Vernon, of Clan Iredale and Clan Innes-Martin. With the stroke of her pen, she would enable Vlod's father to live throughout eternity with the Gods and the Generations. With his agreement, he would damn himself. He would become her man, her servant, her hapless pawn.

For his father's sake.

His choice, then, was between his own damnation or his father's.

"Vlod?"

Ulricka's voice pulled him out of the maze he'd created for himself. He felt stupid and confused, dizzy and nauseous, bereft of clarity and balance.

"Do you agree or not?" she asked.

He made his decision and the words were out of his mouth before he had any chance to reconsider. "Their appeal stands."

"Very well," she said. She held out her hand. "Edmund's appeal, it is my pleasure to consider it."

Vlod produced the document. Oddly, he felt no regret.

She glanced through it. "Nicely worded," she said. "Unfortunately, nice words do not change facts." She scrawled across the bottom of the page and returned it to Vlod.

She'd written her ruling in a single word: "Rejected." Beneath it was her signature: *Ulricka, MM.*

"I'll hold on to your petition," she said. "You might change your mind."

Vlod's nausea gave way to anger.

"Very good, Your Beatitude," he said. He was careful to keep his tone level. He turned toward the door.

"I haven't dismissed you, magus."

"I'm not yours to dismiss," he said, his vision fixed on the door. Its carved panels depicted wheat, fish, apple trees, corn, cattle, and timber.

"Oh, but you are mine, my little wizard. Your duty to Edmund holds you here as surely as an iron chain."

She came around her desk and stood close to him.

He could feel the warmth of her body, smell the mingled scents that clung to her—perfume, soap, costly fabric.

She said, "You're not like other magi."

"In what way?"

"The general run of magi are cowards and prostitutes. You're neither. I'll be interested to see if your proud virtue survives the next few months."

Vlod didn't answer. What was she up to?

"Let's walk together, shall we?" she said.

"As you wish."

She guided Vlod through the solarium and out onto an expansive terrace. Plants in barrel-size tubs stood like sentries along the perimeter and clustered like a floral bonfire in the center. They were an eye-catching assortment: flowering cherry and plum trees, ferns, roses, rhododendrons, azaleas, boxwoods, and dwarf pines. Ulricka's gardener had pruned them into tight, overly nurtured blobs. Not a spontaneous twig remained.

But they looked nice, and they smelled nice.

"I have one last message for Edmund," Ulricka said, "and for you, magus."

"What is it?"

"You'll find out."

They strolled from one end of the terrace to the other. Here and there, she paused to gaze at the plants, to touch a leaf or a flower petal, to bend and inhale the aroma.

"*Heresy* is such an unpleasant word, don't you think?" she said. "*Her-e-sy.*" She lingered on each syllable. "Hare-ah-see. It sounds like a voyaging leporid. Hare at sea."

"*Leporid*?"

"It's a fancy word for hares and rabbits," she said. "*Heresy.* What do you think, hideous word or not?"

"It's an unpleasant word for an unpleasant act."

"With even worse consequences."

She smiled a grave smile, and it reminded Vlod of the girl she had once been, the girl who had handed Thora that first torch at his father's execution.

Ulricka went to the wall and signaled with a wave to someone below, then she beckoned to Vlod. "Come over here, runt," she said. "I want you to see this, and I want you to tell Edmund what you've seen."

Vlod joined her.

Below the terrace was a courtyard. In the middle of it, stood a naked man bound to a tall wooden stake. Burns, bruises, and welts covered his torso. He'd been brutally tortured, and now he was standing on a wooden grate. The grate was no better than a lattice of rough-cut boards, as thick and as wide as a man's hand. It was a burning stand.

Vlod's scalp crawled. With the man's torture, his trial, recently completed, his burning was about to take place.

Black-uniformed guards piled bundles of wood around the man's legs.

The crawling sensation intensified until Vlod became dizzy. His eyes lost focus. The scene appeared as though he were viewing it through a gauze curtain. His legs felt cold.

In an effort to steady himself, Vlod rested his hands on the wall. The stone was cold, the texture smooth. The wall smelled of an aridity so complete that no amount of rain, no amount of snow, no amount of ice could obliterate it.

"Do I have your attention?" Ulricka asked.

Vlod nodded, not trusting his voice.

"It's a fascinating process, burning a man live, viewed mechanically," she said. "First, the wood is air-dried. Then it is soaked in hot pitch, under vacuum to aid in absorption into the wood. That's a recent innovation, by the way. Contrary to what you might think, we're not against progress, but we will stamp out heresy. We will stamp out disorder and chaos. We will crush rebellion."

"Ever the generous and attentive mother, aren't you?"

As though he hadn't spoken, she went on, "Then the pitch is allowed to harden. Finally, a fresh layer of pitch, mixed with turpentine, is applied. That was done just this morning."

Vlod wanted with his entire being to ignore what she was saying, but her words riveted his attention. He had no way to nod his head, and smile politely, and allow what she was saying to drift over him, like a polite teatime chat about yesterday's weather and the prospects for tomorrow.

Ulricka was saying, "See the gloves the guards are wearing? The pitch from the bundles of wood will cover them, like the glaze on a doughnut.

The guards will throw those gloves in among the bundles before they light them. It's part of the ritual. It's said the guards burn their gloves to show their contempt for the condemned. I've also heard it said that they do it because they're afraid the gloves have attracted malevolent forces, demons and the like. Neither is true. Both are peasant piety at its worst. The guards discard their gloves because they're soaked with pitch and would be next to impossible to reuse." She looked at Vlod. "You've seen pitch-soaked wood burn before, haven't you? I can't believe how hot it burns. It can melt iron if a bellows is applied. Did you know that?"

Vlod said, "What's your point?"

"I'd rather it were you tied to that stake," she said, "but, alas, I need you to fill your lord and master's mind with tales of my evil nature and dark intrigues."

"There's no lack of material."

"Now, now, let's have none of that."

"You could have chosen otherwise. You could build rather than burn."

"I am the perfect builder. It's your kind that strapped that man to his stake. He is your victim, not mine."

"You hold the torch," Vlod said.

"Yes, and I intend to use it, too."

By this point, the wood reached well above the condemned man's waist.

The guards stood away.

Then one of them came forward with a wooden bucket and short-handled mop.

"Oh, look," Ulricka said, "they're about to anoint him with the Oil of Grace. Traditionally, it's a mixture of olive oil, linseed oil, aromatic resins, and sulfur, but due to the high cost of olive oil—we have to import it, you see—we have to use a lard-based oil instead. Flares right up, though, despite its base nature."

"It's more than a common heretic deserves," Vlod said, and wondered if the bitch could appreciate true sarcasm when she heard it.

"He isn't the least bit common. I doubt he has a common bone in his body. He's like you, an enthusiastic inventor."

The guard covered the man's torso with the Oil of Grace.

The oil's aroma, not unlike incense before it was burned, billowed up to them. It wasn't an unpleasant smell. The sulfur reminded Vlod of gunpowder, and he wondered if the Cathedral had thought of adding saltpeter to the formula for the Oil of Grace.

"What were his crimes?" Vlod asked.

From what he knew of Cathedral politics, it could have been anything from a failure to pay proper obeisance to the Mother Metropolitan—he hadn't bowed far enough toward the floor—to an effort to revive one of the ancient patriarchal religions—he'd read a forbidden book.

"Can't you guess?" Ulricka asked, a clearly teasing tone in her voice.

The guard with the mop coated the man's head and face. The oil ran down like warm bacon grease, partly congealed and partly liquid. The guard wiped the goo out of the man's eyes and poured the last of the oil over his shoulders. He added the bucket, the mop, and several pairs of pitch-stained gloves to the wood.

The condemned let his head drop toward his chest.

"I've never been much good at guessing games," Vlod said.

"What an old grump you are today," Ulricka said. "He tried to improve the way in which horses are used to pull freight wagons. He said it would lower costs."

"Why is that heretical?"

"It isn't, I supposed, but wherever would his zeal lead him? Into the realm of steam engines? What a misery that would be!"

"A reliable source of motive power," Vlod said. "Machine to provide the brute force rather than animals and people. Why, yes, that would be hell, indeed."

"I ought to show you his file," Ulricka said. "He hitched eight horses to a capstan and used the capstan to drive a wagon's rear wheels. He claimed to have gotten the idea from studying horse-driven flour mills."

"Did it work?"

"What a pragmatist you are!"

"If a teapot can't hold tea, it isn't much of a teapot, is it? No matter how beautiful it is."

"How treacherously evil you are!" she exclaimed. "The vehicle was too wide for the roads, and it exhausted the horses within minutes. He failed to obtain the necessary licenses before building his working prototype."

"He didn't need them, not at that preliminary stage."

"He wasn't condemned on the basis of his prototype, which was a trivial exercise, in any case, but on the basis of his notes and drawings—on the basis of his plans." She smiled again. "Steam-actuated pumps today, a stake of your very own tomorrow."

Vlod arched an eyebrow, but said nothing.

Ulricka smirked at him as though she were chiding him for being hopelessly naive. "His presiding engineer felt differently. He saw the lapse as blatant heresy. Others viewed it as a challenge to established authority. I'm sure Royden would have found the case to be of considerable interest. Wouldn't you agree?"

"I don't report to Royden."

"I'm aware of that, but a precedent is a precedent."

The officer lit a torch. Holding it aloft, she looked up at Ulricka.

"Ah, I see they're ready at last," Ulricka said. She looked at Vlod. "A word to the wise."

"If you would but hear it!" Vlod said.

"I hear them all. All of the words. All of the important ones, anyway."

Ulricka made a chopping motion with her hand.

The officer, a middle-aged woman who was running to fat, grinned like a drunk who's found forgotten money in a coat pocket. She told the condemned that he deserved to roast, and thrust the torch into the wood.

"Well done! Well done!" Ulricka said excitedly. "Did you notice the skill with which she lit the pyre? No fumbling. No hesitation. Every time she does it, too."

"No doubt the condemned find it most reassuring."

"Please. I've told you before. No more jibes and japes. Do you expect me to believe they don't care whether we execute them properly or not? It's better than being executed badly, isn't it?"

"I expect they care more about burning to death than they do about how artistically the torch is wielded."

"Nonsense. A mishandled execution is a horror for everyone. I've seen a few, and believe me, they are not pleasant. Nothing spiritual about them. No transcendence. No remorse. No repentance. No growth. Nothing but death."

The fire spread through the wood, jumping from bundle to bundle.

Yellow and orange flames leapt up and encircled the condemned. Billows of black smoke roiled into the air.

The man's terror and his pain overwhelmed his self-control. Tears ran down his face, and he thrashed from side to side, trying, hopelessly, to avoid the rising flames. The skin-scorching heat clawed up his chest toward his neck.

The officer laughed and called him a spineless coward.

The Oil of Grace caught, and the man became a living torch.

Now the man's screams were not of terror but of mortal agony. The flames blistered and charred his flesh. Black and gray smoke, heavy with pitch and oil, shrouded his face.

He twisted his head from side to side, his whole body writhing. His eyes and mouth were clamped tightly shut. He was holding his breath.

There were those who said it was better, quicker, to gulp down the flames, to sear one's own throat and lungs, thus hastening the end.

"Wriggle, wriggle, you'll not escape," Ulricka taunted.

The wind brought the odors of the burning up onto the terrace: pitch, oil, resin, wood, hair, and human flesh.

"How say you, magus?" Ulricka asked. "You're looking rather pale, almost as though you've seen a sight that doesn't agree with you."

"Shall I faint away?" Vlod asked.

"No. I expect you to remember your father. I expect you to remember that the man down there is your spiritual colleague. I expect you to remember that your body will light up as readily and as delightfully as theirs did."

"Heresy is a dangerous charge to level."

She spared him a glance. "Oh? Why's that?"

The man's body convulsed. It was making a final effort to flee from its torment. Muscle spasm. Nervous spasm. Life holding on and letting go at the same time, driven out by the flames.

"Because definitions change," Vlod said, matter-of-factly. "Today's heretic may be tomorrow's saint. Today's avatar may be tomorrow's heretic."

"A threat? From you?"

"A cautionary reminder. Remember Xiuying the infamous Patriarchal

Deviationist? The synod and the canons of the Cathedral deposed her for heresy, locked her in a cell, and starved her to death."

"She was a dangerous utopian. *Father* metropolitans. Can you imagine such a travesty? Her proposal was as dangerous as it was absurd. How can a man stand as an avatar of the Goddess?"

Abruptly Ulricka pointed down into the courtyard. "His lungs will cook in a moment, and then you'll see something!"

"Xiuying was a mother metropolitan, a theologian, and a prolific writer. Many scholars study her writings. In secret."

"They're fools to run such a risk."

In an explosive rush, the man let out the breath he'd been holding. Reflexively, like a drowning man, he drew in a breath. It must have filled his lungs with pure flame. He was drowning, not in water, but in fire. His body stiffened. His eyes flew open and bulged. He bellowed like an animal in an extremity of pain, a pain that eclipsed the worst imaginable agony.

Vlod held himself as rigid as he could. He commanded himself to watch, not to turn away, to show no weakness, to show no other emotion than indifference.

He owed it to his father and to the man below.

He would not give Ulricka the victory of his own inner pain, his grief, his shame, his powerlessness.

The man stiffened, his body shook, and then he went completely slack. He hung limply in the remnants of his bindings.

The guards cheered and threw fresh bundles of wood onto the flames.

Turn the page for a preview chapter of the next book in The Assassins of Harmony series, *The Heretic's Son*.

ONE

Even before *Morning Victor*'s mooring lines had been secured, Wolfram's messenger leapt across from the dock. He seized whatever handholds and footholds he could find, and grinning broadly, he scrambled up the side. He vaulted over the bulwark, and onto the deck.

He had a spidery build, red hair, and skin that would never tan. It would burn and it would peel, but it would never tan. His teeth were white and fairly straight, no obvious rot.

"You're in one hell of a hurry," the captain groused.

The grin widened.

This wasn't a wise move on the messenger's part.

The captain bellowed, "You could have fallen! You could have been crushed between the ship and the dock!"

"Yes, sir."

"Any idea who'd end up scraping you off the side of the hull with a spatula?"

"No, sir."

"My crew would."

"Yes, sir."

"You're a damn fool and a fucking showoff."

"Sorry, sir."

"Don't 'Sorry, sir' me, you little shit! State your fucking business and then get the hell off of my ship, you selfish moron!"

"Yes, sir."

The message was to the point: Wolfram, Clan Iredale's battlemaster sent his compliments to the captain and asked him to instruct Brenna and Vlod to stay aboard and await his arrival.

In return, via the captain, Brenna and Vlod sent their respects to Wolfram and said they'd be glad to await his arrival.

By this time the ship was secure alongside and the gangway was over.

Standing at the top of the gangway, the messenger waved at the captain. "Welcome back, Grandad. See you tonight for dinner."

"If you live that long," the captain said.

The messenger went ashore, and the captain went below.

To Brenna, Vlod said, "Reminds me of you and your uncle, way back when."

"I lived long enough to grow up, didn't I?"

"We both have," Vlod said.

"No thanks to Ulricka," Brenna said.

Vlod made a dismissive gesture. "She's trapped and looking for a way out. It's bound to throw out the odd misstep."

Brenna made a noncommittal noise. "He's read our reports."

"That's why we sent them on ahead, wasn't it?" Vlod said.

"Your girlish optimism is wearing a trifle thin," Brenna said.

"I do my best to curb it."

"No you don't," she said. She added, "The dispatch riders must have made good time."

"Clever boys, and they're good riders."

"We'll have the devil to pay and no pitch hot."

"Never fear," Vlod said. "Hot pitch will be provided."

"Buckets and buckets of it."

"And a mop, too."

A half hour later, Wolfram slid in behind the captain's worktable and sat on the stern locker. The glare from the windows threw his face into deep shadow. He smelled like leather, oiled steel, and tobacco smoke.

"I'll talk to you later, Brenna," Wolfram said. "Please wait outside and see that Vlod and I are not disturbed."

"I'd rather stay. It was my operation as much as his."

Wolfram slammed his palm down onto the tabletop. The report was deafening in the confined space. "Out!"

"Aye, aye, sir," Brenna said, and left.

To Vlod, Wolfram said, "You've nearly started a war."

Vlod shrugged. It was the response he'd expected, and he had his response rehearsed. "Narmer started it months ago. All I've done, the most I've done, is to force it out into the open."

"Maybe so, you arrogant puppy, but we're not ready for an open war. You've given them an excuse to attack us at will."

"By rescuing Royden?"

"Exactly."

"I thought you sent me upriver to do precisely that."

"I didn't send you up there to pick a fight with the Cathedral Guard!"

"No picking was involved."

"Tell that to the dead!"

Vlod sighed. Beneath the rage and disappointment, Wolfram was frightened. Rightly so. Vlod said, "Narmer seized Royden illegally, and Ulricka took possession of him illegally. We had every right to free him by any and all means necessary."

"*Illegally* be damned. You can't be that stupid. It's the overall look of the thing. It's about the politics. The minor clans don't give a damn about legal niceties."

"About what then?" The question was unnecessary, but Vlod had to ask it. He had to know exactly what the battlemaster was thinking and why.

"What they'll care about is that you stormed in and freed one of Ulricka's prisoners," Wolfram said. "Never mind that she was holding him illegally. That's beside the point. Or had you thought that far ahead? What they'll care about is that you attacked her forces and left several of her people dead. What they'll care about even more is that you violated the sovereignty of their precious cathedral and their revered Mother Metropolitan."

"Meaning?"

"Meaning that you've handed Narmer the perfect pretext."

"Narmer doesn't give a shit about pretexts," Vlod said.

"Perhaps not, but Ulricka does and the clans do. They have an obsessive need to appear as though they're acting within the right."

Where was the right in allowing Narmer to kidnap one of the magi assigned to Clan Iredale?

Vlod had better sense than to pose the question. The clans saw to clan business, and the magi saw to magi business. The overlap muddied the waters in this case, but so be it.

Instead of going down that road, Vlod asked, "Where do things stand here at the manor? What about the project?"

"Edmund and I have shut it down. Call it another casualty of your lack of anticipation."

Edmund and Royden paced along the battlements above Olney Castle's western gate. The sky was clear and the sun shone down as though it were summer instead of spring.

"What did you find out?" Edmund asked.

They had already been through Royden's kidnapping, his treatment at the hands of Narmer's people, his handling at the hands of Ulricka's people, his rescue, Vlod's presentation of the appeal, and what had followed.

Now they were down to whether or not Royden had accomplished his mission, his mission within the mission. What had he ferreted out about the cathedral, about Ulricka's court?

Royden said, "They're a tight-lipped bunch. Touch-me-not to the core. Their wear their piety on their sleeves. No dissatisfaction with Her Beatitude that I could detect, but I did hear a healthy amount of grumbling. They aren't afraid, they're not what I'd call unsettled, but they are aware that not everything is as it should be."

Edmund and Royden reached a corner, rounded it, and walked along the south battlement. The upper reaches of Young's Bay lay spread out at the base of the hill. Farther out, the view presented a patchwork of fields, the bay, Young's River, tide flats, marshes, a winding road, commercial oyster beds, and a scattering of small buildings.

Edmund asked, "What about Narmer?"

"My guess would be that he has agents up and down the bureaucracy."

"How many?"

"Not above a half dozen, but from what I could tell, they're in the right places."

"Is Ulricka aware of them?"

"Yes, and she's worried about them, too. I could tell as much from the questions Narmer's agents asked me."

The sun's warmth was reassuring after the winter they'd had. In the rain-soaked darkness of December, January, and February, day after day of what amounted to twilight, it was second nature to fear that the days would never lengthen again, that spring and summer would never return.

Every year the same question made its unspoken, unacknowledged rounds: Had the Goddess decided to perform a Third Creation? Let there be darkness!

"What about the Cathedral Guard? Compromised or not?"

"No idea. Narmer may have infiltrated it. He'd be a fool not to. Easy enough, too, as far as I could tell. It's wide open."

A cloud passed in front of the sun, and the day turned dark and cold. It was an aftertaste of winter.